PRAISE FOR

LARRY McMURTRY

AND

The Last Picture Show

"Larry McMurtry's *THE LAST PICTURE SHOW* takes on the very real-life denizens of a Texas town that is as tight as a fist."

—*Saturday Review*

"Funny and brutal at the same time."

—Thomas Lask, *The New York Times*

"McMurtry can transform ordinary words into highly lyrical, poetic passages. . . . He presents human dramas with a sympathy and compassion that make us care about his characters in ways that most novelists can't."

—*Los Angeles Times*

"What an imagination he has! When it comes to spinning a good yarn, few writers do it better than McMurtry. . . ."

—*Houston Post*

"Larry McMurtry is the most entertaining novelist in America."

—*Cleveland Plain Dealer*

Books by Larry McMurtry

Buffalo Girls
Some Can Whistle
Anything for Billy
Film Flam: Essays on Hollywood
Texasville
Lonesome Dove
The Desert Rose
Cadillac Jack
Sombody's Darling
Terms of Endearment
All My Friends Are Going to Be Strangers
Moving On
The Last Picture Show
In a Narrow Grave: Essays on Texas
Leaving Cheyenne
Horseman, Pass By

LARRY McMURTRY

The Last Picture Show

POCKET BOOKS

New York   London   Toronto   Sydney   Tokyo   Singapore

This book is a work of fiction. Names, characters, places and
incidents are either products of the author's imagination or are
use fictitiously. Any resemblance to actual events or locales or
persons, living or dead, is entirely coincidental.

POCKET BOOKS, a division of Simon & Schuster Inc.
1230 Avenue of the Americas, New York, NY 10020

ISBN: 0-671-75381-9

First Pocket Books printing May 1992

10 9 8 7 6 5 4 3 2 1

POCKET and colophon are registered trademarks of
Simon & Schuster Inc.

Cover art by Earl Keleny

Printed in the U.S.A.

THE
LAST
PICTURE
SHOW
is lovingly
dedicated
to
my home town.

The Last
Picture Show

CHAPTER I

Sometimes Sonny felt like he was the only human creature in the town. It was a bad feeling, and it usually came on him in the mornings early, when the streets were completely empty, the way they were one Saturday morning in late November. The night before Sonny had played his last game of football for Thalia High School, but it wasn't that that made him feel so strange and alone. It was just the look of the town.

There was only one car parked on the courthouse square—the night watchman's old white Nash. A cold norther was singing in off the plains, swirling long ribbons of dust down Main Street, the only street in Thalia with businesses on it. Sonny's pickup was a '41 Chevrolet, not at its best on cold mornings. In front of the picture show it coughed out and had to be choked for a while, but then it started again and jerked its way to the red light, blowing out spumes of white exhaust that the wind whipped away.

At the red light he started to turn south toward the all-night café, but when he looked north to see if anyone was coming he turned that way instead. No

1

one at all was coming but he saw his young friend Billy, headed out. He had his broom and was sweeping right down the middle of the highway into the gusting wind. Billy lived at the poolhall with Sam the Lion, and sweeping was all he really knew how to do. The only trouble was that he overdid it. He swept out the poolhall in the mornings, the café in the afternoons, and the picture show at night, and always, unless someone specifically told him to stop, he just kept sweeping, down the sidewalk, on through the town, sometimes one way and sometimes another, sweeping happily on until someone noticed him and brought him back to the poolhall.

Sonny drove up beside him and honked. Billy quit sweeping at once and got in the pickup. He was a stocky boy, not very smart, but perfectly friendly; picking him up made Sonny feel less lonesome. If Billy was out the poolhall must be open, and when the poolhall was open he was never lonesome. One of the nice things about living in Thalia was that the poolhall often opened by 6:30 or 7 A.M., the reason being that Sam the Lion, who owned it, was a very bad sleeper.

Sonny drove to the hall and parked and took Billy's broom so he wouldn't go sweeping off again. The air was so dry and dusty it made the nostrils sting and the two boys hustled inside. Sam the Lion was up, all right, brushing one of the snooker tables. He was an old man, but big and heavy, with a mane of white hair; cold weather made his feet swell and he wore his old sheepskin house shoes to work in in the wintertime. He was expecting the boys and barely gave them a glance.

Once they were inside, Sonny let Billy have the broom again and Billy immediately went over to the

2

gas stove to warm himself. While he warmed he leaned on the broom and licked a piece of green pool chalk. Sam the Lion didn't particularly care that Billy licked chalk all the time; it was cheap enough nourishment, he said. Sonny got himself a package of Cheese Crisps and made room for himself at the stove, turning Billy's cap around backward for friendship's sake. It was an old green baseball cap some lady had given Billy three or four summers before.

"Cold in here, Sam," Sonny said. "It's nearly as cold in here as it is outside."

"Not as windy, though," Sam replied. "I'm surprised you had the nerve to come in this mornin', after the beatin' you all took. Anybody ever tell you boys about blockin'? Or tacklin'?"

Sonny ate his Cheese Crisps, unabashed. Crowell, the visiting team, had tromped Thalia 28 to 6. It had been a little embarrassing for Coach Popper, but that was because the local Quarterback Club had been so sure Thalia was finally going to win a District Crown that they had literally jumped the gun and presented the coach with a new .12 gauge Marlin under-over at the homecoming game two weeks before. The coach was quite a hunter. Two of Crowell's four touchdowns had been run over Sonny's guard position, but he felt quite calm about it all. Four years of playing for Thalia had inured him to defeat, and so far as he was concerned the Quarterback Club had been foolishly optimistic.

Besides, he could not see that he had much to gain by helping the coach get new shotguns, the coach being a man of most uncertain temper. He had already shot at Sonny once in his life, and with a new under-over he might not miss.

"Where's your buddy?" Sam asked.

"Not in yet," Sonny said. That was Duane, Sonny's best friend, who besides being an All-Conference fullback, roughnecked the midnight tower with a local drilling crew.

"Duane's gonna work himself into an early grave," Sam the Lion said. "He oughtn't to play a football game and then go out and work all night on top of it. He made half the yardage we made."

"Well, that never tired him out," Sonny said, going to get another package of Cheese Crisps.

Sam the Lion started to cough, and the coughing got away from him, as it often did. His whole body shook; he couldn't stop. Finally he had to stagger back to the washroom and take a drink of water and a swig of cough medicine to get it under control.

"Suckin' in too much chalk dust," he said when he came back. Billy hardly noticed, but Sonny felt a little uneasy. He didn't like to be reminded that Sam the Lion was not as young or as healthy as he once had been. Sam the Lion was the man who took care of things, particularly of boys, and Sonny did not like to think that he might die. The reason Sam was so especially good to boys was that he himself had had three sons, none of whom lived to be eighteen. The first was killed when Sam was still a rancher: he and his son were trying to drive a herd of yearlings across the Little Wichita River one day when it was up, and the boy had been knocked loose from his horse, pawed under, and drowned. A few years later, after Sam had gone into the oil business, a gas explosion knocked his second son off a derrick. He fell over fifty feet and was dead before they got him to town. Sam sold his oil holdings and put in the first Ford agency in Thalia,

4

and his youngest son was run over by a deputy sheriff. His wife lost her mind and spent her last ten years rocking in a rocking chair. Sam drank a lot, quit going to church, and was said to be loose with women, even married women.

He began to come out of it when he bought the picture show, or so people said. He got lots of comedies and serials and Westerns and the kids came as often as they could talk their parents into letting them. Then Sam bought the poolhall and the all-night café and he perked up more and more.

No one really knew why he was called Sam the Lion. Some thought it was because he hated barbers and always went around with a shaggy head of hair. Others thought it was because he had been such a hell-raising cowboy when he was young, but Sonny found that a little hard to believe. He had seen Sam mad only once, and that was one Fourth of July when Duane stuck a Roman candle in the pocket of one of the snooker tables and set it off. When it finally quit shooting, Sam grabbed the pisspot and chased Duane out, meaning to sling it at him. He slung it, but Duane was too quick. Joe Bob Blanton, the Methodist preacher's son, happened to be standing on the sidewalk wishing he was allowed to go in and shoot pool, and he was the one that got drenched. The boys all got a big laugh but Sam the Lion was embarrassed about it and cleaned Joe Bob off as best he could.

When he was thoroughly warm Sonny got one of the brushes and began to brush the eight-ball tables. Sam went over and looked disgustedly at the two nickels Sonny had left for the Cheese Crisps.

"You'll never get nowhere, Sonny," he said. "You've already spent a dime today and you ain't even had a decent breakfast. Billy, you might get the other side of the hall swept out, son."

While the boys worked Sam stood by the stove and warmed his aching feet. He wished Sonny weren't so reckless economically, but there was nothing he could do about it. Billy was less of a problem, partly because he was so dumb. Billy's real father was an old railroad man who had worked in Thalia for a short time just before the war; his mother was a deaf and dumb girl who had no people except an aunt. The old man cornered the girl in the balcony of the picture show one night and begat Billy. The sheriff saw to it that the old man married the girl, but she died when Billy was born and he was raised by the family of Mexicans who helped the old man keep the railroad track repaired. After the war the hauling petered out and the track was taken up. The old man left and got a job bumping cars on a stockyards track in Oklahoma, leaving Billy with the Mexicans. They hung around for several more years, piling prickly pear and grubbing mesquite, but then a man from Plainview talked them into moving out there to pick cotton. They snuck off one morning and left Billy sitting on the curb in front of the picture show.

From then on, Sam the Lion took care of him. Billy learned to sweep, and he kept all three of Sam's places swept out; in return he got his keep and also, every single night, he got to watch the picture show. He always sat in the balcony, his broom at his side; for years he saw every show that came to Thalia, and so far as anyone knew, he liked them all. He was never known to leave while the screen was lit.

"You workin' today?" Sam asked, noticing that

Sonny was taking his time brushing the eight-ball table.

"The truck's being greased," Sonny said. On weekends, and sometimes weeknights too, he drove a butane truck for Frank Fartley of Fartley Butane and Propane. He didn't make as much money as his friend Duane made roughnecking, but the work was easier.

Just as Sam the Lion was about to get back to the subject of the football game they all heard a familiar sound and paused to listen. Abilene was coming into town in his Mercury. Abilene was the driller Duane worked for. He had spent a lot of money souping up the Mercury, and in Thalia the sound of his exhausts was as unmistakable as the sound of the wind.

"Well, we barely got 'em clean in time," Sam said. Abilene not only had the best car in the country, he also shot the best stick of pool. Drilling and pool shooting were things he did so well that no one could decide which was his true vocation and which his avocation. Some mornings he went home and cleaned up before he came to the poolhall—he liked to be clean and well dressed when he gambled—but if it was too early for any of the nine-ball players to be up he would often stop and practice in his drilling clothes.

The Mercury stopped in front of the poolhall and Sam went over and got Abilene's ivory-banded cue out of the padlocked rack and laid it on the counter for him. When the door opened the wind sliced inside ahead of the man. Abilene had on sunglasses and the heavy green coveralls he wore to protect his clothes from the oil-field grease; as soon as he was in he unzipped the coveralls and hung them on a nail Sam had fixed for him. His blue wool shirt and gabardine pants were creased and trim.

"Mornin'," Sam said.

"Mornin'," Abilene replied, handing Sam his expensive-looking sunglasses. He once had a pair fall out of his pocket and break when he was bending over to pick up a piece of pool chalk; after that he always had Sam put the sunglasses in a drawer for him. Though he was the poolhall's best customer, he and Sam the Lion had almost nothing to say to one another. Abilene paid Sam two hundred and fifty dollars a year for a private key to the poolhall, so he could come in and practice any time he wanted to. Often Sonny would come in from some long butane run at two or three o'clock in the morning and see that Abilene was in the poolhall, practicing. The garage where the butane truck was kept was right across the street from the poolhall and sometimes Sonny would walk across and stand by one of the windows watching Abilene shoot. No one ever tried to go in when Abilene was in the poolhall alone.

"Let's shoot one, Sonny," Abilene said. "I feel like a little snooker before breakfast."

Sonny was taken by surprise. He knew he would not even be good competition for Abilene, but he went and got a cue anyway. It did not occur to him to turn down the invitation. Abilene shot first and ran thirty points off the break.

"Duane didn't go to sleep on you last night, did he?" Sonny asked, feeling that he ought at least to make conversation.

"No, the breeze kept us awake," Abilene replied. That was their conversation. Sonny only got to shoot four times; for the most part he just stood back and watched Abilene move gracefully around the green table, easing in his shots with the ivory-banded cue. He won the game by 175 points.

"You shoot pool about like you play football," he said, when the game was over.

Sonny ignored the insult and pitched a quarter on the felt to pay for the game. Abilene insulted everybody, young and old alike, and Sonny was not obliged to take it personally. Sam the Lion came over to rack the balls.

"I hope they hurry and get that truck greased," he said. "The way your fortune's sinking you'll be bankrupt before you get out of here."

"What'd our bet come to, Sam," Abilene asked casually. He busted the fresh rack and started shooting red balls. Sam grinned at Sonny and went over to the cash register and got five ten-dollar bills. He laid them on the side of the snooker table and when Abilene noticed them he took a money clip out of his pocket and put the fifty dollars in it.

"It's what I get for bettin' on my hometown ball club," Sam said. "I ought to have better sense."

"It wouldn't hurt if you had a better home town," Abilene said.

Sam always bet on the boys, thinking it would make them feel good, but the strategy seldom worked because they almost always lost. Most of them only trained when they felt like it, and that was not very often. The few who did train were handicapped by their intense dislike of Coach Popper. Sonny was not alone in considering the coach a horse's ass, but the school board liked the coach and never considered firing him: he was a man's man, and he worked cheap. They saw no reason to hire a better coach until a better bunch of boys came along, and there was no telling when that would be. Sam the Lion went loyally on losing money, while Abilene, who invariably bet against Thalia, cleared about a thousand dollars a season from Sam and others like him.

While Sam and Sonny were idly watching Abilene practice, Billy swept quietly down the other side of the poolhall and on out the door. The cold wind that came through the door when Billy went out woke them up. "Go get him, Sonny," Sam said. "Make him put his broom up for a while."

Billy hadn't had time to get far; he was just three doors away, in front of what once had been the Thalia Pontiac Agency. He was calmly sweeping north, into the cold wind. All his floor-sweep had already blown away, but he was quite content to sweep at the curling ribbons of sand that the wind blew past him. A time or two in his life he had swept all the way to the Thalia city limits sign before anyone had noticed him.

When Sonny stepped out of the poolhall the black pickup that the roughnecks used was stopped at the red light. The light changed and the pickup passed the courthouse and slowed a moment at the corner by the poolhall, so Duane could jump out. He was a tall boy with curly black hair. Because he was a fullback and a roughneck he held himself a little stiffly. He had on Levi's and a Levi's jacket with the collar turned up. Sonny pointed at Billy and he and Duane each grabbed one of Billy's arms and hustled him back down the sidewalk into the warming poolhall. Sam took the broom and put it up on a shelf where Billy couldn't reach it.

10

"Let's go eat, buddy," Duane said, knowing that Sonny had put off having breakfast until he came.

Sam the Lion looked Duane over carefully to see if he could detect any symptoms of overwork, but Duane was in his usual Saturday morning good humor, and if there were such symptoms they didn't show.

"If you boys are going to the café, take this change for me," Sam said, pitching Sonny the dark green coin sack that he used to tote change from one of his establishments to the other. Sonny caught it and the boys hurried out and jogged down the street two blocks to the café, tucking their heads down so the wind wouldn't take their breath. "Boy, I froze my ass last night," Duane grunted, as they ran.

The café was a little one-story red building, so deliciously warm inside that all the windows were steamed over. Penny, the daytime waitress, was in the kitchen frying eggs for a couple of truck drivers, so Sonny set the change sack on the cash register. There was no sign of old Marston, the cook. The boys counted their money and found they had only eighty cents between them.

"I had to shoot Abilene a game of snooker," Sonny explained. "If it hadn't been for that I'd have a quarter more."

"We got enough," Duane said. They were always short of money on Saturday morning, but they were paid Saturday afternoon, so it was no calamity. They ordered eggs and sausage and flipped to see who got what—by the end of the week they often ended up splitting meals. Sonny got the sausage and Duane the eggs.

While Penny was counting the new change into the

cash register old Marston came dragging in. He looked as though he had just frozen out of a bar ditch somewhere, and Penny was on him instantly.

"Where you been, you old fart?" she yelled. "I done had to cook ten orders and you know I ain't no cook."

"I swear, Penny," Marston said. "I just forgot to set my alarm clock last night."

"You're a lying old sot if I ever saw one," Penny said. "I ought to douse you under the hydrant a time or two, maybe you wouldn't stink of whiskey so much."

Marston slipped by her and had his apron on in a minute. Penny was a 185-pound redhead, not given to idle threats. She was Church of Christ and didn't mind calling a sinner a sinner. Five years before she had accidentally gotten pregnant before she was engaged; the whole town knew about it and Penny got a lot of backhanded sympathy. The ladies of the community thought it was just awful for a girl that fat to get pregnant. Once married, she discovered she didn't much like her husband, and that made her harder to get along with in general. On Wednesday nights, when the Church of Christ held its prayer meetings and shouting contests anybody who happened to be within half a mile of the church could hear what Penny thought about wickedness; it was old Marston's misfortune to hear it every morning, and at considerably closer range. He only worked to drink, and the thought of being doused under a hydrant made him so shaky he could barely turn the eggs.

Sonny and Duane winked at him to cheer him up, and gave Penny the finger when she wasn't looking. They also managed to indicate that they were broke, so Marston would put a couple of extra slices of toast on the order. The boys gave him a ride to the county-line liquor store once a week, and in return he helped out with extra food when their money was low.

"How we gonna work it tonight?" Duane asked. He and Sonny owned the Chevrolet pickup jointly, and because there were two of them and only one pickup their Saturday night dating was a little complicated.

"We might as well wait and see," Sonny replied, looking disgustedly at the grape jelly Marston had put on the plate. He hated grape jelly, and the café never seemed to have any other kind.

"If I have to make a delivery to Ranger this afternoon there won't be no problem," he added. "You just take the pickup. If I get back in time I can meet Charlene at the picture show."

"Okay," Duane said, glad to get that off his mind. Sonny never got the pickup first on Saturday night and Duane always felt slightly guilty about it but not quite guilty enough to change anything.

The problem was that he was going with Jacy Farrow, whose folks were rich enough to make them unenthusiastic about her going with a poor boy like Duane. He and Jacy couldn't use her car because her father, Gene Farrow, made a point of driving by the picture show every Saturday night to see that Jacy's car was parked out front. They were able to get around that easily enough by sneaking out the back of the show and going somewhere in the pickup, but that arrangement created something of a courting problem for Sonny, who went with a girl named Charlene Duggs. Charlene had to be home by eleven thirty, and if Duane and Jacy kept the pickup tied up until almost eleven, it didn't allow Sonny much time in which to make out.

13

Sonny had assured Duane time and time again that he didn't particularly care, but Duane remained secretly uneasy. His uneasiness really stemmed from the fact that he was going with Jacy, the prettiest, most desirable girl in town, while Sonny was only going with Charlene Duggs, a mediocre date by any standard. Occasionally the two couples double-dated, but that was really harder on Sonny than no date at all. With all four of them squeezed up in the cab of the pickup it was impossible for him to ignore the fact that Jacy was several times as desirable as Charlene. Even if it was totally dark, her perfume smelled better. For days after such a date Sonny had very disloyal fantasies involving himself and Jacy, and after an hour's sloppy necking with Charlene even the fantasy that he was kissing Jacy had a dangerous power. Charlene kissed convulsively, as if she had just swallowed a golf ball and was trying to force it back up.

Of course Sonny had often considered breaking up with Charlene, but there weren't many girls in the town and the only unattached girl who was any prettier than Charlene was an unusually prudish sophomore. Charlene would let Sonny do anything he wanted to above the waist; it was only as time wore on that he had begun to realize that there really wasn't much of permanent interest to do in that zone. As the weeks went by, Sonny observed that Jacy seemed to become more and more delightful, passionate, inventive, while by contrast Charlene just seemed more of a slug.

When the boys finished eating and paid their check they had a nickel left. Duane was going home to bed, so Sonny kept the nickel; he could buy himself a Butterfinger for lunch. Outside the air was still cold and dusty and gray clouds were blowing south off the High Plains.

Duane took the pickup and went to the rooming house where the two of them had roomed since their sophomore year. People thought it a little strange, because each had a parent alive, but the boys liked it. Sonny's father ran the local domino parlor and lived in a room at the little hotel, and Duane's mother didn't really have much more room. His grandmother was still alive and living with his mother in their two-room house; his mother took in laundry, so the house was pretty full. The boys were actually rather proud that they lived in a rooming house and paid their own rent; most of the boys with real homes envied the two their freedom. Nobody envied them Old Lady Malone, of course, but she owned the rooming house and couldn't be helped. She was nosy, dipped snuff, had a compulsion about turning off fires, and was afflicted with one of the most persistent cases of diarrhea on record. The one bathroom was so badly aired that the boys frequently performed their morning toilet in the rest room of the Texaco filling station.

After Sonny got his delivery orders he jogged up the street to the filling station to get the truck, an old green International. The seat springs had about worn through the padding, and most of the rubber was gone from the footpedals. Still, it ran, and Sonny gunned it a few times and struck out for Megargel, a town even smaller than Thalia. Out in the open country the norther gusted strongly across the highway, making the truck hard to hold. Once in a while a big ragweed would shake loose from the barbed-wire fences and skitter across the road, only to catch again in the barbed-wire fence on the other side. The dry grass in

15

the pastures was gray-brown, and the leafless winter mesquite gray-black. A few Hereford yearlings wandered dispiritedly into the wind, the only signs of life; there was really nothing between Thalia and Megargel but thirty miles of lonesome country. Except for a few sandscraped ranch houses there was nothing to see but a long succession of low brown ridges, with the wind singing over them. It occurred to Sonny that perhaps people called them "blue northers" because it was so hard not to get blue when one was blowing. He regretted that he had not asked Billy to ride along with him on the morning deliveries. Billy was no talker, but he was company, and with nobody at all on the road or in the cab Sonny sometimes got the funny feeling that he was driving the old truck around and around in a completely empty place.

CHAPTER II

Sonny's next delivery after Megargel was in Scotland, a farming community fifty miles in the opposite direction. As luck would have it he arrived at the farm where the butane was needed while the farmer and his family were in town doing their weekly shopping. The butane tank was in their backyard, and so were nine dogs, six of them chows.

Besides the chows, which were all brown and ill-tempered, there was a German shepherd, a rat terrier, and a subdued black cocker that the farmer had given his kids for a Christmas present. When Sonny approached the yard gate the chows leapt and snarled and tried to bite through the wire. It seemed very unlikely that he could bluff them, but he stood outside the gate for several minutes getting up his nerve to try. While he was standing there five little teal flew off a stock tank north of the house and angled south over the yard. The sight of them made Sonny long for a shotgun of his own, and some ammunition money; all his life he had hunted with borrowed guns. The longer he stood at the gate the more certain he became that the dogs could not be bluffed, and he finally turned and walked back to the truck, a little depressed. He had never owned a shotgun, and he had never found a yardful of dogs that he could intimidate, at least not around Scotland. He sat in the truck for almost an hour, enjoying fantasies of himself carrying Jacy Farrow past dozens of sullen but respectful chows.

Just before noon the farmer came driving up, his red GMC pickup loaded with groceries, kids, and a fat-ankled wife. Some of the kids looked meaner than the dogs.

"Hell, you should just 'a gone on in," the farmer said cheerfully. "Them dogs don't bite many people."

Like so many Saturdays, it was a long work day; when Sonny rattled back into Thalia after his last delivery it was almost 10 P.M. He found his boss, Frank Fartley, in the poolhall shooting his usual comical Saturday night eight-ball game. The reason it was comical was because Mr. Fartley's cigar was cocked at such an angle that there was always a small dense cloud of white smoke between his eye and the cue ball. He tried to compensate for not being able to see the cue ball by lunging madly with his cue at a spot where he thought it was, a style of play that made Sam the Lion terribly nervous because it was not only hard on the felt but also extremely dangerous to unwatchful kibitzers, one or two of whom had been rather seriously speared. When Sonny came in Frank stopped lunging long enough to give him his check, and Sonny immediately got Sam the Lion to cash it. Abilene was there, dressed in a dark brown pearl-buttoned shirt and gray slacks; he was shooting nine-ball at five dollars a game with Lester Marlow, his usual Saturday night opponent.

Lester was a wealthy boy from Wichita Falls who came to Thalia often. Ostensibly, his purpose in coming was to screw Jacy Farrow, but his suit was not progressing too well and the real reason he kept coming was because losing large sums of money to Abilene gave him a certain local prestige. It was very important to Lester that he do *something* big, and since losing was a lot easier than winning, he contented himself with losing big.

Sonny had watched the two shoot so many times that it held no interest for him, so he took his week's wages and walked across the dark courthouse lawn to the picture show. Jacy's white Ford convertible was parked out front, where it always was on Saturday night. The movie that night was called *Storm Warning,* and the posterboards held pictures of Doris Day, Ronald Reagan, Steve Cochran, and Ginger Rogers. It was past 10 P.M., and Miss Mosey, who sold tickets, had already closed the window; Sonny found her in the lobby, cleaning out the popcorn machine. She was a thin little old lady with such bad eyesight and hearing that she sometimes had to walk halfway down the aisle to tell whether the comedy or the newsreel was on.

"My goodness, Frank oughtn't to work you so late on weekends," she said. "You done missed the comedy so you don't need to give me but thirty cents."

Sonny thanked her and bought a package of Doublemint gum before he went into the show. Very few people ever came to the late feature; there were not more than twenty in the whole theater. As soon as his eyes adjusted Sonny determined that Jacy and Duane were still out parking; Charlene Duggs was sitting about halfway down the aisle with her little

19

sister Marlene. Sonny walked down the aisle and tapped her on the shoulder, and the two girls scooted over a seat.

"I decided you had a wreck," Charlene said, not bothering to whisper. She smelled like powder and toilet water.

"You two want some chewin' gum?" Sonny offered, holding out the package. The girls each instantly took a stick and popped the gum into their mouths almost simultaneously. They never had any gum money themselves and were both great moochers. Their father, Royce Duggs, ran a dinky little one-man garage out on the highway; most of his work was done on pickups and tractors, and money was tight. The girls would not have been able to afford the toilet water either, but their mother, Beulah Duggs, had a secret passion for it and bought it with money that Royce Duggs thought was going for the girls' school lunches. The three of them could only get away with using it on Saturday night when Royce was customarily too drunk to be able to smell.

After the feature had been playing for a few minutes Sonny and Charlene got up and moved back into one of the corners. It made Sonny nervous to sit with Charlene and Marlene both. Even though Charlene was a senior and Marlene just a sophomore, the two looked so much alike that he was afraid he might accidentally start holding hands with the wrong one. Back in the corner, he held Charlene's hand and they smooched a little, but not much. Sonny really wanted to see the movie, and it was easy for him to hold his passion down. Charlene had not got all the sweetness out of the stick of Doublemint and didn't want to take it out of her mouth just to kiss Sonny, but after a few minutes she changed her mind, took it out, and stuck it under the arm of her seat. It seemed to her that Sonny looked a little bit like Steve Cochran, and she began to kiss him energetically, squirming and pressing herself against his knee. Sonny returned the kiss, but with somewhat muted interest. He wanted to keep at least one eye on the screen, so if Ginger Rogers decided to take her clothes off he wouldn't miss it. The posters outside indicated she at least got down to her slip at one point. Besides, Charlene was always getting worked up in picture shows; at first Sonny had thought her fits of cinematic passion very encouraging, until he discovered it was practically impossible to get her worked up *except* in picture shows.

The movies were Charlene's life, as she was fond of saying. She spent most of her afternoons hanging around the little beauty shop where her mother worked, reading movie magazines, and she always referred to movie stars by their first names. Once when an aunt gave her a dollar for her birthday she went down to the variety store and bought two fifty-cent portraits to sit on her dresser: one was of June Allyson and the other Van Johnson. Marlene copied Charlene's passions as exactly as possible, but when the same aunt gave *her* a dollar the variety store's stock of portraits was low and she had to make do with Esther Williams and Mickey Rooney. Charlene kidded her mercilessly about the latter, and took to sleeping with Van Johnson under her pillow because she was afraid Marlene might mutilate him out of envy.

After a few minutes of squirming alternately against the seat arm and Sonny's knee, lost in visions of Steve Cochran, Charlene abruptly relaxed and sat back. She

21

languidly returned the chewing gum to her mouth, and for a while they watched the movie in silence. Then she remembered a matter she had been intending to bring up.

"Guess what?" she said. "We been going steady a year tonight. You should have got me something for an anniversary present."

Sonny had been contentedly watching Ginger Rogers, waiting for the slip scene. Charlene's remark took him by surprise.

"Well, you can have another stick of gum," he said. "That's all I've got on me."

"Okay, and I'll take a dollar, too," Charlene said. "It cost that much for me and Marlene to come to the show, and I don't want to pay my own way on my anniversary."

Sonny handed her the package of chewing gum, but not the dollar. Normally he expected to pay Charlene's way to the show, but he saw no reason at all why he should spend fifty cents on Marlene. While he was thinking out the ethics of the matter the exit door opened down to the right of the screen and Duane and Jacy slipped in, their arms around one another. They came back and sat down by Sonny and Charlene.

"Hi you all, what are you doin' back here in the dark?" Jacy whispered gaily. Her pretty mouth was a little numb from two hours of virtually uninterrupted kissing. As soon as it seemed polite, she and Duane started kissing again and settled into an osculatory doze that lasted through the final reel of the movie. Charlene began nervously popping her finger joints, something she did whenever Jacy came around. Sonny tried to concentrate on the screen, but it was hard. Jacy and Duane kept right on kissing, even when the movie ended and the lights came on. They didn't break their clinch until Billy came down from the balcony with his broom, and began to sweep.

"Sure was a short show," Jacy said, turning to grin at Sonny. Her nose wrinkled delightfully when she grinned. She shook her head so that her straight blond hair would hang more smoothly against her neck. Duane's hair was tousled, but when Jacy playfully tried to comb it he yawned and shook her off. She put on fresh lipstick and they all got up and went outside.

Miss Mosey had taken the *Storm Warning* posters down and was gallantly trying to tack up the posters for Sunday's show, which was *Francis Goes to the Army*. The wind whipped around the corners of the old building, making the posters flop. Miss Mosey's fingers were so cold she could barely hold the tacks, so the boys helped her finish while the girls shivered on the curb. Marlene was shivering on the curb too, waiting for Sonny to drop her off at the Duggses'. Duane walked Jacy to her convertible and kissed her good-night a time or two, then came gloomily to the pickup, depressed at the thought of how long it was until Saturday night came again.

When they had taken Marlene home and dropped Duane at the rooming house, Sonny and Charlene drove back to town so they could find out what time it was from the clock in the jewelry store window. As usual, it was almost time for Charlene to go home.

"Oh, let's go on to the lake," she said. "I guess I can be a few minutes late tonight, since it's my anniversary."

"I never saw anything like that Jacy and Duane," she said. "Kissing in the picture show after the lights go on. That's pretty bad if you ask me. One of these

23

days Mrs. Farrow's gonna catch 'em an' that'll be the end of that romance."

Sonny drove on to the city lake without saying anything, but the remark depressed him. So far as he was concerned Jacy and Duane knew true love and would surely manage to get married and be happy. What depressed him was that it had just become clear to him that Charlene really wanted to go with Duane, just as he himself really wanted to go with Jacy.

As soon as the pickup stopped Charlene moved over against him. "Crack your window and leave the heater on," she said. "It's still too cold in here for me."

Sonny tried to shrug off his depression by beginning the little routine they always went through when they parked: first he would kiss Charlene for about ten minutes; then she would let him take off her brassiere and play with her breasts; finally, when he tried to move on to other things she would quickly scoot back across the seat, put the bra back on, and make him take her home. Sometimes she indulged in an engulfing kiss or two on the doorstep, knowing that she could fling herself inside the house if a perilously high wave of passion threatened to sweep over her.

After the proper amount of kissing Sonny deftly unhooked her bra. This was the signal for Charlene to draw her arms from the sleeves of her sweater and slip out of the straps. Sonny hung the bra on the rear-view mirror. So long as the proprieties were observed, Charlene liked being felt; she obligingly slipped her sweater up around her neck.

"Eeh, your hands are like ice," she said, sucking in her breath. Despite the heater the cab was cold enough to make her nipples crinkle. The wind had blown all the clouds away, but the moon was thin and dim and the choppy lake lay in darkness. When Sonny moved his hand the little dash-light threw patches of shadow over Charlene's stocky torso.

In a few minutes it became apparent that the cab was warming up faster than either Sonny or Charlene. He idly held one of her breasts in his hand, but it might have been an apple someone had given him just when he was least hungry.

"Hey," Charlene said suddenly, noticing. "What's the matter with you? You act half asleep."

Sonny was disconcerted. He was not sure what was wrong. It did not occur to him that he was bored. After all, he had Charlene's breast in his hand, and in Thalia it was generally agreed that the one thing that was never boring was feeling a girl's breasts. Grasping for straws, Sonny tried moving his hand downward, but it soon got entangled in Charlene's pudgy fingers.

"Quit, quit," she said, leaning her head back in expectation of a passionate kiss.

"But this is our anniversary," Sonny said. "Let's do something different."

Charlene grimly kept his hand at navel level, infuriated that he should think he really had license to go lower. That was plainly unfair, because he hadn't even given her a present. She scooted back toward her side of the cab and snatched her brassiere off the mirror.

"What are you trying to do, Sonny, get me pregnant?" she asked indignantly.

Sonny was stunned by the thought. "My lord," he said. "It was just my hand."

"Yeah, and one thing leads to another," she complained, struggling to catch the top hook of her bra. "Momma told me how that old stuff works."

Sonny reached over and hooked the hook for her, but he was more depressed than ever. It was obvious to him that it was a disgrace not to be going with someone prettier than Charlene, or if not prettier, at least someone more likable. The problem was how to break up with her and get his football jacket back.

"Well, you needn't to get mad," he said finally. "After so long a time I get tired of doing the same thing, and you do too. You wasn't no livelier than me."

"That's because you ain't good lookin' enough," she said coldly. "You ain't even got a ducktail. Why should I let you fiddle around and get me pregnant? We'll have plenty of time for that old stuff when we decide to get engaged."

Sonny twirled the knob of his steering wheel and looked out at the cold scudding water. He kept wanting to say something really nasty to Charlene, but he restrained himself. Charlene tucked her sweater back into her skirt and combed angrily at her brownish blond hair. Her mother had given her a permanent the day before and her hair was as stiff as wire.

"Let's go home," she said. "I'm done late anyway. Some anniversary."

Sonny backed the pickup around and started for the little cluster of yellow lights that was Thalia. The lake was only a couple of miles out.

"Charlene, if you feel that way I'd just as soon break up," he said. "I don't want to spoil no more anniversaries for you."

Charlene was surprised, but she recovered quickly. "That's the way nice girls get treated in this town," she said, proud to be a martyr to virtue.

"I knew you wasn't dependable," she added, taking

the football jacket and laying it on the seat between them. "Boys that act like you do never are. That jacket's got a hole in the pocket, but you needn't ask me to sew it up. And you can give me back my pictures. I don't want you showin' 'em to a lot of other boys and tellin' them how hot I am."

Sonny stopped the pickup in front of her house and fished in his billfold for the three or four snapshots Charlene had given him. One of them, taken at a swimming pool in Wichita Falls, had been taken the summer before. Charlene was in a bathing suit. When she gave Sonny the picture she had taken a ballpoint pen and written on the back of the snapshot, "Look What Legs!", hoping he would show it to Duane. The photograph showed clearly that her legs were short and fat, but in spite of it she managed to think of herself as possessing gazellelike slimness. Sonny laid the pictures on top of the football jacket, and Charlene scooped them up.

"Well, good-night," Sonny said. "I ain't got no hard feelings if you don't."

Charlene got out, but then she bethought herself of something and held the pickup door open a moment. "Don't you try to go with Marlene," she said. "Marlene's young, and she's a good Christian girl. If you try to go with her I'll tell my Daddy what a wolf you was with me and he'll stomp the you-know-what out of you."

"You was pretty glad to let me do what little I did," Sonny said, angered. "You just mind your own business and let Marlene mind hers."

Charlene gave him a last ill-tempered look. "If you've given me one of those diseases you'll be sorry," she said.

She could cheerfully have stabbed Sonny with an ice pick, but instead, to impress Marlene, she went in the house, woke her up, and cried for half the night about her blighted romance. She told Marlene Sonny had forced her to fondle him indecently.

"What in the world did it look like?" Marlene asked, bug-eyed with startled envy.

"Oh, the awfulest thing you ever saw," Charlene assured her, smearing a thick coating of beauty cream on her face. "Ouuee, he was nasty. I hope you don't ever get involved with a man like that, honey—they make you old before your time. I bet I've aged a year, just tonight."

Later, when the lights were out, Marlene tried to figure on her fingers what month it would be when Charlene would be sent away in disgrace to Kizer, Arkansas, to have her baby. They had an aunt who lived in Kizer. Marlene was not exactly clear in her mind about how one went about getting pregnant, but she assumed that with such goings on Charlene must have. It was conceivable that her mother would make Charlene leave the picture of Van Johnson behind when she was sent away, and that thought cheered Marlene very much. In any case, it would be nice to have the bedroom to herself.

CHAPTER III

After he let Charlene out Sonny drove back to town. He was amazed that breaking up with her had been so easy: all he felt was a strong sense of relief at having his football jacket back. It was the jacket he had earned in his junior year when he and Duane had been cocaptains, and it had "Cocaptain" stitched across the front in green thread. He was proud of it, and glad to have it safely out of Charlene's hands.

When he got back to the square it was midnight and the town looked just as deserted as it had looked that morning. The night watchman's old white Nash was parked where it always was, and the night watchman, a man named Andy Fanner, was asleep in the front seat, his heels propped on the dash. As usual, he had his motor running and his windows rolled up; the town thought Andy a very likely candidate for monoxide poisoning and expected any morning to find him a purplish corpse, but he slept comfortably through hundreds of winter nights with no apparent ill effects. Sonny didn't share the general worry: he had ridden in the Nash and knew there were holes enough in the floorboard to provide ample ventilation.

He drove to the all-night café and started in, but when he looked through the window he saw that his father, Frank Crawford, was sitting at the counter, sipping defensively at a cup of coffee and talking to Genevieve Morgan, the night waitress. His father liked Genevieve and Sonny liked her too, but they couldn't both talk to her at the same time so Sonny returned to the pickup and backed down the street to the square to wait for his father to come out. Waiting made him a little uneasy; somehow he couldn't help begrudging his father the nightly conversations with Genevieve. She was a shapely black-headed woman in her mid-thirties whose husband had been busted up in a rig accident almost a year before. He was not yet well enough to go back to the oil fields, and since they had two boys and were paying on a house, Genevieve had to go to work. The waitressing job was ten at night to six in the morning, and she didn't like it, but in Thalia there were not many jobs open at any hour. When she took over the night shift Sam's business had improved enormously: half the truckers and roughnecks and cowboys in that part of the country would hit the café at night, hoping to make out with Genevieve. She was beginning to thicken a bit at the waist, but she was still pretty, high-breasted, and long-legged; men accustomed to the droopy-hipped plod of most small town waitresses liked the way Genevieve carried herself. Sonny liked it himself and had as many fantasies about Genevieve as he had about Jacy Farrow.

He hadn't been parked long when he saw his father leave the café and come walking up the empty street toward the square, shivering and shaking. All he ever wore was summer slacks and a thin cotton jacket, too short at the wrists. Sonny felt briefly guilty for not offering him a ride to the hotel. He would have, but his father would only try to give him ten dollars and that would make them both nervous. It would not be worth it to either of them to get in a money argument that late at night. Money arguments often upset them for hours. Frank couldn't help offering it and Sonny couldn't help refusing to take it. Sonny did not want it, nor could he see how his father could possibly do without it, as high as his prescriptions were. Frank Crawford was not the town's only drug addict, but he was the one with the best excuse: he had been high-school principal in Thalia, until his car wreck. One night he was coming home from a high-school football game and sideswiped a cattle truck. Sonny's mother was killed and Frank was injured so badly that six operations failed to restore him to health. He couldn't stand the strain of teaching, tried to learn pharmacy and failed, and finally had to settle for the job at the domino hall. He got through life on prescriptions, but the prescriptions didn't make him feel any better about the fact that his son was living in a rooming house rather than in a proper home.

Sonny was a little afraid his father might spot the pickup, but Frank Crawford had his chin tucked down and the cold wind made his eyes water so badly that he hardly even saw the street. He passed under the blinking traffic light and went into the hotel, and Sonny quickly started the pickup and drove back to the café. Five soldiers had just come out and were standing around their car flipping quarters to see who

31

drove the next stint. Their car had Kansas license plates and the boy who lost the toss looked depressed at the thought of how far there was to go.

When Sonny went in Genevieve was back in the kitchen cleaning off the grill. He sat down at the counter and tapped the countertop with a fifty-cent piece until she came out of the kitchen to see who the customer was.

"Surprise," he said. "I guess I'll have a cheeseburger to go to bed on."

"You would," Genevieve said, far from surprised. She went back to the kitchen and slapped a hamburger patty on her clean grill. When the burger was ready she carried it right past Sonny and set it down at one of the red leatherette booths. Then she got a glass of milk for him and a cup of coffee for herself.

"If you'll sit in that booth I'll keep you company," she said.

Sonny was quick to obey. The steam from her coffee rose between them as he ate his cheeseburger. The window by the booth was all fogged over, but the misted glass was cold to the touch, and the knowledge that the freezing wind was just outside made the booth seem all the cozier. Genevieve sat quietly, her hands on the coffee cup; the warmth against her palms was lovely, but it made her a little too nostalgic for all the winter nights she had spent at home, sleeping against her husband. Then her whole body had felt as warm and comfortable as her palms felt against the cup.

"Your dad was in a few minutes ago," she said, raising her arm to tuck a strand of black hair in place.

"Guess I just missed him," Sonny said quickly.

"Where'd you hide?" she asked, giving him a perceptive grin. Her teeth were a little uneven, but strong. Sonny pretended he hadn't understood her and tried to think of a way to change the subject. Charlene was the only thing that occurred to him.

"I guess you'll have to be my girl friend now," he said. "Me and Charlene broke up tonight."

"It was about time. I better take advantage of the situation while I can. Come on back in the kitchen and have a piece of pie while I do some dishwashing."

Sonny gladly went with her, but he was painfully aware that she was only joking about being his girl friend. He sat in a chair and ate a big piece of apricot pie while Genevieve attended to a sinkful of dishes. For a minute, lost in her work, she forgot Sonny completely and he felt free to watch her. Gallons of hot water poured into the sink and working over it soon had her sweating. Her cheeks and forehead shone with it; there were beads on her upper lip, and the armpits of her green uniform darkened. The errant strand of hair hung over her forehead when she bent to fish the knives and forks out of the water. As always, Sonny found himself strongly affected by her. Sweat, if it was Genevieve's, seemed a very intimate and feminine moisture. Even Jacy didn't affect him quite as strongly; beside Genevieve, Jacy seemed strangely diminished, and apparently Jacy knew it. She always made Duane take her to the drive-in rather than the café when they ate together.

When Genevieve finished her dishes she glanced over at Sonny and saw that he seemed rather melancholy.

"Honey, you shouldn't be down in the mouth about Charlene," she said. "You put up with her long enough. She didn't even have a good disposition."

"I ain't blue about her," Sonny said, handing her the pie dish.

When she asked him why he was blue, he shrugged, not knowing what to say. He was blue because he wanted her and knew he would never have her, but that wasn't something he could talk about. "There ain't nobody to go with in this town," he said finally. "Jacy's the only pretty girl in high school, and Duane's got her."

Genevieve squeezed out her gray dishrag. "I'd call that his tough luck," she said. "She'll bring him more misery than she'll ever be worth. She's just like her grandmother. Besides, I doubt Lois and Gene want her marrying a poor boy."

"What's the matter with them?" Sonny asked. "Why do they think everybody has to be rich?"

"Oh, I don't guess they do," Genevieve said. "I oughtn't to even talk about them. We were all good friends once. Gene and Dan roughnecked together when we first moved here and we all went to dances together. Lois' mother had disowned her and she and Gene were livin' in a little one-room place over the newspaper office. She couldn't even afford a flour-sack apron, much less a mink coat."

Genevieve untied her own apron, which was damp from having been pressed against the sink. She stared at the floor a moment, her look full of memory.

"I'll always have a soft spot for Lois," she said. "Lois is some woman. Gene just never could handle her. Since he started making his strikes we haven't seen much of one another. When folks get rich all of a sudden it makes them feel sort of guilty to be around folks who've stayed poor."

"I hate people like that," Sonny said.

Genevieve sighed and got herself a fresh apron. "You oughtn't to," she said. "It's perfectly natural. I've always wondered what would have happened if Dan had bought the rig and made the strikes. They offered that rig to Dan first. In fact, Gene Farrow tried to get Dan to go partners with him on it, but when it comes to money Dan Morgan never took a chance in his life. If we had made the money we might be just as touchy about it now as they are. It can change people, you know."

Sonny looked at her curiously. He could not imagine Genevieve rich.

"Do you wish you all had made it?" he asked.

"Oh sure," she said, smiling tiredly. "I wish we'd made it."

Sonny handed her a ten-dollar bill in payment for the cheeseburger.

"Your dad give you this?" she asked.

He shook his head. "I never take money from him if I can help it. He needs all he's got."

Genevieve frowned, and Sonny nervously began popping toothpicks out of the toothpick machine. "It wouldn't hurt you to take a little something from him once in a while," she said. "You're the only boy I know who won't even let his own father give him money."

But Sonny had his mind on other things. "I hear Dan's goin' back to work soon," he said. "I guess you'll be quittin' work before long."

Genevieve slapped at his hand to make him let the toothpicks alone, but she was touched by the question. Of all the boys who had crushes on her, Sonny

35

was her favorite. Also, he had the worst crush, and was the most vulnerable. She watched a moment as he walked over to the brightly lit jukebox and stooped to catch his reflection in the shiny plastic dome. He got out his pocket comb and began to comb his brown hair. He was so young and so intent on himself that the sight of him made her feel good about life for a moment; she almost wanted to cry, and since her husband's accident that was something she only dared do in moments of optimism.

"Honey, we got four thousand dollars' worth of doctor bills to pay," she said finally. "I'll probably be making cheeseburgers for your grandkids."

Sonny shoved his comb back in his hip pocket. Four thousand dollars in debts was something he couldn't really imagine; it was a misfortune, of course, but somehow he felt lighter about things. He went back and got one more toothpick to show Genevieve he wasn't intimidated.

She ignored him and drew herself another cup of coffee. It was such a cold night that there probably wouldn't be any more customers until the bus came through at 3 A.M., and then it would only be the bus driver. The only time anyone ever got on or off in Thalia was when some soldierboy was coming home on leave or else going back to his base. The two hours before the bus came were the loneliest of the night.

"See you," Sonny said. "If I knew how to cook I'd stay and substitute for you."

Genevieve was idly peeling the polish off a fingernail, while her coffee cooled. "If you knew how to cook I'd let you," she said.

When he got within a block of the rooming house,

36

Sonny killed his motor and let the pickup coast up to the curb. Sometimes just the sound of a pickup would waken Old Lady Malone. He tiptoed in, trying to miss all the squeaky boards. When Old Lady Malone woke up she always came slopping down the hall in her dead husband's house shoes to tell Sonny to be sure and turn out his fire. Then she frequently went in the bathroom and made bad smells for half an hour.

His room was discouragingly cold, and smelled dusty. Things always smelled dusty after the wind had been blowing for a day or two. He considered reading for a while, but there was nothing there to read except a couple of old *Reader's Digest*s and a few sports magazines. He had read them all so many times he had them practically memorized.

That morning he hadn't bothered to make his bed and the quilts were all in a heap. He undressed and snuggled under the heap, his mind returning at once to Genevieve. Not Genevieve at the café, though— Genevieve naked, just out of her bath, with the ends of her black hair dampened and drops of water on her breasts. In a room so dry, with the dusty air chafing his nostrils, the thought of Genevieve dripping water was very exciting; but unfortunately the fantasy was disturbed by his feet poking out from under the ill-arranged covers into the cold air. For a moment he attempted to kick the covers straight but they were too tangled. He had to get up, turn on the light, and make the bed, all the while somewhat embarrassed by his own tumescence. Like most of his friends he went through life half-convinced that the adults of Thalia would somehow detect even his most secret erections

LARRY McMURTRY

and put them down in the book against him. The chill of the room and his own nervousness were distracting, and by the time the quilts were spread right his only thought was to get under them and get warm. Before he could reestablish his picture of Genevieve naked he was asleep.

CHAPTER IV

The one really nice thing about high school in Thalia was that it gave everybody a chance to catch up on their sleep. Sonny and Duane habitually slept through their three study halls and were often able to do a considerable amount of sleeping in class. Working as hard as they did, school was the only thing that saved them. Occasionally they tried to stay awake in English class, but that was only because John Cecil, the teacher, was too nice a man to go to sleep on.

When they got to English class on Monday morning Jacy was already there, wearing a new blue blouse and looking fresh and cheerful. Mr. Cecil sat on his desk, and he also looked happy. He had on a brown suit and an old green tie that had been knotted so many times the edges were beginning to unravel. His wife Irene kept the family accounts and had decided the tie was good for one more year. She was a fat bossy woman and their two little girls took after her. Yet somehow, despite his family, Mr. Cecil managed to keep liking people. When he wasn't actually teaching he was always hauling a carload of kids somewhere, to a fair

39

or a play or a concert. In the summertime he often hauled carloads of boys over to an irrigation ditch where they could swim. He didn't swim himself but he loved to sit on the bank and watch the boys.

"Well, I wonder what my chances are of interesting you kids in John Keats this morning," he said, when the class was settled.

"None at all," Duane said, and everybody laughed. Mr. Cecil laughed too—it was all in fun. The kids didn't hold it against him that he liked poetry, and he didn't hold it against them that they didn't. He read them whatever poetry he felt like reading, and they dozed or got other homework done and didn't interrupt. Once in a while he told good stories about the poets' lives; Lord Byron and all his mistresses interested the boys in the class a good deal. They agreed among themselves that Lord Byron must have been a great cocksman, but why he had bothered to write poetry they couldn't figure.

While Mr. Cecil was trying to decide what poetry to read that day Sonny got Joe Bob Blanton's algebra homework and began to copy it. For a year or two it had been necessary to threaten to whip Joe Bob before he would hand over his problems, but in time he began to want to be popular and handed them over willingly. That morning, to everyone's surprise, he held up his hand and got in an argument with Mr. Cecil over one of Keats's poems.

"I read the one about the nightingale," he said. "It didn't sound so good to me. It sounded like he wanted to be a nightingale, and I think it's silly of all these poets to want to be something besides what the Lord made them. It's criticizing the Lord."

Everybody snickered except Mr. Cecil. Joe Bob was sort of religion crazy, but nobody could blame him for it, considering the family he had. He was even a preacher himself, already: the summer before he had gone to church camp and got the call. Everybody figured Joe Bob had just done it to get a little extra attention from the girls at the church camp, but if that was it it sure backfired. So far as Brother Blanton was concerned the Lord's call was final: once you heard it you were a preacher forever. He started Joe Bob preaching sermons right away.

Mr. Cecil never quite knew what to do when Joe Bob got started. "Oh, I don't really think he wanted to be a nightingale, Joe Bob," he said. "Maybe he just wanted to be immortal."

Joe Bob was not satisfied with that either; he took out his pocket comb and slicked back his blond hair.

"All you have to do to be immortal is lead a good Christian life," he said. "Anybody can do it if they love the Lord, and you can't do it by writing poems anyway."

"Maybe not, maybe not," Mr. Cecil said, chuckling a little. "Here, now let me read you this."

He started reading the "Ode on a Grecian Urn," but the class was not listening. Joe Bob, having said his say, had lost interest in the whole matter and was doing his chemistry. Duane was catching a little nap, and Jacy was studying her mouth in a little mirror she kept behind her English book—she had been considering changing her lipstick shade but didn't want to do so hastily. Sonny looked out the window, and Mr. Cecil read peacefully on until the bell rang.

Civics class was next, a very popular class. Sonny

and Duane had taken the precaution to sit in the back of the room, so they could cheat or sleep or do whatever they wanted to, but actually, in civics class, they could have done about as much if they had been sitting in the front row. Coach Popper taught civics— if what he did could be called teaching—and he could not have cared less what went on.

Not only was the coach the dumbest teacher in school, he was also the laziest. Three days out of four he would go to sleep in class while he was trying to figure out some paragraph in the textbook. He didn't even know the Pledge of Allegiance, and some of the kids at least knew that. When he went to sleep, he never woke up until the bell rang, and the kids did just as they pleased. Duane usually took a nap, and Joe Bob made a big point of reading the Bible. The only girl in class was a big ugly junior named Agnes Bean; the boys who didn't have anything else to do teased her. Leroy Malone, Old Lady Malone's grandson, sat right behind Agnes and kept the class amused by popping her brassiere strap against her back. Once he made her so mad popping the strap that Agnes reached under the desk, slipped off her brogan shoe, and turned and cold-cocked him with it before he could get his guard up. His nose bled all over his desk and he had to get up and sneak down to the rest room and hold wet towels on it until it stopped.

Another time, for meanness, the boys all ganged up on Joe Bob and stuck him out the window. They hung on to his ankles and let him dangle upside down a while, assuring him that if he yelled and woke up the coach they would drop him. Nobody was sure whether they really would have dropped him or not, but Joe Bob was sensible and kept quiet. The classroom was just on the second floor, so the fall might not have hurt him much even if they had dropped him.

After civics there was a study hall, and then lunch, a boring time. One year Duane and Jacy had been able to sneak off to the lake and court during lunch, but it was only because Lois Farrow was drinking unusually hard that year and wasn't watching her daughter too closely. Lois was the only woman in Thalia who drank and made no bones about it. That same year Gene Farrow gave a big barbecue out at a little ranch he owned, and all his employees were invited. Duane was roughnecking for Gene then and took Sonny along on his invitation. Lois was there in a low-necked yellow dress, drinking whiskey as fast as most of the roughnecks drank beer. She was also shooting craps with anyone who cared to shoot with her. That was the day that Abilene won over a thousand dollars shooting craps, six hundred of it from Lois and the other four hundred from Lester Marlow, who was Jacy's official date. Lois thought Abilene cheated her and wanted Gene to fire him on the spot, but Gene wouldn't. She cussed them both out, got in her Cadillac, and started for town, but the steering wheel got away from her as the Cadillac was speeding up and she smashed into a mesquite tree. Lois just got out, gave everybody a good hard look, and started to town on foot. Nobody stopped her. Gene Farrow got drunk and Abilene kept gambling. While he was rolling dice with Lester, Duane took Jacy over behind some cars and in the excitement almost got her brassiere off. Sonny himself won $27 in a blackjack game, and he was not even an employee. That night somebody busted Lois' lip and blacked her eye; some thought Gene Farrow did it but others claimed it was Abilene. He had known the

43

Farrows before they were rich, and he wasn't a man to put up with much name calling, and nobody but Lois would have had the guts to call him names in the first place; if there was anything in the world she was scared of nobody knew what it was. She was a tall, rangy blonde, still almost as slim as her daughter, and she was not in the habit of walking around anyone.

If you didn't have someone to sneak off and court with, all there was to do at lunchtime was play volleyball. The one alternative amusement was watching the Melly brothers, George and Ed, who ordinarily spent their lunch hour jacking off in the boys' rest room. The Melly boys lived on a broken-down farm in the western part of the county, and had very few pleasures. Freshmen and sophomores got a kick out of watching them go at it, but it was really beneath the attention of seniors like Sonny and Duane.

As classes were being dismissed that afternoon Coach Popper announced that anyone interested in coming out for basketball should be in the gym in fifteen minutes. Basketball was not a big deal sport in Thalia; Sonny and Duane only went out because they were seniors and felt obligated. Also, the road trips were nice because the boys' and girls' teams rode on the same school bus. When all candidates were assembled in the boys' dressing room there turned out to be only nine boys there, not even enough for two teams. It was no real surprise: Thalia was generally conceded to have about the most miserable basketball team in the state. On a few spectacularly dismal occasions they had managed to lose games by over a hundred points.

The nine boys began to get into their jockey straps

and shorts, and were rubbing foot toughener on their feet when Coach Popper came in from the equipment room. He wore a green fatigue jacket that he had swiped from the army and he was dragging two big sacks of basketballs. He was big and he was proud of it: two hundred and thirty-five pounds, at least half of it gut.

As soon as he got to the dressing room he stopped and took a quick tally. His countenance darkened.

"Goddammit!" he said. "Ain't there but nine of you little farts? Forty-six boys in this high school, ain't but nine come out? If this ain't a piss-ignorant place to have to coach. Where's Joe Bob, anyhow? The least that little piss-ant can do is come out for basketball."

"He's home jackin' off," Leroy said. "Or else he's readin' the Bible. That's all he does, one or the other."

"You all take ten laps and get out there and shoot some free throws," the coach said. "I'm going down to the church and get him. He ain't worth a shit but he's easy to find and I ain't gonna drive all over this country looking for basketball players. I ain't gonna hold no practice unless we got at least two teams, either."

He hitched his pants up over his big, sagging belly and went out the door.

All but two or three of the boys ignored the ten-lap command and began shooting whatever kind of shots came into their heads. The only one who actually ran all ten laps was Bobby Logan, the most conscientious athlete in school. Bobby liked to stay in shape and always trained hard; he was smart, too, but he was such a nice kid that nobody held it against him. He was the coach's special favorite.

45

When the coach came back he had Joe Bob at his heels. By that time all the boys were throwing three-quarter court peg shots, like Ozark Ike in the comics. Balls were bouncing everywhere. Once in a game Sonny had seen an Indian boy from Durant, Oklahoma, actually make a three-quarter court peg shot in the last five seconds of play. It didn't really win the game for Durant, because they were already leading Thalia by about sixty-five points, but it impressed Sonny, and he resolved to start trying a few himself.

"Hey, quit chunkin' them balls, you little dumbasses," Coach Popper yelled. "Just for that we'll have some wind sprints."

Joe Bob was standing just behind the coach, combing his hair. The coach happened to turn around and the sight made him so mad he grabbed Joe Bob's comb and threw it up in the stands as high as he could. "Get your skinny ass suited out," he said. All the boys grinned when Joe Bob went into the dressing room because while the coach was gone they had mixed a little glue in with the foot toughener. If Joe Bob used any of the foot toughener he would probably have to keep his socks on for about three weeks.

The coach divided the boys into two teams and put them to running simple plays. He sat in a bridge chair with a blue towel around his neck and watched them, yelling from time to time. He had a little paper cup for his tobacco juice sitting by the chair. The loudest he yelled all afternoon was when a freshman who hadn't yet learned to dribble let a ball knock the cup over. They spent the last twenty minutes of practice running wind sprints up and down the gym. Joe Bob's feet were so badly blistered by that time that he had to hop the last two wind sprints on one leg. Some of the freshmen were no better off, and Coach Popper thought it was a hilarious sight.

"Tough it out, boys, tough it out," he yelled. "You got to be men like the rest of us, ain't none of you pretty enough to be women."

In the dressing room there was a great laugh when it turned out Joe Bob had used the foot toughener after all. The only reason he could get his socks off at all was that he had almost solid blisters and the blisters peeled loose a lot easier than the glue. When Coach Popper saw the sight he laughed till he cried. "You might try boilin' 'em off, Joe Bob," he said. "It wouldn't be no harder on your feet."

In fact, the coach made matters even worse for Joe Bob by horsing around and trying to grab his pecker.

"Look at that little worm there," he said, making a grab. "What kind of female you ever gonna get with that thing for bait, Joe? Wouldn't do for a six-year-old girl."

He kept laughing and grabbing, backing Joe Bob around the room until finally Joe Bob couldn't stand it anymore and ran to the showers with one sock still on.

"Another minute and I'd have had him bawling," the coach said jovially, sitting down to take off his tennis shoes.

It was all pretty funny, the boys thought, but when they came out of the shower something happened that wasn't so funny. Everybody was horsing around, popping towels and grabbing at one another's nuts, like they usually did after practice. Duane and Sonny and Bobby Logan were having a little three-way towel fight, and the trouble started when Duane caught Bobby a smacker on the hip. It was just a flat pop and didn't hurt Bobby at all, but the coach happened to be coming out of the shower about that time and for some reason it made him furious. He was naked except for a whistle around his neck, but he grabbed a towel and laid into Sonny and Duane. He let one fly at Duane that would have castrated him on the spot if it had landed. "I'll show you little fuckers some towel fightin'," he said. The boys were too surprised to fight back: they just retreated into a corner where there were benches and clothes hangers to block some of the coach's shots. His wet hair was down in his face and he was snorting and puffing like a mad boar hog.

In a minute or two he got over it, though, and threw the wet towel at Sonny. "No more goddamn towel fightin'," he said and went over and looked closely at Bobby Logan's hip. The freshmen were scared almost to death—one was so nervous he put his shoes on the wrong feet and wore them home that way, too scared to stop and change. The older boys had seen the coach flare up before and knew it was just a matter of surviving until he cooled off. The time he shot at Sonny it was because he thought Sonny had scared away a dove he was sneaking up on. Fortunately, Sonny was a hundred yards away and wasn't hit.

"I don't understand how Mrs. Popper's lasted," Duane said, as he was dressing.

"She ain't the healthiest looking woman in town," Sonny reminded him. Mrs. Popper's name was Ruth; she was a small woman, pretty but tired and nervous looking. No one saw much of her. At Christmastime she sometimes made Sonny and Duane cookies and brought them around. Sam the Lion had known her all her life and said that she had been lovely when she was young.

48

Jacy was waiting for the boys when they came out. "My folks are gone to Wichita," she said. "Let's go get a hamburger."

They got in the convertible and drove to the drive-in, a place called The Rat-Hole. The boys were starved and ordered two hamburgers apiece; while they were cooking, Jacy and Duane smooched a little and Sonny cleaned his fingernails and looked out the back window. About the time their order came Abilene drove up in his Mercury and parked beside them. They all waved at him and he nodded in reply, barely moving his head. He was drinking a can of beer.

"You need a haircut," Jacy said, putting her hand lightly on the back of Duane's neck. They were sitting very close together, and were feeding one another French fries when the Farrows' big blue Cadillac pulled in and parked beside them. Lois Farrow was driving. She had her sunglasses on, even though it was a cloudy day. Duane scooted back to his side of the car as quickly as he could, but the Farrows gave no indication that they even noticed him. In a minute Mrs. Farrow got out and walked around to Jacy's window.

"We're having supper at home tonight," she said. "As soon as the boys get through with their hamburgers you take them to town and get yourself home, you hear?"

Mrs. Farrow looked bored, even with her sunglasses on. For some reason Sonny felt scared of her, and so did Jacy and Duane. All three were nervous. Mrs. Farrow noticed Abilene sitting there and she calmly thumbed her nose at him. He gave her a finger in return and took another swallow of his beer. Lois went

49

back to the Cadillac and the three kids hastily finished their meal, Jacy dripping tears of annoyance into her strawberry milk shake.

"She didn't have to look so hateful," Jacy said, sniffling. "I just wish my grandmother was alive. She'd see we got married even if we had to run away and do it."

CHAPTER V

At the Farrow supper table an hour later, Lois and Jacy politely ignored one another, while Gene made conversation with desperate good cheer. After supper, though, he gave up, watched Groucho Marx, and then got in bed and quickly drank himself to sleep. He just wasn't built to withstand the quality of tension Lois and Jacy could generate.

The one thing Lois envied Gene was his ability to drink himself to sleep quickly. He went to sleep on so little alcohol that he was never bothered with hangovers the next day, whereas Lois had to drink for hours before the liquor would turn her off. If she just had to sleep, she took pills.

When it was almost Jacy's bedtime Lois stopped at her door for a minute, knocked, and went in. Jacy had already showered and was sitting on the bed in pink pajamas, rubbing cleansing cream into her face. Occasionally, despite her precautions, Jacy got what she called a blemish, but she took great pains with her complexion and didn't have many.

"Go on, don't let me interrupt your facial," Lois

51

said. She walked around the room, frowning. Almost every object in the room annoyed her; she couldn't decide whether Jacy simply had bad taste or had deliberately chosen ugly objects as a means of affronting her. There were five or six stuffed animals, all of which Duane had won for her at ball-throwing booths in the State Fair; they were grouped in one corner, around a large Mortimer Snerd doll, also a gift from Duane. One wall was mostly bulletin board, and every picture of Jacy or Duane that had ever appeared in the *Thalia Times* was tacked on it. In addition to the pictures there were football programs, photographs of Jacy as cheerleader (sophomore year) and as Football Queen (junior year), the menu of the junior dinner dance, the program of the junior play, and many other mementos. On the bedside table there was a framed picture of Duane, and on the wall, a framed picture of Jesus. Next to the picture of Duane was an alarm clock and a white zipper Bible, and on the other side of the bed was Jacy's pile of movie magazines, most of them with Debbie Reynolds on the cover. Debbie Reynolds was Jacy's ideal.

"Well, I guess you hate me tonight, right?" Lois said.

"Oh, Momma, you know I love you," Jacy said, wiping the cream off. "But I love Duane too, even if you don't like it."

"Like it? Liking it or disliking it hasn't entered my head, because I don't believe it. Who you love is your own pretty self and *what* you really love is knowing you're pretty—I'm sure he tells you how pretty you are all the time so I don't doubt you're fond of him. Even your grandmother learned that much about you. And you *are* pretty, you ought to enjoy it. I'd just sort of hate to see you marry Duane, though, because in about two months he'd quit flattering you and you wouldn't be rich anymore and life wouldn't be near as much fun for you as it is right now."

"But I don't care about money," Jacy said solemnly. "I don't care about it at all."

Lois sighed. "You're pretty stupid then," she said. "If you're that stupid you ought to go and marry him—it would be the cheapest way to educate you."

Jacy was so shocked at being called stupid that she didn't even cry. Her mother knew she made straight-A report cards!

"You married Daddy when he was poor," she said weakly. "He got rich so I don't see why Duane couldn't."

"I'll tell you why, beautiful," Lois said. "I scared your daddy into getting rich. He's so scared of me that for twenty years he's done nothing but run around trying to find things to please me. He's never found the right things but he made a million dollars looking."

"If Daddy could do it Duane could too," Jacy insisted, pouting.

"Not married to you, he couldn't," Lois said. "You're not scary enough. You'd be miserable poor but as long as you had somebody to hold your hand and tell you how pretty you are you'd make out."

"Well you're miserable and you're rich," Jacy countered. "I sure don't want to be like you."

"You sound exactly like your grandmother," Lois said, looking absently out the window. "There's not much danger you'll be like me. Have you ever slept with Duane?"

It was undoubtedly the most surprising conversation Jacy had ever had!

"Me?" she said. "You know I wouldn't do that, Momma."

"Well, you just as well," Lois said quietly, a little amused at herself and at life. She never had been able to resist shocking her mother; apparently it was going to be almost as difficult to resist shocking her daughter.

"Seriously," she added. "There's no reason you shouldn't have as much fun as you're capable of having. You can come with me to the doctor sometime and we'll arrange something so you won't have to worry about babies. You do have to be careful about that."

To Jacy what she was hearing was almost beyond belief.

"But Momma," she said. "It's a sin unless you're married, isn't it? I wouldn't want to do that."

"Oh, don't be so mealymouthed," Lois shouted. "Why am I even talking to you? I just thought if you slept with Duane a few times you'd find out there really isn't anything magic about him, and have yourself some fun to boot. Maybe then you'd realize that pretty things and pretty people are what you like in life and we can send you to a good school where you'll marry some good-looking kid with the wherewithal to give you a pleasant life."

"But I don't want to leave," Jacy said plaintively. "Why can't I just stay here and go to college in Wichita?"

"Because life's too damn hard here," Lois said. "The land's got too much power over you. Being rich here is a good way to go insane. Everything's flat and empty and there's nothing to do but spend money."

She walked over to Jacy's dresser and picked up the big fifty-dollar bottle of Chanel No. 5 that Gene had given his daughter the Christmas before.

"May I have some of your perfume?" she asked. "I suddenly feel like smelling good."

"Help yourself," Jacy said, suddenly wishing her mother were gone. "Don't you have any?"

"Yes, but this is right here, and I feel like smelling good right now. Do you ever feel like doing anything right now?"

She wet her palms and fingertips with perfume and placed her hands against her throat, then touched her fingers behind her ears. The cool scent was delicious. She dampened her hands again, touched her shoulders, and then stooped and ran her palms down the calves of her legs.

"That's lovely," she said. Almost at once the perfume made her feel less depressed, and when she looked at Jacy again she noticed how young she was. Jacy's hair was pulled back by a headband, and her face, clean of makeup, was so clearly a girl's face that Lois ceased to feel angry with her.

"This is the first time in months I've seen your eyelids," she said. "You should leave your face just like that—it would win you more. Makeup is just sort of a custom you've adopted. All you really need right now is an eyebrow pencil."

Jacy looked blank and sleepy and Lois knew her advice was wasted.

"Okay," she said. "I'll let you alone. I probably confused you tonight and I do hope so. If I could just

55

confuse you it would be a start. The only really important thing I came in to tell you was that life is very monotonous. Things happen the same way over and over again. I think it's more monotonous in this part of the country than it is in other places, but I don't really know that—it may be monotonous everywhere. I'm sick of it, myself. Everything gets old if you do it often enough. I don't particularly care who you marry, but if you want to find out about monotony real quick just marry Duane."

With that she left and walked down the thickly carpeted hall to her bedroom. As she walked through the door she heard her husband snoring; the only light in the room was the tiny orange glow of the electric blanket control. Lois sat down on the bed and rubbed her calves wearily. To kill the morning she had gone to Wichita Falls and spent $150; to kill the afternoon she had had three drinks and several rubbers of bridge at the country club. It seemed unjust that after all that work she should still have the problem of how to kill the night. She got up and went out in the hall, where she could see her wristwatch. It was only a little after ten.

After considering a moment she went to the kitchen and got a whiskey glass out of the cabinet. Bourbon was her night drink. She picked up the wall phone and dialed the poolhall and Sam the Lion answered.

"Hi, friend," she said. "How are you?"

"Hi, honey," Sam said. "I'm winterin' fairly well. How about you?"

"Oh, I won't complain," Lois said. "I wish you'd come and see me sometime. Has your number one customer left for the night?"

"No, he's here shootin'," Sam said. "I'll let you talk

to him as soon as he finishes his run. You come and see me, you got a car."

In a minute or so Abilene took the phone. "Yeah," he said.

"Hey. Feel like a night off?"

"Depends on the salary," he replied.

"Well, drill hard," she said. "You're better at oil wells anyway."

She took her bourbon into the den and switched the TV on. A Claudette Colbert movie was just starting. She pulled her bathrobe around her and settled back in Gene's big leather chair to watch. From time to time she rubbed her calves. When the third commercial came on she went back to the kitchen and refilled her whiskey glass.

CHAPTER VI

After civics class Tuesday morning Coach Popper stopped Sonny in the hall. There had been an assembly that morning and the coach had on a necktie, an article of dress he seldom wore.

"Like your tie, Coach," Sonny said jokingly. It was a bright orange necktie and it stuck out from under the coach's shirt collar in the back.

"Purty, ain't it," the coach said distractedly. "Need you to do somethin' for me. Ruth's been sick the last couple of days and needs somebody to drive her to Olney to the doctor. She's afraid they might drug her or something so she wouldn't be able to drive home. If you'll drive her down and back I'll get you out of your afternoon classes."

Sonny immediately accepted the offer. He was for anything that would get him out of algebra class. The Poppers' house was only a couple of blocks from school and as soon as he finished lunch he walked over. He looked through the doorpanes before he knocked and saw that Mrs. Popper was ready to go. She was sitting in the living room, her purse in her lap.

"Oh hello, Sonny, what do you want?" she asked, when she came to the door.

"Coach said you needed a driver," he said. "I thought he told you I was coming."

Mrs. Popper looked disappointed but she tried hard to hide it. "No, he didn't mention it," she said. "I thought he was going to drive me himself. I guess he just couldn't get off."

She handed Sonny the keychain and he went and got the car out of their garage. It was a black '53 Chevy. When Mrs. Popper got in she had a Kleenex in her hand and was daubing at her eyes with it. Sonny felt like he ought to say something to cheer her up, but he couldn't think of anything. The Chevy didn't have much pickup but it ran smoothly once they got on the road. The wind was rustling dust in the dry bar ditches beside the highway.

"I'm sorry to be all this trouble," Mrs. Popper said. "You're very nice to drive me."

"It sure beats sittin' through algebra," he said.

Mrs. Popper smiled, but neither of them spoke again, all the way to Olney. Sonny watched the road, only glancing at her occasionally; she was looking out the window at the gray pastures. Her hair was brown with just a few traces of gray, and she wore it long, almost shoulder length. There was something about her that was really pretty. She was a little too thin, and her skin was too fair for the country she lived in: wind and sun freckled her on her cheekbones and beneath her eyes. Just before they got to the clinic she opened her purse and got out her lipstick, but she just held it a minute and put it back in her purse without using any.

While she was with the doctor Sonny sat in the

59

waiting room of the clinic, reading magazines. There were lots of copies of *Outdoor Life* around, with good hunting stories in them. The only trouble was that the people in the waiting room made him so gloomy he could hardly read. A shaky old man sat next to him on the green waiting-room couch. He had had his voicebox taken out and had a little screen where it ought to be; every third breath he wheezed so loud that Sonny couldn't concentrate on his reading. Then a little boy came over and spat his bubble gum in the pot of a rubber plant next to Sonny. It was a pink, wet hunk of bubble gum and Sonny kept wanting to cover it with dirt. Across the room from him there was a farmer and his wife with an old old lady between them. They were very nervous, and Sonny knew why because he had seen them there several times before: if they had to wait too long the old lady would start going to the bathroom right in her chair. It was very embarrassing, but then something about the waiting room was always embarrassing. When his father had still been getting regular shots Sonny had had to wait there often, and it hadn't changed a bit.

Finally the wheezing and the bubble gum and the old old lady got on his nerves so much that he went out and waited in the car. The coach was too tight to have a radio put in the car, so there was nothing to do but sit and look out the long empty street toward the west. Someone in a passing car threw out an empty ice-cream carton and the wind skittered it across the street to the far curb.

When Mrs. Popper finally came out she was walking so stiffly that Sonny thought they must have given her the drug after all; then when she got close he saw that she walked that way because she was crying. The wind blew her hair across her face and a few strands stuck to her wet cheek. She tried awkwardly to brush them back. Sonny got out and opened the door for her, wondering what he ought to do. He knew nothing at all about crying women.

He got in and drove back through Olney, thinking surely she would quit, but she didn't. She was not crying loudly, but she was crying.

"Would you like for me to take you to the hospital?" he asked. "I don't have to be back to school by any special time."

"Oh no," Mrs. Popper said, straightening up. She shook the tears out of her eyes so hard that two or three drops splattered on the dashboard. "I'm just scared," she said. "I have to have an operation tomorrow for a tumor in my breast."

The rest of the way home she sat quietly, but it wasn't really that she was just sitting, either. It seemed to Sonny that in some way she was pulling at him, trying to get him to say something to her. He would have been glad to say something to her, only he had no idea what to say. Even algebra class would have been better than what she was doing: nobody had ever pulled at him in such a strange way. It made him so nervous that he grew careless and let the car edge off the shoulder of the road. After that he concentrated very hard on his driving.

When they got to her house Sonny drove the car on into the garage. He got out, relieved that it was over, but Mrs. Potter kept sitting in the front seat as if she didn't know she was home or in her garage or any-where. She wasn't crying, just sitting there. After a minute Sonny went around and opened the door for her.

"Oh," she said. "Thank you."

"Here's the car keys," Sonny said. "I guess I better go back to school."

"No, not yet," Ruth said. "If you can stand me for a few more minutes I'd like you to come in and have cookies and a Coke." She looked at him apologetically, but she didn't take the car keys.

Sonny knew he couldn't get out of going in. Somehow or other Mrs. Popper had got in control and he didn't know anything to do about it. Reluctantly he followed her through the back door and into the kitchen. The yellow kitchen linoleum was old and worn out.

"Just sit at the table," Mrs. Popper said. There was something wild in her face that made Sonny think of his father—when she smiled at him there was a pressure behind the smile, as if something inside her were trying to break through her skin.

"Would you like milk or a Coke?" she asked. "I'm really sorry I made you come in—you can go right now if you like. For a minute I was just scared to be alone."

Sonny said he would take a Coke. She got one, and set a plate of thin Nabisco cookies on the table with it. For a minute of two, watching him eat, she seemed to be getting all right, and then to his amazement and disgust she burst out crying again, loudly. She put her head in her arms and sobbed, her body shaking as if she had the heaves. Sonny was sure she must be crazy and he wanted to be away from her. He didn't even want to swallow the bite he had in his mouth. Mrs. Popper seemed to know what he was thinking; she looked up at him and tried to quit crying.

"You'll never forgive me, I know," she said. "You

think I'm pitiable, you're disgusted. Go on away if you want to, you don't have to stay any longer."

"Thank you for the Coke," Sonny said hastily, taking her at her word. "Maybe you'll get to feeling better after your operation."

"Oh no, it's not the operation," she said, wiping her face with a yellow table napkin. "It's not the operation at all. The tumor probably won't be dangerous. It's just that thinking about it makes me so lonely I can't stand it."

"Well, I guess you'll be glad when basketball season is over," Sonny said, feeling a little more kindly toward her. "Coach probably doesn't get to stay home much during football and basketball season."

Mrs. Popper laid down her napkin and looked at Sonny as if she were seeing him for the first time. She quit crying and became completely calm. "My God," she said. "You don't know a thing about it, do you?"

Then she did a thing which he would never forget: she got up, came around the table, put out her hand, and traced her fingers down his jaw almost to his mouth. Her fingers were cool. She put her hand on his head for a minute, felt his hair against her palm and between her fingers, and then quickly reached down for one of his hands and pressed it against her cheek and throat. She held his hand there for a moment and then laid it back on the table as carefully as if it were a piece of china.

"I know I mustn't be that way," she said, and again it looked as if something were pushing at the inside of her skin. Sonny felt very confused, but no longer particularly scared or particularly anxious to get away. From the way she touched him and looked at him he knew she had thought about kissing him when she put her hand on his face. He didn't know what would have happened, because he had no idea how it would feel to kiss someone older than himself, someone who was married. But when he looked at Mrs. Popper's mouth he wished that she had gone ahead, or that he had done something. He was sure it would have been nice to kiss her, much nicer than it had been to kiss Charlene.

But Mrs. Popper went back to her own chair and looked at the splotch on the tablecloth her tears had made.

"Here I am wanting to tell you I'm sorry again," she said, smiling a little. "I know I've given you a bad afternoon. For ten seconds there I was ready to try and seduce you, if you know what that means. To tell you the honest truth, I don't know what it means myself. I've never seduced anyone and I've never been seduced, but I've always liked the word. I thought if I was ever going to find out what it meant it had better be now."

She sighed. "I don't guess you can imagine being seduced by the wife of your coach. I'm not so terribly pretty and I don't think you even like me. It probably wouldn't be best for you to be seduced by a forty-year-old woman you don't even like. Do you have a girl friend?"

"I did have," Sonny said. "We broke up last Saturday night."

"Why did you break up?" she asked. "Do you mind talking? I wish I wasn't so avid. You don't really have to answer my questions if you don't want to."

"I was going with Charlene Duggs," Sonny said. Something had changed; he felt more comfortable with Mrs. Popper than he had all afternoon.

"Charlene thought I got fresh with her, but I never did, really. I guess the reason we broke up was because we didn't like one another much to begin with."

"I shouldn't be sad about it, if I were you," Ruth said. "I know Charlene and I don't think she's nearly nice enough for you. Even I would be better for you than she would."

She put her fingers to her temples and smoothed back her hair. "Besides, she must be a dumb creature, not to appreciate you. I can't even imagine how it would be to be young and have someone like you get fresh with me."

Sonny decided she really was a little crazy, but he liked her anyway. He even wanted to compliment her in some way, say something that would make her feel nice.

"I already like you better than I ever liked her," he said, wondering if it was a wrong thing to say.

Mrs. Popper's face lightened—she looked glad that he had said it. They were silent for a moment and Sonny finished his cookies and Coke. There was no longer a reason for him to stay, but he kept sitting, hoping that Mrs. Popper might want to come around the table again.

She knew that was why he was staying, too, and she did stand up, but not to come to him. She went to the sink and looked out the back window a moment before she spoke. She was not crying, but her face was sad. "Maybe you better go on to basketball practice," she said. He stood up and she walked with him to the front door.

"I see you feel you've missed a chance," Ruth said, when they were at the door. She looked at him frankly. "You see, I'm very confused, even if I look like I'm not. That's why you must go. I've got on a great many brakes right now—what I was thinking about a while ago is nothing I've ever done except with Herman, and for a long time I haven't even believed a man could want me that way. I don't know if I believe it now, even though I see you do. But then I think it isn't really *me* you want, it's only *that* . . . sex. Not that there's anything wrong with you wanting that, it's perfectly natural. . . ." She was talking faster and faster, but suddenly she stopped.

"You must really think I'm crazy," she said. "I am crazy I guess."

"Why's that?" Sonny asked.

"What?" Ruth said, caught by surprise.

"I mean why do you feel crazy? I guess I shouldn't be askin'."

"Of course you should," she said. "I was just surprised you had the nerve. The reason I'm so crazy is because nobody cares anything about me. I don't guess there's anybody I care much about, either. It's my own fault, though—I haven't had the guts to try and do anything about it. It took more guts for me to put my hand on your face than I ever thought I had, and even then I didn't have enough to go on."

She shut the screen door and they stood for a moment looking through the screen at one another. Sonny hated to leave; in some funny way he had come to like Mrs. Popper and he knew that the minute he left she would go in the house and cry again.

"Maybe I never will know what seduce means," she said quietly. "Thank you for putting up with me. You don't need to tell Herman about the operation. I'll tell him when he gets home."

Sonny was trying to think of something appropriate to say that would let her know that he really liked her, but he couldn't think of anything that didn't sound corny. Ruth noticed, and to spare him further embarrassment she shut the living-room door. When she heard his footsteps on the sidewalk she began to cry.

Basketball practice was so far along that Sonny didn't bother to suit out, but he did check in with the coach. Joe Bob and one of the freshmen had done something wrong and the coach was sitting on his bridge chair watching them run punishment laps.

"Come on, run 'em," the coach yelled. "Be men. I don't want no sissies on this team. Quit flapping your hands, Joe Bob, you look like a goddamn goose."

Sonny slipped his shoes off and took some free-throw practice with the rest of the team. He expected the coach to ask about Mrs. Popper, but he just sat on the bridge chair, chewing tobacco and occasionally scratching his balls. When he did ask, after practice, it was not exactly about Mrs. Popper—he wanted to know if the doctor had given her any prescription.

"I don't think so," Sonny said. "We didn't get any filled."

"Good," the coach said. "Damn doctors. Every time she goes over there they prescribe her ten dollars' worth of pills and they don't do a fuckin' bit of good. I tell her to take aspirin, that's all I ever take. If she's got a sore place she can rub a little analgesic balm on it—that's the best thing for soreness there is."

He didn't say so, but analgesic was also free. The school bought it by the case and the coach took what he needed.

"She wasn't feeling too good when I left her," Sonny

67

said, thinking the coach might be worried enough to hurry on home. Instead, the news seemed merely to disgust him.

"Hell, women like to be sick," he said. He was on his way to the showers, but he stopped long enough to grab a cake of soap from a passing freshman. "Ruth had rather be sick than do anything. I could have bought a new deer rifle with what she's spent on pills just this last year, and I wish I had, by God. A good gun beats a woman any day."

CHAPTER VII

I guess she just couldn't get out of it," Sonny said, chalking his cue. It was Saturday night and Duane had just found out that Jacy wasn't going to be at the picture show that evening: she was going to a country club dance with Lester Marlow.

"She wasn't sheddin' no tears over the telephone," Duane said bitterly. "She may be getting to like country club dances, that's what worries me."

He was in such a terrible mood that the pool game wasn't much fun. Jerry Framingham, a friend of theirs who drove a cattle truck, was shooting with them; he had to truck a load of yearlings to Fort Worth that night and asked them to ride along with him, since neither of them had dates.

"We might as well," Duane said. "Be better than loafin' around here."

Sonny was agreeable. While Jerry went out in the country to pick up his load he and Duane walked over to the café to have supper. Sam the Lion was there, waiting for old Marston to bring out his nightly steak. Penny was still at work and Marston was hopping to

69

get the orders out. Penny had taken to wearing orange lipstick.

The boys sat down with Sam the Lion and ordered chickenfried steaks. "Sam, how's the best way to get rich?" Duane asked.

"To be born rich," Sam said. "That's much the best way. Why?"

"I want to get that way. I want to get at least as rich as Lester Marlow."

"Well, of course," Sam said, buttering a cracker. "You're really too young to know what's good for you, though. Once you got rich you'd have to spend all your time staying rich, and that's hard thankless work. I tried it a while and quit, myself. If I can keep ten dollars ahead of the bills I'll be doin' all right."

"How much do you think Gene Farrow's worth?" Duane asked. "How rich would I have to get to be richer than him?"

"How much cash you got?" Sam asked.

"Fifty-two dollars right now. Fifty-one after we eat."

"Then cashwise I imagine you're as rich as Gene," Sam said, looking suspiciously at his salad. Marston was always sneaking cucumbers into his salads, against strict orders. Sam the Lion regarded cucumbers as a species of gourd and would not eat them.

"I doubt if Gene could lay his hands on fifty dollars tonight," he added.

Both boys were stunned. Everyone thought Gene Farrow was the richest man in town.

"Why Sam, he's bound to have lots of money," Duane said. "Mrs. Farrow's fur coat is supposed to be worth five thousand dollars."

"Probably is," Sam said. "That's five thousand he

don't have in cash, though. He's got lots of trucks and equipment and oil leases, too, but it ain't cash and there's no way of tellin' how much of it's his and how much is the bank's."

He broke a biscuit in two and wiped his gravy bowl clean. "There ain't no sure-nuff rich people in this town now," he said. "I doubt there'll ever be any more. The oil fields are about to dry up and the cattle business looks like it's going to peter out. If I had to make a guess at who was the richest man in town I'd say Abilene. He may not own nothing but his car and his clothes, but I've never seen the day when he couldn't pull a thousand dollars out of his billfold. A man with a thousand dollars in his pocket is rich, for Thalia."

Duane cheered up suddenly and began to go after his steak with good appetite. "Well that's all good news," he said. "Maybe if the Farrows go broke they won't mind my marrying Jacy."

Sam grunted his disagreement. "Penny, bring me a dish of that cobbler," he said. "Apricot. Nope, Duane, you're wrong. I don't know about Lois, but if Gene was to even think he was going broke he wouldn't want you to get within a mile of that girl. There ain't nobody snootier than an oilman who's had to sell one of his Cadillacs."

"Aw, Sam, it's not him," Duane argued. "I get along with him all right. It's Mrs. Farrow who don't like me. I bet it's her fault Jacy's off with Lester tonight."

"Well, Lois has got a lot of judgment; maybe she's doin' you a favor," Sam said. "That little girl is goin' to be a hard one to please."

Talk like that made Duane huffy. "I please her well enough," he said. Sonny wished the meal were over. It

71

was getting so Duane wanted to talk about Jacy half the time, and for some reason the conversations always left Sonny depressed.

Outside, after they had all finished, Sam the Lion slapped them on the shoulder. "Well, have fun in Cowtown," he said. "If I didn't have all these businesses to run I'd ride along with you. Ain't been to Fort Worth in fifteen years." The night was cold and sleety and he hobbled on back to the poolhall on his sore feet.

The boys walked over to the courthouse where they could wait out the wind. While they were waiting they saw Lester and Jacy drive by in Lester's Oldsmobile. Jacy wasn't sitting very close to him but as they passed under the street light the boys could see that she was laughing at something. Her hair was rolled up on her head in a fancy way.

"You don't need to look so blue about it," Sonny said. "This time next year you'll probably be married to her. Look at me, I ain't got no date either."

"Yeah, but you ain't in love," Duane said.

Finally Jerry's cattle truck screeched up to the stoplight, jam-packed with Hereford yearlings. When it stopped they all began to bawl and shove around and shit through the sideboards. The boys ran over and climbed up in the high cab—Jerry whanged the truck in gear and they were off.

"Break out the beer," Jerry said. "There's two six-packs there on the floor somewhere."

Sonny found an opener in the glove compartment. When he popped into a can the cold beer spewed all over him, its smell filling the cab. "The coach would have a shit fit if he knew we were breakin' trainin'," he said happily. For a moment Mrs. Popper crossed his mind—what would she be doing on a Saturday night? —but it was so much fun to be going down the road in a high, bouncy cattle truck that he soon forgot her. All he and Duane had to do was drink beer and watch the fence posts and the culverts whiz by; before the first six-pack was finished their troubles were forgotten and they were happily reminiscing about old times in Thalia High School, reliving all the ball games they had played and the fights and adventures they had had. Jerry Framingham enjoyed the conversation: most of the kids he had graduated with were in the army and he seldom had any company at all on his cattle hauls.

Sonny and Duane found that they were a little out of shape for beer drinking. By the time they reached Fort Worth they were both fairly drunk, and the anecdotes they were telling seemed so funny to them that it would sometimes take them three or four miles to quit laughing. One classic story simply broke them up: it was about the time they had persuaded Billy to come out for football, although he wasn't even enrolled in school. Billy knew nothing about football and hadn't thought it at all strange when they put his shoulder pads on backward, daubed foot toughener in his ears, and made him wear a jockey strap for a noseguard. When he trotted out on the field with his jockey strap on his nose the whole team had hysterics and Coach Popper laughed so hard he almost ruptured himself.

Jerry Framingham was not drunk and thus did not become uncontrollably amused when he heard such stories retold—in fact the boys' laughter seemed to irritate him a little. "You drunk bastards can't do anything but laugh," he said.

Jerry's turn came later, after they had unloaded the cattle. They were having a beer or two in a honky-tonk on North Main and Jerry talked them into putting up five dollars apiece toward a fifteen-dollar whore he knew about. They could all three have easily found five-dollar whores, but Jerry insisted on flipping to see who got the more expensive one, and he won the flips. The whore was in a dinky little North Main hotel. Sonny and Duane walked around outside, freezing their tails, while Jerry went up to have fun. They stepped inside a cheap dance hall a few minutes to warm up and watched a lot of sideburned stockyard hands dance their skinny girl friends around the room.

As soon as Jerry was done and they were back in the truck the boys went to sleep. Jerry was somewhat weakened himself and on the home side of Jacksboro he pulled the truck off the road and went to sleep himself. About four in the morning Sonny woke up, practically frozen to death. Jerry and Duane were both mashed on top of him, trying to keep warm, and the door handle was about to bore a hole in his back. The windshield was completely sleeted over. Sonny pushed around until he woke the others up and he and Jerry got out and scraped the sleet off the windshield with an old Levi jacket. While they were doing that Duane crawled over and vomited in the bar ditch. Coming back from Fort Worth was never as much fun as going.

While they had rolled around trying to sleep they had kicked the heater wires loose, so the rest of the trip home was miserably cold. The café looked like the most comfortable place in the world when they finally pulled in. Genevieve was sitting at the counter reading an old paperback of *Forever Amber* that everyone who worked at the café had read several times. When she saw what bad shape Sonny and Duane were in she put it away and fixed them some toast and coffee; as soon as they ate a little they dozed off and slept with their heads on the counter while she filled the coffee maker and got things ready for the morning business. Asleep they both had the tousled, helpless look of young children and she kept wanting to cover their shoulders with a tablecloth or something. When Marston came in she woke them up. She put on her heavy blue coat and the boys stumbled outside behind her, trying to keep their eyes open. The cold air snapped them out of it a little. Genevieve had an old gray Dodge that was hard to start and by the time she got it to kick off the boys were wide awake.

"What do you think about a woman that would make her daughter go with Lester Marlow?" Duane asked, remembering that he had a grievance.

"I don't know much about Lester, but if I had a daughter I don't know that I'd want her going with either one of you boys, the way you all cut up," she said, treating the whole matter lightly. She pulled up in front of their rooming house and raced her motor, so the old car wouldn't die.

The boys got out, thanked her, waved as the car pulled away, its exhaust white in the cold air. "Well, at least we got to go *somewhere*," Sonny said, picking up a beer can somebody had thrown out on the lawn. Fort Worth, after all, was a city, part of the big world, and he always came back from a trip there with the satisfying sense that he had traveled. They flipped to see who got the bathtub first and he won.

CHAPTER VIII

The first basketball game of the season was with Paducah, a town well over a hundred miles from Thalia. It was the longest trip of the year and usually the wildest: in Paducah they played basketball as if it were indoor football, and they had everything in their favor, including a gym so small that the out-of-bounds lines were painted on the walls. The Paducah boys were used to the gym and could run up the walls like lizards, but visiting teams, accustomed to normal-sized courts, had a hard time. Every year two or three Thalia players smashed into the walls and knocked themselves out.

This time it happened to Sonny, and in the very first minutes of play. Leroy Malone managed to trip the gangly Paducah center and while the center was sprawled on the floor Sonny ran right along his back, in pursuit of the ball. Just as he was about to grab it somebody tripped *him* and he hit the wall head first. The next thing he knew he was stretched out beside the bench and one of the freshmen players was squeezing a wet washrag on his forehead. Sonny tried to keep his eyes closed as long as he could—he knew Coach Popper would send him back into the game as soon as he regained consciousness. He feigned deep coma for about five minutes, but unfortunately the coach was experienced in such matters. He came over and lifted one of Sonny's eyelids and saw that he was awake.

"Possuming," he said. "I thought so. Get up and get your butt back in there. We're forty points behind and it ain't but the second quarter."

"I think I got a concussion," Sonny said, trying to look dangerously ill. "Maybe I ought to stay out a little while."

"Get up," the coach insisted. "We just quit football practice ten days ago, you ain't had time to get that out of shape. If you want to rest, by God go in there and foul out first. Knock the shit out of that forward two or three times—he's the one doin' all the scorin'. Hell, we come all this way, let's make a showing."

Sonny reluctantly got up and went back in. He managed three fouls before the half, but he was too weak to hit anybody very hard and none of the fouls was really satisfactory. The half-time score was Paducah 62 and Thalia 9. During the half the coach called them over for one of his little pep talks, this one very brief.

"You ten boys have got the shortest little peckers of any bunch of kids I've ever coached," he said sincerely. "By God, if you don't stomp some asses this next half I'll stomp a few tomorrow afternoon when we start practicing."

He scowled fiercely and strolled off to the concession stand to have some coffee.

In the second half things began to look really ominous. Sonny felt strangely lightheaded and went out on the floor not much caring what he did. Paducah defense had become virtually impenetrable: for one thing, they had started openly tackling whichever Thalia player had the ball. It seemed to Sonny that at last the time had come to shoot peg shots—there was not much chance of moving the ball down the court any other way. Whenever they tried, Paducah tackled them, tripped them, threw body blocks into them, or had the referee call fouls on them.

Actually, the refereeing was another very bad aspect of basketball in Paducah. Unusual as it was, Paducah had a male home economics teacher, a frail little man named Mr. Wean. The school board felt that teaching home ec was really too light a job for a man so they made Mr. Wean basketball referee. He had never managed to learn much about the game, but he was quite docile and called whatever the Paducah team told him to call. Also, he was in bad shape and couldn't possibly run up and down the court for forty-eight minutes. Instead of following the ball, he just stood on the center line and made all his calls from there.

After considering the matter for half a quarter or so Sonny concluded that peg shots were the only feasible tactic. He was simply too weak to dodge the blocks the Paducah boys were throwing. From then on, every time he got the ball he threw it at the backboard he was attacking. At the very worst it slowed down Paducah's scoring. The other Thalia players were quick to see the wisdom of such an offense and in five minutes they were all doing it. Whoever caught the throw-in after a Paducah score would immediately whirl and throw a full-court peg shot. The only one it didn't work for was Leroy Malone: the big Paducah center anticipated him, caught the ball, and threw a ten-yard peg shot right at Leroy's groin. It hurt so bad he later told Sonny he was unable to jack off for two weeks.

The groin shot drew such sustained applause from the Paducah bleachers that Sonny was angered. Mr. Wean had failed to see that it was a deliberate foul: indeed, Mr. Wean was seeing less and less all the time. Thalia's peg-shot offense confused him—he had to keep turning around and around to keep up with the ball. After a while this made him so dizzy that he simply stopped and stood facing the Thalia goal—most of the Paducah team was down there anyway, catching the peg shots and throwing them back. Mr. Wean felt that he had somehow got involved in a game of ante over, and he didn't like it. He had a fat wife and all he really wanted to do was stay in the home ec classroom and teach young, small-breasted girls how to make pies. Instead he was standing on the center line, sweating and wishing the quarter would end. Suddenly, Sonny had an irresistible urge to chunk somebody. He unleashed a flat, low peg shot that caught Mr. Wean squarely in the back of the head and sent him sprawling.

The Thalia bench, boys and girls alike, arose with shrieks and cheers, their jubilation all the more noticeable because of the moment of total silence in the Paducah bleachers. The shot instantly made Sonny a celebrity, but it also scared hell out of him and his teammates who were on the floor at the time. They rushed over and tried to help Mr. Wean up, but his legs were like rubber. He had to be dragged off the floor. Paducah's assistant football coach was called in to referee the rest of the game—by the time he got his tennis shoes on, the hometown bleachers had recovered from their shock and were clamoring for Sonny's blood. He knew his only hope was to foul out immediately and get to the bench. While he was trying to decide on the safest way to foul, Coach Popper came to his rescue and took him out.

"Good lick," the coach said. "Nobody but a queer would teach home ec anyway."

From there on things were dismal for the Thalia five. Duane fouled out before the quarter ended, leaving no one but Joe Bob and the freshmen to play the fourth quarter. Paducah was ahead 88 to 14. Coach Popper got so mad at the freshmen that he couldn't see; he almost strangled himself tugging at the towel around his neck. He sent Sonny in again but Sonny quickly threw a couple of light body blocks and fouled out. That left Joe Bob and the freshmen to do the best they could. For the remainder of the game they never once managed to get the ball into their end of the court. As soon as they threw it in, the Paducah players took it away from them and made another goal. In five minutes the score was 110 to 14 and Coach Popper called time out. A huddle was in order.

"I tell you," the coach said philosophically, "let's just forget about winning and try to hold the score down. We're gonna get beat over a hundred points if we ain't careful. Oaks, you throw the ball into Joe Bob and Joe Bob, as soon as you get it lay down with it. That way they'll have to tie it up and jump for it every time. That'll slow 'em down a little."

The tactic worked fine the first time it was tried. Joe

Bob swallowed the ball and Paducah had to tie it up to get possession. It took them about forty seconds to score. Thalia tried it again and three Paducah players gang-piled Joe Bob as he went down. He had to be carried off. The freshman who shot his free throw for him was so scared he barely got the ball halfway to the basket.

Joe Bob's injury left the four freshmen alone on the field for the last few minutes of the game. None of them wanted to swallow the ball and get pang-piled so they did what they could to cooperate with Paducah. The final score was 121 to 14.

"Well, hell, at least my B team got some experience," Coach Popper said. "Might as well look on the bright side. Let's go to the bus."

Basketball defeats weighed very lightly on the coach: football was the only sport that really counted. Ten minutes later he was flopped down in his bus seat, sound asleep.

The boys sat in a stupor for the first twenty miles or so, trying to get used to feeling safe again. Besides, Old Lady Fowler, the girls' coach, was still awake and they could not start to work on the girls until she dropped off. She went to sleep as they were pulling out of Vernon, and from there on it was dog-eat-dog.

The four little freshmen had no chance with the girls and had to get what amusement they could out of tormenting Joe Bob. They crowded him in a seat, took his underpants off, and threw them out the window. Joe Bob was too weak from the gang-piling to fight back, and he might not have bothered anyway. He lost so many pair of underwear that his mother bought them wholesale. He was the only boy on the team who wore his regulars, rather than a jockey strap: Brother Blanton wouldn't hear of him wearing anything so immodest.

"What if you got hurt and were taken to a hospital wearing a thing like that?" Brother Blanton said. "Our good name would be ruined."

Most of the kids had seen Joe Bob's underwear often enough to be thoroughly bored with it. The freshmen attracted no notice at all, and soon went to sleep.

Sonny started the return trip sitting by Leroy Malone, whose balls were so sore that the mere thought of girls made him writhe. After a little bargaining Sonny managed to switch with the kid in front of him, which put him next to the pretty but prudish sophomore he had had his eye on. Knocking Mr. Wean down gave him so much status that he was able to hold the girl's hand almost immediately. Martha Lou was her name. By the time they reached Electra she was willing to let him kiss her, but the results were pretty discouraging. Her teeth were clenched as tightly as if she had lockjaw, and even Sonny's status couldn't unlock them. His only reward was a taste of lipstick, in a flavor he didn't much care for.

The only real excitement on the bus ride home involved Jacy and Duane, the star couple. That was usually the case. None of the other kids excited one another much. There was a fat blonde named Vida May who would feel penises, but the teachers knew about her and made her sit so close to the front that it was dangerous to fool with her even when the teachers were asleep.

Jacy and Duane, as a matter of course, were sitting in the very back seat. Duane didn't like the back seat much because there was a little overhead light above it that the bus driver refused to turn off. The bus driver's name was Wilbur Tim and he wasn't about to trust any kids in a totally dark bus. One time years earlier his wife Jessie had found two prophylactics when she was sweeping out the bus, and it just about sent her into hysterics. She was the apprehensive type and went around for months worried sick that some nice little girl had got pregnant on her husband's bus. After that Wilbur installed the light.

It was a small bulb that didn't really give any light, just a nice orange glow. Jacy loved it and wouldn't sit anywhere else, despite Duane's protests. She thought the light was very romantic and suggestive: everyone in the bus could tell when the couple in the back seat were kissing or doing something sexy, but the light wasn't strong enough for them to see too clearly. Courting with Duane when all the kids on the school bus could watch gave Jacy a real thrill, and made her feel a little like a movie star: she could bring beauty and passion into the poor kids' lives.

Because Jacy enjoyed them so much, the kissing sessions in the back seat had become a sort of regular feature on basketball road trips. All the kids watched, even though it made them itchy and envious. Jacy, after all, was the prettiest girl in school and watching her get kissed and played with was something to do on the long drives home. The element that made it really exciting to everyone was the question of how far Jacy would go. Once Duane got started kissing he was completely indifferent to whether he had an audience or not: all he wanted was more. The dim light made it impossible to tell precisely how much more Jacy allowed: everyone caught shadowy glimpses, and occasionally a gasp or a little moan from Jacy indicated that Duane was making some headway at least, but no one ever knew how much or what kind.

Only Jacy and Duane knew that he was making a great deal of headway indeed. Jacy would kiss and play around any time, but she seldom got excited past the point of control unless she was on the school bus, where people were watching. Being in the public eye seemed to heighten the quality of every touch. On the bus seat she never had to feign passion—she was burning with it. It was easy for Duane to get his hands inside her loose uniform and touch her breasts, and she loved it. Also, since she was in shorts, it was easy for him to do even more abandoned things to her. She loved to have him slide his hands up the underside of her legs, and sometimes she would even get to the point where she wanted him to touch her crotch. It was a matter that took very delicate managing, but if Duane's hand were cupped against her at the right time so she could squeeze it with her legs, something nice would happen. That was not for the audience, however: she didn't want the kids to see that. When the moment came near she would try to get Duane to crowd her back in the corner, so they couldn't be seen so well. Sometimes it worked beautifully. The younger and more naïve kids were sure Duane went all the way; the juniors and seniors knew better, but felt he must be going a pretty significant distance, anyhow. Every trip added to Jacy's legend. The following day at school she would be on every tongue. Some of the girls said bitter things about her, but the boys took notice when she walked by. The only one seriously discommoded by bus-seat sessions was Duane, who frequently ached painfully by the time the bus reached home. He didn't like it, but he supposed such frustration was something he would simply have to bear until they were married.

Just before the bus got back to Thalia Coach Popper woke up and looked around. Most of the kids were asleep by that time, Jacy and Duane among them, but Jacy had gone to sleep with her legs across Duane's and when the coach saw that he was infuriated. It would put him in an awful spot if Lois Farrow somehow found out he had let her daughter go to sleep with her legs across Duane's. Gene Farrow was on the school board, and an incident like that could cost a coach his job. He stormed back and shook Jacy until she was awake enough to stumble down the aisle to the front seat, where she stayed the rest of the way home.

When all the kids had been delivered to their houses the coach got to thinking about it and began to cuss. There was no end to the trouble a couple of silly-ass kids might cause, particularly if one of them was Lois Farrow's daughter. Lois Farrow was the one person in Thalia who didn't give a damn for the fact that he was football coach.

Wilbur Tim dropped him off at his home, and he stomped inside, still angry. When he turned on the light in his bedroom closet it woke Ruth up. She had just had her breast operation a few days before and was still taking pain medicine. As he was taking off his shoes she sat up in bed.

"Herman, could you bring me a pain pill?" she asked. "It's hurting a little and I'm too groggy to get up."

"You sound goddamn wide awake to me," the coach

said, fed up with women. "I bet if I let you you could lay there and talk for two hours. Get up and get your own pills, I ain't no pharmacist."

After a moment, Ruth did. She was dizzy and had to guide herself along the wall, holding her sore breast with one hand. She had washed that day and her white cotton nightgown smelled faintly of detergent. The coach ignored her and flopped on the bed. So far as he could tell, it had not been enough of an operation to make a fuss about. The scar on her breast was barely three inches long. He had cut himself worse than that many times, usually when he was hurrying through a barbed-wire fence to get to a covey of quail. The only thing that worried him about Ruth was the chance that they hadn't removed all the tumor and might have to operate again, in which case there would be no end to the expense. The cheapest and most sensible thing would have been for them to take the whole breast off while they were at it. The breast wasn't doing Ruth any good anyway, and if they had taken it all that would have been the end of the matter. He had told them so, too, but the doctor had ignored him and Ruth had gone off in another room and bawled. A woman like her would try the patience of a saint.

The next day at basketball practice the coach gave Duane a dressing down in front of the whole squad. He told him if he ever again so much as sat with Jacy on a basketball trip he would give him fifteen licks with a basketball shoe. A basketball shoe was the only thing the coach ever whipped boys with, but since he wore a size thirteen that was enough. He also told Duane to run fifty laps around the outside of the gym, and at that point Duane rebelled.

"I ain't runnin' no fifty laps all at one time," he said. "I'll do ten a day."

"You'll do fifty right now or check your suit in, by God," the coach said. "If you check it in you don't need to come out for track or baseball, neither. We can get along without you."

Duane went to the locker room, took his suit off, and left. It was just what the coach had hoped for. Any mess the boy got into with Jacy Farrow could no longer be laid at his door. It put him in such good spirits that he worked the boys until seven o'clock that night. The next day he commandeered a sophomore, and the team had ten players again.

CHAPTER IX

In Thalia, winter was always duller than summer, at least for the boys. In the winter it was too cold to sit around on the square and think up meanness to do—if they wanted to sit around they had to do it in the café, and that cost money. When the square became empty because of the cold, the town seemed emptier than ever.

A senior year was supposed to be exciting but with winter setting in Sonny's suddenly began to look very dull. When Duane quit basketball, the game became a sort of tiring chore that Sonny went on with because he didn't have a legitimate excuse to quit. Thalia lost every game by thirty points or more. Even teams that were as bad as they were beat them thirty points on sheer morale. No team had less in the way of morale than Thalia.

Besides that there was his work. It was an unusually cold winter, and the demand for butane was high. Often, after practice or after a game, Frank Fartley would be waiting for Sonny at the gym and Sonny would have to spend half the night driving over the dark, ice-rutted roads looking for a farmhouse with an empty butane tank. Sometimes he could only find them by the mailboxes, usually old-fashioned Sears and Roebuck models stuck on posts beside the road.

Sonny took to drinking coffee to stay awake, and Genevieve didn't approve. "You've got to get you another job," she told him one time. He had come stumbling into the café at two-thirty in the morning, half-frozen. The heater in the old International only worked about half the time.

The trouble was, there weren't any other jobs, and Genevieve was scarcely in a position to give that kind of advice. Her husband was not improving as rapidly as he had been—it looked like it would be summer before he got back to work. The strain had begun to tell on Genevieve: her uniform no longer fit so snugly at the shoulders, and often she was so tired she couldn't sleep even when she had the time.

Everybody seemed to have the winter doldrums, including Sam the Lion. He was taking daily naps for his heart condition and his cough was still just as bad. Duane's grandmother took the flu and was in the hospital two weeks; everyone expected it to carry her off but all it did was destroy what was left of her mind. Since he didn't have basketball to wear him out, Duane had taken to working a double shift. It was cold work, but it paid, and he could count on having Saturday nights off to spend with Jacy.

The strange conversation Jacy had had with her mother threw Jacy temporarily into a state of uncertainty. For a time she had been convinced that she knew exactly what her mother wanted of her, and exactly how to get around it; but since the conversation she hadn't been so sure. It seemed incredible that her mother would actually give her license to sleep with Duane. For a day or two she was rather tempted, just to see what sex felt like, but then she decided that would merely be walking into her mother's trap. Advice like that was bound to be a trap.

For a time the conversation had the effect of inhibiting Jacy drastically. After she and Duane had concluded they were in love she had taken to allowing him considerable freedom with her body. She had even let him feel inside her panties on a few occasions, but when her mother told her to go ahead and sleep with him she immediately put a stop to that. She felt she had to if she were going to protect their love from her mother's subtle treacheries. Besides, the only times she really enjoyed letting him touch her there was on the school bus.

She even tried to quit letting him take off her brassiere, but Duane complained so bitterly about the loss of that privilege that she finally let him start doing it again. There were a few awkward dates, but in time Jacy became rather proud of herself for the mature way she was handling the situation. She could let Duane kiss her and play with her breasts and yet remain quite cool about it all, protecting them from his passion and her own. Her mother was outwitted and Duane had as much fun as was good for him. Sometimes in church she felt a little like a martyr because of the effort it cost her to keep the two of them morally upright. Her grandmother would have approved if she had been alive and known about it—her grandmother had been a woman of virtue.

Besides, sexual intercourse was supposed to be

painful at first, and she knew Duane wouldn't want to hurt her until it was absolutely necessary. There was a time and a place for everything, as her grandmother had always said.

The week before Christmas there was a big countywide dance held at the American Legion Hall, an annual affair that everybody looked forward to. About the only people that stayed away were the hardshell Baptists and a few of the smaller, eccentric denominations who, like the Baptists, believed that dancing was sinful. In the old days, before the church women of the town had organized, eggnog had been served at the dance, and the men who couldn't tolerate dilution brought their whiskey bottles inside and kept them in their coat pockets while they danced. But when the church women finally organized, they saw to it what drinking was done, was done outside.

This year Lester Marlow was one of the first people to arrive at the dance. He stood around the almost empty hall for an hour, practicing looking rakish and devil-may-care. Lester was temporarily a celebrity in Thalia by virtue of the fact that, only the night before, he had lost a record amount of money to Abilene in an all-night nine-ball game. He had come out the loser by some $820, winning only 11 of 181 games, but that fact did not dismay him at all. Instead he felt almost legendary for having lost so much, and as he strolled around the silent dance floor he continually adjusted the hang of his cashmere sports coat. He wanted to look like the sort of fellow who was ready to accept all risks. He had not bothered to bring a date, but had a plan involving Jacy that he meant to put into effect at the proper time.

Half an hour later, when Jacy drove up in her convertible, Lester was waiting at the curb, bourbon flask carelessly in hand.

"Why hi, Lester," Jacy said nervously. She knew Sonny and Duane would be coming along any minute.

"I hear you lost some money last night," she added. The sum *had* been impressive.

"Duane coming?" Lester asked at once. Jacy nodded. Any other time Lester would have taken the nod as final, but he had had enough whiskey to be able to set aside his normal caution.

"You know Bobby Sheen, in Wichita?" he asked. "He's going to have a midnight swimming party tonight in his indoor pool. A lot of kids from the club are going to be there. I guess you heard about the last one: his folks were gone to Miami and everybody swam naked. I was there and it was really something. I don't know what they'll do tonight, but his folks are gone again and it's probably going to be pretty wild. If you want to run over there with me after the dance, why don't you? Bobby has great parties."

Lester was smart enough to leave it at that. He rakishly took another sip of bourbon and went back into the dance. Just as he was walking away Sonny and Duane rattled up. They parked the pickup and immediately got in Jacy's car. Duane had noticed Lester talking to her and asked about it.

"Oh, he just wanted to tell me about losing all that money," Jacy said, a little on edge. She had been all primed to enjoy the dance, but Lester's invitation upset her timing a little and Duane came along before she could think things out.

In a few minutes Sonny got out of the car and went in the dance to see what Mr. and Mrs. Farrow were doing. They were on the sponsoring committee and Jacy felt she and Duane probably ought to go in separately unless her father was already drunk enough not to notice them.

While Sonny was reconnoitering Jacy made a quick decision: clearly she would have to go to the swimming party with Lester. It took a rich, fast crowd to go swimming naked, and Jacy always prided herself on belonging to the fastest crowd there was, moral or immoral. Indeed, for a rich, pretty girl like herself the most immoral thing imaginable would be to belong to a slow crowd. That would be wasting opportunities, and nothing was more immoral than waste.

Then too, when word got around that she had gone swimming naked with a lot of rich kids from Wichita Falls her legend would be secure for all time. No girl from Thalia had ever done anything like that.

It was clear that she had to go: the only problem was Duane. He had the night off and was expecting to devote it entirely to her—if she left him at eleven o'clock to go somewhere with Lester it would make him so mad he might even break up with her, and that was to be avoided. She quickly decided that her best bet would be to spend a couple of hours being extremely nice to him, so he would be too much in love with her to be mad when she left. If he was mad anyway she would have to blame it all on her mother —that always worked.

She turned to Duane and started to kiss him, but then stopped and looked at him fondly a moment. "I love you so much tonight," she said. "I wish we could stay together all night."

As soon as they settled into the kiss Jacy turned so that one of her breasts nudged Duane's hand. He was

93

astonished, but not too astonished to take advantage of what was offered him. He pulled her brown sweater out of her skirt and slipped his hand beneath it. Her belly was warm but the brassiere was a cold barrier. It was frustrating to come up against the stiff, cold material when Jacy's warm breasts were just underneath. Duane had experienced that frustration many times before, but it was nothing Jacy usually cared to help him out with; anyway he could hardly expect her to undress right in front of the Legion Hall. Then Jacy broke the kiss with a soft sigh. "Wait a minute," she said. "I don't want to go in right now—let's get in the back seat a few minutes." As soon as they had she edged both her bra straps off her shoulders. Duane slipped the bra down a few inches and her breasts were free. She didn't seem to mind that the tight straps more or less imprisoned her arms. She kissed Duane lingeringly while he touched her breasts and nipples.

Sonny came out to report a minute or two later, meaning to tell the two that it was perfectly safe for them to come in together. Lois and Gene were at the other end of the hall, and both fairly tight besides. When he got to the car and saw what Jacy and Duane were doing, he hated to interrupt, but he wanted to let them know about Jacy's parents. Finally he rapped on the windshield a time or two and went hastily back inside.

Duane was annoyed that Sonny had even knocked. He was deliriously caressing Jacy's bosom, and gladly would have given up the dance for another hour with Jacy in her present mood. For her part, Jacy was quite ready to go in, though she was careful not to show it. The evening ahead would require delicate timing, and it would be unwise to allow Duane too many goodies right at the beginning. She straightened up and smiled at him, her arms still imprisoned by the bra straps.

"We better go in while we can," she said, turning so her back was toward him. "Would you put my bra back on? I can't manage it without taking off this sweater."

Her request was a perfect touch. She had never even used the word "bra" in Duane's presence before, and her willingness to let him put the garment on her added a quality of intimacy to the proceedings that more than compensated for the interruption. He reached under her sweater from behind and slipped the straps up over her slim shoulders—when her arms were free she raised them and let Duane put her breasts back in their cups. When he had the bra hooked he held her a moment, feeling very tender and protective.

A square dance was in progress as they entered the hall and Gene and Lois were dancing. All the men loved to square dance with Lois Farrow because if she was in a good mood she was tolerant of a little free-and-easy feeling around. She might be heavier at the waist than she had been once, but she was still a much prettier woman than most of the men saw at home, and they hovered around her.

During the course of the evening Jacy noticed that more people at the dance paid attention to her mother than to her—an annoying fact that she had never noticed before. Her mother was the belle of the ball, and she wasn't. She could tell by the men's faces that they found her mother very attractive, and the same men hardly noticed her at all. Lois was wearing a loose white dancing dress with a low neckline; her hair was combed out long and shook about her shoulders as she danced. Jacy noticed, too, that her mother was wearing some sort of very brief, fashionable bra. The men could see her breasts move as she danced. It wasn't that Lois' breasts were overly large or indecently exposed, exactly; it was just that they were shaped right and exposed just enough to excite the men in the hall. The more she saw the men watching her mother the more annoyed Jacy became. Not only were the respectable men like the bankers and the doctor watching her mother, but the unrespectables were, too: the farmers and oil-field hands and filling-station men. When her mother danced their faces lit up; when she danced they didn't even notice. It was very insulting. Jacy decided that the next day she would point out to her mother that highnecked dresses would be more becoming for a woman her age. She could say it had to do with facial structure and all that, but it might not work. Her mother knew a good bit about facial structure too.

Jacy was somewhat let down to discover that she had fewer admirers among the male community than she had supposed. A close count revealed that she had only two admirers who really counted: Lester and Duane. Sonny admired her extravagantly, but he had no money and had not been in the backfield, so he really just didn't count. Of course almost all the sweaty little sophomores admired her, but they counted even less than Sonny.

Since there was clearly nothing she could do about her mother, Jacy turned her attention back to the swimming party and guided Duane back to the farthest, darkest corner of the Legion Hall, where the couples most in love always danced. In that corner it was possible to dance very close, and an hour or so of really close dancing fitted in perfectly with Jacy's plan. She had known for a long time that boys had erections on dance floors, at least when they danced with her—apparently it was just one of the little common-places of life that pretty girls had to put up with. It had never occurred to her that such a phenomenon could be useful until she began laying plans to get away to the swimming party, when she concluded that the thing to do was make Duane simply delirious with love. If he were delirious, and convinced she was on the verge of giving herself to him, then he couldn't be too mad when she made ready to leave. The quickest way to convince him was by dancing as close as it was possible to dance; so grimly Jacy did it, pressing herself right against him. It was so creepy it almost set her teeth on edge, but the effect on Duane was very strong indeed.

"Let's sneak out to the car a minute," he said, his breath hot in her ear.

Jacy knew that wouldn't be sensible. Much better to hold out the promise of a brief trip to the car after she had his reaction to her leaving. Then if he just had to be pacified some way, she could let him put his hand inside her panties. After all, he *was* very sweet, and had given her a fifty-dollar wristwatch for Christmas.

"I'll go talk to Mother a minute," she said. "Maybe I can talk her into letting me stay out a little later tonight."

She left the dance floor and found her mother in the front foyer, but the circumstances were extremely surprising. Abilene had just come in the door and her mother was kissing him, right there in the Legion Hall. Not only was it a shock to Jacy, but even more of

97

one to the short, pretty brunette Abilene had come in with. Lois was kissing him right on the mouth, and though he seemed a little flushed he was not trying to make her quit. Even when her mother broke the kiss she kept her hands locked around Abilene's neck.

"Merry Christmas," she said, glancing at the brunette, whom she had not noticed. The girl was angry, but she was shorter than Lois and much younger and didn't quite know what to do with her anger.

"Uh, this here's Jackie Lee French," Abilene said. "Jackie Lee, this is Lois Farrow, my boss's wife."

"Hello, Jackie," Lois said.

"I don't have to talk to her," Jackie Lee said, turning angrily to Abilene. "I think she's just awful. What do you mean kissin' her like that, I'm embarrassed to death. I ought to slap her face."

"You can't even reach it, honey," Lois said, smiling at her. "Is your name really French or is that just something you like to do?"

Jackie Lee was absolutely stunned. Her mouth fell open. Nobody had ever talked like that to her before —she was the star barmaid in the tavern where she worked, and all the cowboys and airmen treated her very much like a lady.

Abilene made an amused face and took Jackie Lee by the elbow. "I never come here to referee no fight," he said, moving toward the dance floor. Jackie Lee went with him, holding her butt in indignantly.

Lois snorted in amusement. "I know what I did wrong," she said. "You're supposed to have mistletoe." When she noticed Jacy she snorted again and went into the coatroom. She had a flask of bourbon in her coat pocket and took a neat nip, fishing in her purse for some Kleenex. The dancing had made her sweaty.

"My goodness, Mother," Jacy said, "you oughtn't to behave like that. What would Daddy say if he saw you?"

"Nothing," Lois replied. She took another nip and put the cap back on the flask. "He wouldn't say a damn thing and there's no reason he should. Kissing one another at Christmastime is a custom among civilized peoples. Besides, why are *you* lecturing *me*? What have you been doing back in that dark corner for the last hour, telling secrets?"

Jacy was taken aback. For a moment she couldn't think how to reply. "I was just coming to ask you something," she said finally. "Lester wants me to go with him to a swimming party in Wichita Falls. Is it okay if I go?"

"Sure," Lois said. "Have a good time. And let's you and me just leave one another alone so far as men are concerned, okay? We compete about enough things as it is."

After Lois went back to the dance floor Jacy decided her feelings were hurt and stayed in the coatroom, sniffling a little. It seemed to her her mother had no sense of responsibility at all, and it was very confusing. Then she grew angry, jerked the bourbon flask out of her mother's coat and took a tiny sip of whiskey in defiance. Like mother, like daughter, people would say if they saw her. She put the flask back and hurried in to Duane before the tears could dry on her cheeks. "Oh I'm just sick," she said. "Mother says I have to go to a swimming party with Lester. I can't get out of it now. It's all her fault and I could just kill her."

Ten minutes later she and Duane were in the front

seat of the pickup, kissing. The pickup was parked in a darker place than the convertible. Duane had been furious and it had taken all Jacy's coaxing to get him out of the Legion Hall without some kind of scene taking place. Even when they got to the pickup he kept wanting to go back in and drag Lester out and fight him. Jacy quickly saw that she would have to go to desperate lengths to keep him with her. She sprawled across his lap, kissing him, and she didn't bother to cross her legs and trap his arms with her own, like she usually did. He could dimly make out her white, half-exposed legs in the dark cab. When he touched her lightly above the knee she didn't stop him. Wildly encouraged, he at once forgot Lester and leapt to the attack: he put his hand right on the warm slick band of silk that passed between her legs. She still didn't stop him! It was a miracle of generosity!

Jacy thought so too. She had never left herself quite so wide open before and she hoped Duane appreciated it. After a few nervous minutes of tracing his fingers delicately along the edges of her panties he got up enough nerve to slip his hand inside a leghole and touch the real place, which was surprisingly slippery. He had not really expected to arrive at that destination that evening and he was not quite sure what to do next. Jacy gave no clues. She quit kissing him and pressed her face tightly against his neck, not exactly sure if she liked what was happening or not. She was determined to go on with it a few minutes, though: it would never do to go to a naked swimming party in total ignorance of such matters. Once in a while Duane hit on the right spot and she couldn't help gasping and squirming a little, but most of the time he seemed to be fumbling around in a rather pointless way and that made her impatient. She went a little out of it for a few minutes, waiting for Duane to hit the right spot and quivering with pleasure when he did. It was not until he took his hand away and tried to lay her down on the seat that she realized she had pacified him quite enough. He was actually trying to get on top of her! It was terrible of him to try such a thing when her head wasn't completely clear—it was hard enough for her to finish the evening in the proper tone without him doing that.

"No, no, Duane, I've got to go," she said. "Lester will be coming any minute."

She struggled up, gave Duane a quick kiss to show she wasn't mad at him, and then got herself out of the pickup and into Lester's Oldsmobile. She wanted a minute or two to calm down before Lester came out—the dancing and the courting had left her wet with sweat, and she wasn't even sure but what she smelled.

To her great annoyance, Duane got out of the pickup, his hair all tousled, and stood right on the porch of the Legion Hall, obviously waiting for Lester. After all she had given him, it was infuriating! When Lester came out he bumped right into Duane and Duane grabbed him. They had words, that was clear, but Lester managed to shake loose and came on to the Olds. The sleeve of his sports coat was torn.

"What'd he say?" Jacy asked.

"God he's mad," Lester said, panting. He was visibly scared, but he did his best to make light of it. "He called me names, hoping I'd hit him."

"Oh, he's so silly," Jacy said. "I don't know what I'm going to do about him. He's just so crazy about me he doesn't have good sense."

"I'm not saying anything against Duane, but that's a roughneck for you," Lester said. "They never are very sophisticated about these things."

The farther he got from the scene the easier it was for Lester to believe he would have come out well in a fight with Duane. His emotions became mixed, and so did Jacy's. It occurred to her belatedly that it wouldn't have been so bad if Lester and Duane *had* fought over her. At the very least it would have taken a few people's minds off her mother.

They rode to Wichita in silence, each of them thinking out the kind of fight scene they wished had taken place. Lester imagined that he had fought to a standstill, contemptuous of pain, while Jacy saw it differently: Lester would win by dishonorable means, like kicking Duane in the groin, and she would weep on the sidelines. Then she would go and comfort Duane and drive away with him, contemptuous alike of money and parental displeasure, content to be ruined for love.

It seemed a pity to her that Lester hadn't had the guts to start the fight.

The Sheen home, where the party took place, was a two-story, twenty-room mansion near the Wichita Falls country club. When they drove up several sports cars were parked in the long curved drive.

"This may be the wildest thing yet," Lester said, smiling at Jacy a little nervously.

No one answered the doorbell, so they went on in. Lights were on and there were girls' coats and boys' coats and glasses and liquor bottles all around, but no people. A Dave Brubeck album was lying next to the phonograph.

Once they opened the basement area it was obvious from the yelling and splashing where everyone was.

"Yep, they're naked," Lester said when they arrived downstairs. He left Jacy in the ping-pong room a minute and peeked into the pool. She found the prospect of walking into a room full of naked city kids somewhat frightening, but she determined to do it and look delighted, whatever she might feel. She let Lester hold her hand when they walked in, and that was something she didn't permit very often.

At first it was not especially startling, because all the Wichita kids were in the water, having water fights and cutting up. You couldn't see what ordinarily you were not supposed to see. There were about six boys and six girls, most of them kids Jacy knew slightly from dances at the country club. One rather famous rich girl was there—her name was Annie-Annie and she was black-headed and notoriously wild. She was only seventeen and had been sleeping with boys for years. Her boy friend was Bobby Sheen, the kid whose parents owned the house. He was a very good-looking boy and had owned the first Ford Thunderbird in that part of the country.

"Hey, look," he yelled, when he saw Lester and Jacy. "New victims."

To Jacy's embarrassment all the kids immediately stopped their water fights and swam right over to the side of the pool where she and Lester were standing. Bobby Sheen made a big show of jumping out of the water and shaking Lester's hand, just as if he had been properly dressed.

"Hi, Jacy," he said, grinning and sluicing the water off his hair with one hand. "Glad you made it to the party. We're dressed informally, as you see."

That brought a big laugh from the kids in the pool, and Bobby cocked his leg in acknowledgment. Jacy laughed too, though a little thinly. She was trying not to look at Bobby's penis, or at anybody's penis.

Annie-Annie got out of the pool too and walked over to them. She was a tall, willowy girl, very graceful. Having her out of the water embarrassed Jacy almost as much as having Bobby out. Streams of water dripped off Annie-Annie's breasts and ran down her stomach into her black pubic hair. She didn't even bother to dry herself, and Jacy thought that most indecent. Letting drops of water shine in one's pubic hair was certainly not a ladylike thing to do.

"You two will have to join the club," Annie-Annie said. "We're the Senior Nudists, and we'll let you join if you want to."

"Sure," Lester said. "How much does it cost? I'll pay for both of us."

"Oh it doesn't cost money," Annie-Annie said, grinning and still dripping. "You just have to be initiated. You walk out on the diving board and take all your clothes off, while we watch. You all willing?"

"Sure," Lester said, not looking at Jacy. "We were just fixing to get undressed anyway."

When he asked Jacy if it was okay, she nodded. She didn't know what else to do. She certainly wasn't anxious to go out on the board and take her clothes off, but she couldn't very well stand around with them on while everybody else was naked.

"I'll go first," Lester said.

All the kids got out of the pool and sat on the edge, kicking their feet in the water. One little kid surprised Jacy no end. He was by far the youngest, littlest kid there; he had freckles and a burr haircut and looked about thirteen, and he had on a green diving mask. While they were all waiting for Lester to untie his shoes the kid walked right past Jacy to get a towel. What surprised Jacy was his penis, which stuck straight out. It wasn't very big or anything but it certainly was sticking out and Jacy thought it was just awful that he would walk around with it like that. A couple of the other girls giggled.

"That's my little brother Sandy," Bobby Sheen said. "Don't pay any attention to him—he's not in the club. He just likes to swim under water with his mask on and look at girls while he fiddles with himself. If he gooses you or anything tell me and I'll make him go to bed."

When Lester got out on the diving board, Jacy expected everybody to yell and whistle, but instead they just sat quietly on the side of the pool, watching. The room was so quiet that they could hear the gentle slap of water against the tile poolside. Lester had expected yelling too, and the silence unnerved him. He decided that speed was of the essence, and his disrobing was incredibly speedy. He peeled off his shirt, yanked down his pants and underwear at the same time, and in a second was in the water. Jacy was amazed at how quickly he did it. He swam over and pulled himself up on the side with the others, no longer the least embarrassed.

When Jacy saw how unselfconscious he had become she grew terribly annoyed with him for having gone first. If he had offered to let her be first, like a gentleman should have, she would be sitting calmly on the side and it would be over with. But everybody in the room was watching her and there was simply nothing to do but bluff it out.

"Goodness, I hope I don't fall off this thing," she said, when she got on the diving board. Diving boards always looked a lot higher up when you were on them.

"Sandy will fish you out if you do," Annie-Annie said.

Sure enough, that hideous little Sandy had slipped into the pool again and was swimming around like a frog about ten feet from the diving board. He had his mask on. Jacy decided she was with the most brazen bunch of kids she had ever seen, and she didn't like one of them.

She took her shoes off first, and then pulled her sweater off over her head. It was not as easy for her to undress fast as it had been for Lester. Once the sweater was off the question was whether she should take her skirt off first and then her bra and panties, or her bra off first and then her skirt and panties. She decided the skirt should come off first and she got out of it without looking up. It was embarrassing to have to reach back and unhook a bra in front of so many kids, but she had so much off already that she couldn't afford to dawdle. It seemed as though she had been out on the board about thirty minutes, as compared to five seconds for Lester. Once she got the bra off she started to yank her panties down and jump, but just as she bent over to slide them down Sandy frogged right under the board and peered up at her through his goggles. Jacy lost her balance and had to sit down very quickly to keep from falling in. At that all the kids burst out laughing and whistling and pointing at Sandy, who was becalmed just beneath her, his tiny little mast sticking up out of the water. It was plainly degrading. Angrily Jacy jerked the panties off her ankles and dropped them right on Sandy's mask.

Instantly the crowd became hers: they all began to laugh *at* Sandy, who frog kicked off toward the shallow end of the pool. Jacy let herself off the board and swam to the poolside to much acclaim—two boys helped her up on the side.

For an hour she swam and giggled, and the longer she stayed with them the more she came to like the crowd. They seemed like the wildest, most intelligent kids she had ever seen, and she determined then and there to throw in her lot with them. Before the night was over she could stand by the pool talking to some boy or other and feel perfectly at ease—the drops of water shining in her pubic hair soon ceased to disconcert her and began to seem rather becoming. At last she could even look at boys' penises without embarrassment.

Only one thing upset her: her new wristwatch, Duane's Christmas present. She had forgotten to take it off when she jumped into the pool. The kids all pooh-poohed her and told her not to worry so much about a fifty-dollar watch and she saw that they were right. It was just a wristwatch, and she could always make it up to Duane some other way.

CHAPTER X

Jacy and Lester had not been gone from the dance ten minutes before word got around that they were going to a swimming party where everyone would be naked. The reason word got around so fast was that Lester told several of the younger kids about it just before he left. He told them he and Jacy were going to swim naked, just like everybody else. It was almost past belief, but when the kids saw him actually drive away with Jacy they instantly believed it and began to talk about it. Nothing wilder had ever been heard of in Thalia—it was even wilder than actually making out, because that was customarily done in the dark and nothing much could be seen.

In no time there were groups of excited boys standing around, speculating about the look of Jacy's breasts. They even had a hot argument over whether or not blond girls really had blond hair underneath their panties. Some of the younger, illiterate kids thought that all women had black hair in that particular place, but the better-read youths soon convinced them otherwise by reference to the panty-dropping

108

scene in *I the Jury,* a book the local drugstore could never keep in stock.

The news about Lester and Jacy did not surprise Sonny much. He knew that any time Lester came to Thalia he was likely to end up taking Jacy somewhere, and since he had heard for years that Wichita kids were always having orgies it was only natural that sooner or later Lester would take Jacy to one. The worst thing about it was that it would depress Duane something fierce.

While he was waiting for Duane to get the news, Sonny wandered into the refreshment room. There had been a big table full of plates of cookies, with a huge bowl of punch for the kids and the grown-ups who didn't drink. All the punch was gone and the only cookies left were a few rubbery, inedible brownies. Empty paper cups were strewn all around and a lady in a black dress was bent over picking them up and putting them in a big wastebasket. It was Mrs. Popper. The school teachers' wives always fixed the refreshments for the Christmas dance, but somehow Sonny was surprised to bump into Mrs. Popper just then. Coach Popper never came to dances, and especially not to Saturday night dances. He would not have missed *Gunsmoke* for all the dances in Texas.

"Hello, Sonny," Mrs. Popper said. "Want to help me pick up these cups, since you're not dancing? I'm tired."

She looked tired, too—at least her face did. She was not wearing any makeup and had apparently just come down to do her part with the refreshments.

"Sure, be glad to," Sonny said, picking up a cup. The punch had been a sweet, grape mixture and the rims of the cups were sticky. Sonny gathered about twenty and went to drop them in the wastebasket.

"I guess you still haven't found a new girl friend, have you?" Mrs. Popper asked quietly. Sonny was very startled. He had forgotten she knew about his old girl friend.

"No ma'am, but I'm looking hard," he said.

"Are you?" Ruth said, even more quietly. "It seems to me that if you were really looking hard you might look at me."

Surprised, Sonny did look at her, and remembered that they had become a little fond of one another the afternoon he had driven her to the hospital. He remembered wishing they had kissed, and when he looked at her mouth he wished it again, a very strange wish to be having in the refreshment room of the Legion Hall, during the Christmas dance. But there was something fresh about Mrs. Popper's mouth, as if what was left of the softness and beauty she was said to have had as a girl still lingered there. Sonny was mute. Suddenly he wanted Mrs. Popper and he didn't have the slightest idea what to do about it. He was simply mute, and his silence filled Ruth with despair. She waited a moment, hoping he would say something; when he didn't she felt something slip out of line inside of her and she turned away, holding the wastebasket full of dirty cups. She was afraid she might cry. Sonny saw the look of sadness come in her face and realized he had to say something if he wanted anything to happen between them.

"I'll help you carry that out to the trash barrel," he said.

Then it was Ruth's turn to be mute—mute with

110

relief. They went out the back door together and walked to the group of barrels at the edge of the alley. When they had dumped the cups into one of the barrels, Ruth hesitantly came close to Sonny and then came very close. Her cheek was warm against his throat, and he smelled the thin, clean smell of her perfume. For a minute they were too silent—Sonny looked over her head, beyond the town. Far across the pastures he saw the lights of an oil derrick, brighter than the cold winter stars. Suddenly Mrs. Popper lifted her head and they kissed. Their mouths didn't hit just right at first and she put her fingers gently on each side of his face and guided his mouth to hers. The touch of her cool fingers startled and excited him and he pulled her to him more tightly. Her breath was warm across his cheek. Near the end of the kiss she parted her lips and teeth for a moment and touched him once with her tongue. Then she took her mouth away and for several minutes pressed her lips lightly against his throat.

"You're not as scared as you were the first time I wanted to do this," she said.

It was true: Sonny didn't feel at all scared, though his legs were trembling just a little from excitement. He liked to feel Mrs. Popper's lips moving against his throat. This had been the first time in his life when kissing someone had been as pleasant as he imagined kissing should be. It was never that pleasant with Charlene.

"Maybe we're going to have something, after all," Ruth said. "Will you drive me to the hospital again next week, if I arrange for Herman to ask you?"

"You bet," Sonny said. "The sooner the better, as far as I'm concerned." He bent down to find her

111

mouth and Ruth put her hands on his cheeks again. They kissed slowly and luxuriously. At first the kiss was as soft as the first one had been, but then Ruth discovered that Sonny had awakened and was thrusting at her, not so much with his mouth as with himself, wanting more of her. He kissed so hard her head was pushed back and when she opened her eyes for a moment she was looking straight up, toward the stars. Sonny tried to get even closer to her, pulling her against him with his arm. In years nothing had thrilled her so much or touched her so much as he did, simply by wanting her—the rush of her blood made her almost dizzy. She took his tongue into her mouth and touched it lightly for a second with her tongue and the edges of her teeth. Then she took her face away quickly, pressing it against his neck again.

"I'm going home now," she said. "This is no place to dawdle. Tuesday we'll do this more. I really want to do it more, don't you?"

"You bet," Sonny said, bending to kiss her neck. He didn't want to talk—what he wanted was more of the delicate, delicious sensations her mouth had given him. It seemed to him it might just be best if he said so.

"I want to kiss you one more time before you go home," he said.

"Goodness," Ruth said. "Okay." She lifted her hand and traced the edges of his lips with one finger before she kissed him. Again, when they kissed, he pressed against her with an insistence that thrilled Ruth: it was if he were trying to find her very center, her deepest place. While they were kissing, a car turned into the other end of the parking lot and the lights arced in their direction. It was simply some teenagers turning around, but it scared them and they broke apart immediately.

"In three days I'll see you," Ruth said, picking up the wastebasket.

Sonny felt it wouldn't do for him to follow her in, so he walked around the building and entered at the front door. When he came in Duane was standing by the coatroom, obviously furious. Leroy Malone and two or three other boys were standing there too.

"I guess you heard the news," Duane said. "My girl's gone swimming naked with Lester Marlow. That's about the damnedest thing I ever heard. It's enough to make a man go get drunk."

"I guess Mrs. Farrow forced her into it," Sonny said.

"Let's go get drunk," Leroy suggested. "I know where we can steal a couple of bottles of vodka—I saw a man put two in his car just a minute ago."

The suggestion had much appeal, and Sonny immediately seconded it. Getting drunk would be the only way to save Duane from a gloomy night, and besides he felt a good bit like getting drunk himself. Kissing Mrs. Popper had left him excited and confused.

Leroy swiped the vodka and the three of them drove to the poolhall, which generally stayed open until one or two o'clock on Saturday nights. A good many of the younger kids trailed up also, hoping to get a swallow or two of vodka.

They all bought Cokes and took them back to the john one at a time and spiked them. None of them were used to vodka and it was not long before it began to have an effect on their behavior, not to mention their pool shooting. They shot so badly that it took them thirty minutes to finish an eight-ball game.

"Boys, from the way you all are shootin' a feller would think you were drunk," Sam the Lion said innocently, breaking them all up.

Leroy Malone was very inventive when it came to pestering Billy, and when eight-ball began to get tiresome it occurred to him that it might be fun to get Billy drunk. He drew Sonny and Duane aside.

"Let's take Billy somewhere and get him drunk," he said. "Think how funny he'd be drunk."

The boys were not against it. Anything for mischief and adventure. They grabbed Billy and waltzed him outside. Several of the younger boys got wind of the plot and tagged along.

"We could go on down to the stockpens," Leroy suggested. "There's a blind heifer down there we could fuck. She belongs to my uncle. There's enough of us we could hold her down. It'd be as good a place as any to get Billy drunk."

The prospect of copulation with a blind heifer excited the younger boys almost to frenzy, but Duane and Sonny, being seniors, gave only tacit approval. They regarded such goings on without distaste, but were no longer as rabid about animals as they had been. Sensible youths, growing up in Thalia, soon learned to make do with what there was, and in the course of their adolescence both boys had frequently had recourse to bovine outlets. At that they were considered overfastidious by the farm youth of the area, who thought only dandies restricted themselves to cows and heifers. The farm kids did it with cows, mares, sheep, dogs, and whatever else they could catch. There were reports that a boy from Scotland did it with domesticated geese, but no one had ever actually witnessed it. It was common knowledge that the reason boys from the dairy farming communities were so reluctant to come out for football was because it put them home too late for the milking and caused them to miss regular connection with the milk cows.

Many of the town kids were also versatile and resourceful—the only difficulty was that they had access to a smaller and less varied animal population. Even so, one spindly sophomore whose father sold insurance had once been surprised in ecstatic union with a roan cocker spaniel, and a degraded youth from the north side of town got so desperate one day that he crawled into a neighbor's pig pen in broad daylight and did it with a sow.

"I say a blind heifer beats nothing," Leroy said, and no one actively disagreed with the sentiment. They all got in the pickup and headed for the stockpens, eight or nine of the younger boys shivering in the back.

The stockpens were a mile or two north of town, surrounded by mesquite. When they got there all the boys in the back piled out and went to locate the heifer, but Sonny and Duane stayed in the cab a minute and took a final drink of vodka to warm them up. They gave Billy a Coke that was about a third full of vodka and he drank it happily.

"We better slow him down," Duane said. "If he gets too drunk he may want a turn at the heifer. I doubt old Hank Malone would want an idiot screwin' his livestock."

Sonny got out, not saying anything. It bothered him when people called Billy an idiot. Billy didn't seem *that* much dumber than other people, and he was a lot friendlier than most.

When they got to the lots Leroy was sitting on the fence watching the younger kids chasing the scared, sightless heifer around the dark pen.

"They're after her," he said. "They'll get her in a minute."

The little heifer didn't weigh over three hundred pounds and in a few minutes the boys cornered her by the loading chute and wrestled her to the ground. She struggled for a while but finally gave it up and lay still. A freshman was sitting on her head and her frightened breath raised little puffs of dust from the sandy lot. Sonny, Duane, and Leroy got off the fence and went over to watch. Billy had climbed up on the fence, but he didn't know what was going on and just sat there sucking the empty Coke bottle.

"You boys are holding her wrong," Leroy said in a superior tone. "Ain't you ever fucked a heifer before? You little piss-ants must be virgins. Let her up on her knees."

The younger boys thought that was bitter news: the heifer had been trouble enough to get down. Leroy was a senior, however, and they respected his authority. When they let her up she almost got away, but there were nine of them and they managed to hang on and stop her.

It had come time to decide who went first, and the younger boys, nearing exhaustion just from holding the heifer, pressed for a decision. It would be one of the three seniors, of course.

"You all decide," one of them pleaded. "We can't hold her all night."

At that point Sonny surprised everyone, even himself, by suddenly withdrawing from the competition.

116

"You all help yourselves," he said hastily. "I drunk too much, I think I'm gonna have to puke."

It was the best excuse he could think of. When he agreed to come to the stockpens he supposed he would naturally be a participant, but the moment he saw the little blind heifer he knew he didn't want to. It had something to do with Mrs. Popper, though he was not certain just what. It didn't seem right to kiss Mrs. Popper and still fiddle around with heifers, blind or not blind. Not only did it not seem right: it no longer seemed like fun. Kissing Mrs. Popper even once was bound to be more fun than anything he could possibly do with the skinny, quivering little heifer. He suddenly felt like he had graduated, and it was an uneasy feeling. He knew Duane and the other boys would think it awfully strange of him not to take a turn, so to fool them he went off in the mesquites and pretended to be sick.

When he came back to the fence the orgy in the lot was in full progress. Duane was attacking the heifer, and Leroy, who had already finished, was helping hold. Two or three of the younger boys had their pants down and were parading lustfully around the lot. One sophomore was in something of a predicament because, by an unexpected stroke of luck, he had actually made out with a girl that night, a pig from Holliday who had come to the dance. As a consequence of that success the boy was feeling somewhat enervated and was attempting to restore himself by beating his member against a cold aluminum gate. When the freshmen started in on the heifer it was even more hilarious: many of them were too short to reach the target comfortably and had to struggle on tiptoe.

Then in the midst of it all the heifer finally broke loose and went dashing across the lot with one of the freshmen hanging furiously to her tail. Sonny was just as glad. Somehow it wasn't as exciting as it had been when he was a freshman.

"Look at ol' Billy takin' that in," Leroy said. "What we ought to do is buy him a piece. We could get the carhop for a dollar, if it was just Billy."

"Hell, if she's that cheap we ought to gone to her ourselves," Duane said. "I heard she was a five-dollar whore."

"Naw," Leroy said. "Anybody with five dollars can do better than Jimmie Sue. That heifer's got prettier legs than she has. She'd be okay for Billy, though. I've heard that idiots die when they're fifteen or sixteen— we oughtn't to sit around and let Billy die a virgin."

"I don't know if we ought to try anything like that," Sonny said. "What if it upset Billy and Sam the Lion found out about it? I'd just as soon not get crosswise with Sam."

"Aw don't be a chickenshit, Crawford," Leroy said. "It might do Billy good to get a little."

"Not if he gets it from Jimmie Sue it wouldn't," Sonny said, very ill at ease.

"You don't have to chip in if you're so stingy," Duane said. "Let's go on and get her."

Sonny quit arguing—he really didn't know how to argue against a whole crowd. He never had even wanted to before. They piled back in the pickup and he drove to the back entrance of the town's one little hotel. Leroy and Duane went up to make arrangements with Jimmie Sue Jones, the available girl, and Sonny sat in the cab with Billy, who was still sucking on the empty Coke bottle. It was almost the first time in Sonny's life that he had not been willing to go on and do whatever the crowd was doing. Before, it had always seemed like fun, whether it was getting drunk or screwing heifers, but he didn't think it would be any fun at all to make Billy do it with Jimmie Sue. Billy was in a perfectly peaceful mood, sucking on the bottle and glad to be along with all the boys, and it seemed a pity to disturb him.

In a minute the boys came out with Jimmie Sue, who was a sort of drive-in version of Penny, only dirtier. She had been car-hopping in Thalia for nine years and everyone in town was tired of her. She had been married once, to a mechanic with rat-tail sideburns, but he soon left her and went back to Bossier City, Louisiana, where he came from. The drive-in paid Jimmie Sue next to nothing and she seldom got tips, so she had to peddle herself when she could to make ends meet. She dyed her hair red and had no eyebrows except those she painted on in the morning, and she was so absentminded that sometimes she only painted on one eyebrow and went around like that all day. For Billy she didn't bother to paint on even one. When she got in the cab it immediately began to smell so oniony that Sonny had to roll his windows down. Jimmie Sue looked at Billy disgustedly.

"Why that thing's just a kid," she said. "You all oughtn't to woke me up for a thing like that. I ought to get at least two dollars."

"Hell no, you said a dollar and a half," Duane reminded her.

"Well, I'd just as soon it was an idiot as not," Jimmie Sue said, unpeeling a stick of chewing gum. "The only thing I draw the line at is Mixicans and niggers. I guess I told you about the time that nigger

119

man in high heels stole my suitcase right out of the bus station, that time I went to Los Angeles. . . ."

It had been Jimmie Sue's one adventure. She saved her money and went to Los Angeles to work, but the very hour she arrived in the Los Angeles bus station a black man wearing high heels stole her suitcase and all her possessions. Jimmie Sue had never been so disappointed in all her life as she was with Los Angeles. She couldn't get a job and had to turn around and hitchhike back to Thalia, to keep from starving. Hitchhiking across the desert without any eyebrows proved a slow business, too. If it hadn't been for a carful of horny Mexicans she never would have got out of Needles, California, and bad as that was, Lordsburg, New Mexico, was worse. Tired of eating dust, she let a Negro pick her up. By the time she got back to Thalia she had nothing good to say about minority groups.

Billy looked at her with mild curiosity, but was obviously neither disturbed nor excited by her presence in the cab. Sonny drove back over the narrow, one-vehicle road that cut through the mesquite to the stockpens.

"You all just get that thing out while I get ready," Jimmie Sue said. "This ain't the ideal dressin' room."

Billy was happy to get out: he wondered if they were going to sit on the fence and watch the boys chase the cow again. To his surprise, no sooner was he out than six or seven of the boys grabbed him and unceremoniously threw him down on the cold hard ground. They took off his shoes, pants, and underwear. Groups of boys were always taking his pants off, and that alone wouldn't have bothered him. It was having them off so
120

late at night and at the stockpens that puzzled him. Also his legs were cold.

"All right," Jimmie Sue said. "Let the stupid little thing in."

"Wait a minute," Duane said. "There's a flashlight there in the glove compartment. We want to show him where to go."

He got the flashlight and flashed it over Jimmie Sue, who was laying back in the pickup seat, as spraddle-legged as the narrow pickup would permit her to be. All the boys looked, and for a moment, paused in amazement. None of them had realized quite how fat Jimmy Sue was until the flashlight played over her huge hams and flabby stomach; nor had they considered how unappetizing the female anatomy could be when presented in its most unappealing light. They were all quiet for a moment, staring. It was only after they had looked for a while that they began to feel a little stirred up. Jimmie Sue was so ugly it was almost exciting—it was as if they were finally being shown the nasty things parents and preachers had always whispered about. It wasn't exactly what they had expected, because they persisted in thinking about it in terms of pretty girls, movie stars like Elizabeth Taylor, but it was precisely what they had been taught to expect, and after the shock wore off it was exciting.

"Shove that thing in here with me," Jimmie Sue said. "I never hired out for no peep show."

The boys shoved Billy in, more or less between Jimmie Sue's legs, and tried to shut the door. They couldn't get it completely shut but there were so many of them there was not much chance it would come open.

Billy grunted with surprise and tried to back out, but he was trapped.

"Why this is the dumbest thing I ever saw," Jimmie Sue said. "It don't even know what to do."

The boys flashed the light long enough to see that Jimmie Sue had managed to catch Billy with her legs, but she yelled at them to turn it off and they did. Apparently Billy got close enough to the object of it all that he caught on, because he stopped pushing backward and in a moment the pickup began to rock a little from side to side. Everybody yelled encouragement.

"Quit that yellin' and get hold of this thing," Jimmie Sue said irritably. "He ain't in."

The flashlight was brought into play again and it was discovered that Billy, cramped as he was, had completely missed his natural target and was poking energetically at a deep wrinkle in the folds of Jimmie Sue's stomach. Duane and Leroy laughed until they could barely stand up, but the younger kids were more fascinated than amused. None of them had ever seen so strange a sight, and they made no effort to correct Billy's aim. Jimmie Sue was getting madder by the minute.

Sonny stood by the rear end of the pickup, determined not to look. It wasn't that he thought Billy would mind him looking—it was just that he didn't really want to look. Jimmie Sue was uglier than Charlene, and the pickup would smell like onions for weeks.

"Why goddamn you, you little thing!" Jimmie Sue yelled furiously. "Now look what a mess you made!"

Sonny knew from the tone of her voice that it was time to get Billy out, so he hurried around to the door.

122

The boys still had the flashlight on and were cackling and giggling: Billy had reached the end of his journey while still in the wrinkle, and Jimmie Sue was pounding at his face, trying to back him out of the pickup. Sonny managed to scatter the crowd enough to get the door open and help Billy out, but calming him down was something else. He was scared and confused and shivering, and Jimmie Sue had bloodied his nose. Sonny helped him get dressed and even found the empty Coke bottle for him, but Billy no longer wanted it.

"Well, now I know idiots is just as bad as Mixicans," Jimmie Sue said. "Don't you wake me up for that crazy thing no more. I wouldn't mess with him again for less than three-and-a-half."

By the time they got back to the poolhall the front of Billy's shirt was all covered with blood. Sonny couldn't get the nosebleed completely stopped. He knew Sam the Lion was going to be furious, and he didn't blame him: it was no way to treat Billy. He wished he had known how to stop the whole business, but the only possible way would have been to offer to fight if they didn't let Billy alone, and he couldn't very well offer to fight when his own best buddy was one of the crowd. If Lester and Jacy hadn't run off to the swimming party none of it would have ever happened.

As soon as the pickup stopped Billy jumped out and ran in the poolhall. It was officially closed, but they could all see Sam the Lion inside, reading a newspaper he had spread out on one of the tables. All he was really doing was waiting for Billy to come in. They lived in a plain little three-room apartment above the poolhall, and Sam never went to bed until Billy was in safe.

Billy ran right on past him, up the stairs, and Sam left his paper and followed him. The boys waited nervously outside, wondering if they would be able to narrate the episode in such a way that Sam the Lion would see the humor in it. Sonny knew they couldn't and waited miserably for Sam to come down, but the boys who thought they might strutted around on the sidewalk talking with great bravado. Duane was sleepy and lay down in the cab of the pickup and went to sleep. The boys could have left, but none of them really wanted to go home until Sam the Lion came down and bawled them out. His bawling them out would relieve their minds of whatever minor guilt feelings they had about Billy, and would leave them free to enjoy the celebrity of having participated in such an event.

Finally the light went out in the upstairs apartment and Sam the Lion came down. He opened the door and stood quietly a minute, looking at the boys. Sam the Lion was not the type who yelled and cussed about the pranks boys pulled. They could not see his face, but the light from the poolhall touched his white mane of hair.

"Who's got his underwear?" he asked, after a minute.

Sonny had them, and it put him on a terrible spot. He had been so anxious to get Billy back in his pants that he had forgotten to put the underwear on him— he picked them up later and stuffed them in his pocket. For a moment he was tempted to say nothing and pretend the underwear was lost—if he pulled them out and handed them over it would make him seem more of a participant than he had been. Sam didn't withdraw the question and the other boys began to look at Sonny nervously, so he took the underwear out of his pocket and awkwardly handed them over.

"When I was helpin' get his pants on I couldn't find them," he said. "I just forgot to hand them to him."

"Who went and bloodied his nose?"

"Jimmie Sue Jones," Leroy said. "We thought he was getting tired of being a virgin so we chipped in and bought him a piece. Jimmie Sue got mad about somethin' and gave him that nosebleed."

"Jimmie Sue?" Sam said, startled. "You what?" He had supposed it was just a simple case of the boys taking Billy's pants off, something that happened all the time. When he realized what Leroy said he was stunned, and sat down in the doorway of the poolhall.

Sonny became really worried. "Is Billy all right?" he asked. "We're sorry, Sam."

"He went to sleep," Sam said, a little absently. "Did he want to go with Jimmie Sue?"

"Not hardly," Leroy said. "He didn't even know what he was supposed to do."

Sam scratched his ankles for a minute and then stood up again. He didn't look particularly mad, just tired and discouraged.

"Boys, get on home," he said. "I'm done with all of you. I don't want to associate with you anymore and I don't want Billy to, either. Scaring an unfortunate creature like Billy when there ain't no reason to scare him is just plain trashy behavior. I've seen a lifetime of it and I'm tired of putting up with it. You can just stay out of this poolhall and out of my picture show and café too."

With that he closed and locked the door and went upstairs to bed. The boys were thunderstruck. They had been prepared for Sam to rage and storm and instead he had simply closed the door and locked them out. No one knew what to say. They stood on the cold sidewalk a minute, confused.

"We're his best customers," Leroy said. "He can't run us off, can he?"

Sonny and the other boys knew very well he could. It made Sonny feel a little sick. They all crawled back into the pickup and Sonny delivered them to their homes. Duane didn't fully wake up until they were back at the rooming house, and when Sonny told him what Sam the Lion had done he thought it was hilariously funny. Since he had been lying down and Sam had not seen him it was clear to Duane that he was not included in the banishment.

"Good thing I went to sleep when I did," he said. "I'd hate to have to eat at that drive-in all the time."

He went in and contentedly went back to sleep, but Sonny stayed awake and reread most of an old copy of *Outdoor Life*. Duane taking the news the way he had made the evening even more depressing, and it had been depressing enough as it was.

Kissing Mrs. Popper had been the only good thing that happened all night, and Sonny had no idea what would come of that. It occurred to him that at least it would be something exciting to think about in bed, so he turned the light off and tried it. Her face and the touch of her lips were fresh in his mind and it worked pretty well, though occasionally, before he finished, a few old images of Jacy and Genevieve slipped in. Jacking off was an old game, monotonous, but a good way to get to sleep when all else failed.

CHAPTER XI

When Sonny kissed Mrs. Popper outside the Legion Hall it seemed to him that a whole spectrum of delicious experience lay suddenly within his grasp. No kisses had ever been so exciting and so full of promise, neither for him nor for Ruth. She felt as if she were finally about to discover something she had somehow missed discovering twenty years before. Neither of them foresaw any great difficulties, just the minor difficulty of keeping it all secret.

Both, in fact, were so excited that they longed to talk about it to someone, but that they couldn't do. In Thalia sex was just not talked about. Even Genevieve would go to considerable lengths to keep from calling a spade a spade. Everything acknowledged the existence of sex: babies were born now and then, and things to prevent them were sold at the drugstores and one or two of the filling stations. The men told dirty jokes and talked all the time about how they wished they had more pussy, but it didn't really seem to bother many of them so long as the football team was doing well. The kids were told as little about sex as

127

possible and spent most of their time trying to find out more. The boys speculated a lot among themselves and got the nature of the basic act straight when they were fairly young, but some of the girls were still in the dark about it when they graduated from high school. Many girls simply refused to believe that the things the boys peed out of could have any part in the creation of babies. They knew good and well that God wouldn't have wanted any arrangement of His to be *that* nasty.

The only thing everyone agreed on was that the act itself could only be earthly bliss. Once the obstacle of virginity was done away with, mutual ecstasy would be the invariable result. One or two of the bolder girls knew differently, but they didn't want to be thought freaks so they kept quiet about their difficulties.

When Sonny and Ruth met again, the Tuesday after the dance, they both expected things to be simple and wonderful, and they were both disappointed. For one thing, they both felt compelled to go through with the unnecessary trip to the doctor; both of them were nervous and tense and they rode to Olney in silence. The dusty air had given Ruth a sniffle, and Sonny could see the bluish shadows under her eyes. The wait in Olney was short, but on the way back they found themselves even more at a loss for conversation than they had been coming. Ruth could not imagine what had possessed her to think she could bring off such a thing as a love affair. They each concluded that they were not as appealing in the daylight as they had been in the dark, so they sat looking out their separate windows at their separate sides of the road. There was little in the leafless winter landscape to cheer them.

It was only when Sonny drove the Chevrolet into

the dimness of the garage, with Herman's lawn tools and hedge shears hanging neatly on the walls, that they regained some hope. They both realized they were about to miss the chance they had been counting on. Sonny reached for Ruth's hand and she quickly scooted over toward him and they kissed. The kiss was awkward but warm and they didn't think of moving apart—for several minutes they let their mouths and faces touch.

Both would have been just as happy to stay in the garage all afternoon, but they felt obligated to complete the experience, and for that they had to go in the house, where things were not so good. The wallpaper in the bedroom was light green, and blotched in places. It was the bedroom where Ruth and Herman had spent virtually all their married nights: on one wall there was a plaque Herman had been given for taking a troop of Boy Scouts to the National Jubilee. Two or three copies of *High School Athletics* lay on the bedside table.

"Are you sure he won't come?" Sonny asked. The room seemed full of the coach.

"You know he won't," Ruth said. "He's just starting basketball practice."

She took his hand again and they kissed standing up. Neither of them really believed what she said: as they kissed both of them kept imagining the coach walking in. They were so conscious of him they hardly felt the kiss, but Ruth was determined to go on however dangerous it was, even if Herman did walk in.

They were unable to think of a smooth way to undress—it would have been better to do it while they were still kissing, but neither of them was expert enough for that. Ruth had on a dress and a slip, both of which had to come off over her head. Sonny could not even get her bra unhooked with the dress still on. Both of them wished for something to say, something that would break the tension, but neither could think of anything. Finally they simply broke apart and hurried about their own undressing. Ruth got her dress off, but when she bent to pull the slip over her head one of the straps caught on a bobby pin—for an awkward moment she could not get the slip loose. Her face was hidden in the silk. Sonny moved to help her, but just as he did she tore it loose and looked up at him with a wry smile, as if to comment on her awkwardness. They took their undergarments off at the same time, both of them choked with embarrassment. Ruth glanced at Sonny's body, curious and a little frightened. He was two or three steps away from her and for a moment they did not know how to get to one another. Sonny was too self-conscious about his erection to move. Finally, with another wry smile, Ruth sat down on the bed and he sat down with her. When she lifted her arms to embrace him he saw the small scar on her breast. They fell over in an embrace but in a moment scrambled up again: the room was cold and they needed to be under the covers.

When they were covered and warm they felt better and kissed again with pleasure. They were amazed at the feel of one another's skin, but in a minute or two they began to be nervous again. It seemed to them they must have been lying there kissing for half an hour at least. Ruth touched her hand to Sonny's throat and chest now and then, but other than that she didn't move. He felt very unsure: it occurred to him that perhaps his experience was inadequate. There might be some way of doing it that was especially suitable to ladies, some way he knew nothing about.

Ruth had her eyes closed and was waiting trustfully for a beautiful thing to happen to her. She knew that Herman knew nothing about the beautiful thing, or that if he did he had no interest in giving it to her. But she supposed Sonny would know: she would only have to wait and receive it. His body was very warm against her. It was only when she opened her eyes and looked at him that she remembered how young he was and realized he didn't know what to do.

"It's all right," she said, opening her legs. Sonny gratefully moved about her, but there was another long moment of awkwardness when they tried to join. Sonny was not absolutely sure of the target, and when he found it Ruth could not at first accommodate him easily. When he moved she gasped and Sonny's face was so close to hers that he could not tell whether she felt pain or pleasure. She said nothing, so he kept moving—in a moment it became easier and pleasure made him move faster and more surely.

For Ruth the discomfort was only momentary, but even once it ceased she could not manage to cross over into pleasure. The bed had begun to squeak. As Sonny moved more confidently it squeaked louder, and Ruth could not help hearing it. She would never have imagined it could squeak so loudly. Soon the squeaking drove all hope of pleasure from her mind. The noise made her fearful that someone outside the house might hear it; anyone walking on the sidewalk in front of the house could hear it, she was sure.

In a few moments she was near panic: she was convinced that everyone in Thalia could hear the squeaking bedsprings. If all the cars stopped, if the housewives came to their doors and listened, they could all hear the squeaking bed and would know what she was doing. It was a horrible bed; she felt it had betrayed her. No one could receive a beautiful thing with such a squeaking going on beneath her. She tried to lie very still, but Sonny's movement went on, and the sound was constant. Finally she began to cry, and when the tears dripped down her cheeks and wet Sonny's neck he realized that something was wrong after all. He raised his head and saw that Ruth's eyes were flooded with tears. She was ashamed that she had stopped him and quickly hooked her arm over his neck so he wouldn't raise up and see her face again. Sonny felt she must want him to stop but his body didn't want to and in a moment he went on, hearing the springs only as a faint background to his pleasure. Soon he finished and lay still upon her.

As soon as the squeaking stopped Ruth felt better. She kept her arms around Sonny, holding him so he could not see her face and now and then wiping the tears out of her eyes with the back of one hand. Once Sonny became still it was very pleasant to have his body upon hers—he was so warm and young, almost like a child. She had always wanted a child more than anything, but Herman wouldn't hear of it—he didn't want the expense. On the rare occasions when he took his pleasure of her he was always careful to wear a condom, even though they made Ruth's bladder hurt. Having Sonny upon her was very different, and deeply pleasant. She ran her hands up and down his back, and when she felt composed again lifted her arms so he could raise his head.

"I'm sorry I cried," she said. "I guess I was just scared."

"Aw, he isn't going to come," Sonny said, no longer worried. "They're runnin' plays right now, I bet."

"No, not scared of that," Ruth said, touching his mouth softly with her fingers. "I was scared I could never do this, I guess. I wanted to be wholehearted about it, but I wasn't."

She was silent a moment. "Do you know what it means to be heartbroken?" she said. "It means your heart isn't whole, so you can't really do anything wholeheartedly."

Sonny wanted to leave, but he didn't think he should, quite so soon. Mrs. Popper was sad, but at least she seemed calm and she kept touching him softly with her hands. He kissed her lightly and her cheeks were warm; then he stretched and drew the covers back a little, so he could see more of her body. She was very slim and smallbreasted, her arms a little too thin. When Ruth saw he was looking at her she grew frightened. She had never considered her body attractive, and she was afraid that if Sonny looked too long he would not want to be with her anymore. She turned on her side and curled toward him, her head on his thighs. Her shoulder bones stuck out, making her look even thinner. Sonny rubbed her back a minute and then got out of bed and quietly dressed. When he sat down on the edge of the bed to tell her good-bye she was on the verge of tears again.

"I was right the first time, wasn't I?" she said hopelessly. "I'm too old and ugly for a young man like you. I don't know how to do this anyway and maybe I'm too old to learn. I can't do anything without crying about it—how could you like me?"

"I like you," Sonny said awkwardly—actually he was not sure. All her crying upset him and made him nervous about himself, and she was certainly not as pretty as a movie star or as pretty as Jacy. Still, he did like her some. Since they hadn't got caught he had begun to feel elated about the whole thing. It was an adventure to have slept with somebody's wife. He didn't know if he would tell anybody or not, but it was sort of a feather in his cap, nonetheless.

Ruth sighed. "If you like me then you decide what to do about me," she said. "I'm not going to chase after you anymore. If you really like me you figure out how to come and see me—I sure don't want you to drive me to the doctor. I think right now you just like what you can do with me. That's fine, but now that you've found out women think you're good looking you'll probably want to go do it with somebody younger and prettier. I wouldn't blame you one bit."

Suddenly she wanted him to leave. She had become embarrassed about her body and didn't want him to see her naked anymore. She stayed curled up on the bed, her breasts and loins hidden from him.

"Track starts pretty soon," Sonny said. "I just won't go out. I can sneak up the alley and in the back door."

He sounded like he really wanted to, and Ruth changed back to hoping. What if he did only want her for sex? It was more than anyone else had ever wanted her for. Suddenly she felt like doing something a little wanton and she sat up and kissed him, her naked breasts against his shirt. Sonny liked that, and when he left he looked back through the doorway and saw her, still naked, bending over the bed to strip away the sheets. It would be well worth giving up track to come and see her, even though the coach would rage and storm at losing his only decent hurdler.

* * *

The second time Sonny came, Ruth wanted to tell him that the squeaking bedsprings bothered her, but she didn't quite have the nerve. She really wanted them to lie down on the floor, but she was afraid if she told Sonny he would think her depraved or something. She knew men were curious when it came to women's desires. Nothing revolted Herman more than to think that she was enjoying him that way. Once or twice in their marriage she had felt something good, but when she began to move or wiggle beneath him to make it feel even better it made Herman furious. "Lay still," he said. "What kind of woman do you think you are, anyway?" After that she lay still, and if she happened to feel something a little good she didn't let him know. Herman was so heavy that most of the time she just felt mashed.

She had not really expected Sonny to come again; when he slipped inside the back door she was filled with delight, and determined not to make any mistakes that might scare him away. They were both still very nervous, and the bedsprings bothered Ruth even more than they had the first time. They were almost too much. She felt something a little good but the springs kept her from concentrating on it; every time she felt it the grinding of the springs drove it away, and finally she simply endured them, waiting for the quiet lovely time when he was still, dozing on her body.

Sonny knew something was wrong because Ruth's body was cold and her arms and legs were tensed— she was trying to hold herself in such a way that the springs would be silent. She managed not to cry, but it took a long time for the tension to drain out of her—she was so tense that even the aftermath was not so enjoyable. Neither of them spoke—they simply had no words. Ruth was not sure she wanted him to come anymore; it was not working out at all like she had imagined. But when she felt a little better she began to stroke his back and to play with the shaggy hair at the back of his neck, and she decided she did want him again. Something about it was good, even if much was bad.

On his third visit she gathered up her nerve and told him, as they were undressing, that the noise of the bedsprings bothered her. She asked if they could lie on a quilt on the floor. Sonny was mildly surprised, but it was okay with him. When Ruth saw that he didn't think it was wrong of her to want it all to be nice she was so relieved she couldn't speak. She walked to the hall closet, naked, and got an old blue quilt that she and Herman had quit using years ago.

They spread the quilt on the floor by the little gas stove and sat a moment watching the flicker of the blue gas flames as they touched one another. They still couldn't talk, but they had ceased to be nervous, and they quit trying to conceal their loins from one another. For Ruth the quiet was wonderful. All she could hear was Sonny's breath and her own and she knew no one in the street could hear them breathing. She realized too that Sonny was enjoying her keenly and that made her glad. He was in no hurry and Ruth had moments of pleasure that were stronger than any she had ever known before. She discovered that Sonny didn't mind at all if she moved: in fact, he liked it. She became excited enough that her breath was ragged, but it was all still new to her and she could not pull the moments of pleasure together into one that was complete. For her the beautiful time was still afterward. Sonny was still inside her when he went to sleep, and Ruth found that lovely. It was almost as if he were a child inside her, and she put her calves over his legs to keep him there. When he finally came out she slipped upward on the quilt so that his warm cheek was against one of her breasts. It was so lovely that she wanted it not to change. That day, for the first time, she was regretful when he had to leave.

By the time Sonny had paid her a half-dozen visits he was everything to Ruth: he was what made the days worth confronting. The thought that he might quit coming filled her with terror. The thought of going back to the existence she had had before he came was too much to face.

Sonny allowed her to love him, though it was strange to him and he had to get used to it slowly. They were soon able to spend four or five hours a week on the old blue quilt. Ruth learned a great deal about Sonny and also a great deal about herself. After the first weeks she did nothing that would frighten him. She learned that he liked to be naked around her—it gave him a sense of adventure. She gladly let him, often mending his shirts or patching his pants after they had made love. She discovered that she had no particular modesty about her loins, only about her breasts, which seemed to her too small. Also she was afraid the small scar might disgust Sonny, since apparently it disgusted Herman. She took to wearing one of Herman's old hunting shirts while they talked. Sonny didn't like for her to wear anything while they were making love, but she always put it on afterward. She learned gradually how to play with him and how to tease him. One day she got a brush and comb and showed him a way to comb his hair that she felt was more becoming. Sonny was delighted. She would have liked to cut his hair for him, but there wouldn't have been time.

She soon made terms with lovemaking itself, though for a time they were not the best possible terms. She thought that once they relaxed with one another the beautiful thing would happen, the whole moment toward which all the sharp little individual moments tended. She had read about it, she expected it, she longed for it, and came very close to it, but it eluded her. For a week or two she was sure, every time, that it would happen. Once or twice she came so close that she was desperate for it to happen, and when she missed it after all her agitation was very intense. The violence of her excitement surprised Sonny and disturbed him a little: despite her weeping spells he thought of her as a quiet, rather timid woman. Her movements were sometimes so strong and unexpected that he was thrown off balance—once when she missed she was beside herself with disappointment. "Oh please," she said. "Please keep going." Sonny was already gone, but she continued to struggle against him until they were both soaked with sweat; he could not call himself back, and she gave up.

After that Sonny didn't come back for three days and Ruth was fearful she had ruined it all. When he did come she was so thrilled and relieved that she resolved not to seek the moment if it was going to put everything else in danger. If he would keep coming, keep wanting her, that would be enough. They sat on the blue quilt and she opened his shirt and rubbed his chest with her palm. When she looked past him, at the green wallpaper and Sears and Roebuck furniture she realized that she had lived for years in a room that was terribly drab.

Sonny was hesitant about making love, worried that he could cause Ruth disappointment again. "No, look," she said, taking his hand and kissing his palms and fingers. "Nothing was your fault. You have to remember that I've been lonely for a long time. Loneliness is like ice. After you've been lonely long enough you don't even realize you're cold, but you are. It's like I was a refrigerator that had never been defrosted at all—never. All these years the ice has just been getting thicker. You can't melt all that ice in a few days, I don't care how good a man you are. I didn't even realize it, like I didn't realize till just now how ugly this room is. I don't know, maybe at the center of me there's some ice that never will melt, maybe it's just been there too long. But you mustn't worry. You didn't put it there." She moved her hand up to his shoulders.

The talk of ice and refrigerators meant little to Sonny, but he was relieved that she wanted him to make love to her again. That day she was very warm and amenable, but much calmer—calmer than he had ever known her. He recognized that in a way she had withdrawn from the struggle, but his own pleasure was so strong that he merely felt grateful, not responsible. She saw to it that he didn't feel responsible, and for herself, had no difficulties except at the very end— then, for a wistful, regretful moment, she felt like crying.

After that, for more than a month, she concentrated on making Sonny welcome. He came often, sometimes just to make love, sometimes staying to drink some hot chocolate or to let her mend his clothes. He tolerated the chocolate and the clothes mending, but Ruth knew very well that what they did on the quilt was what he really liked, what he enjoyed doing with her. It thrilled her that that, of all things, would be what made a person want to come and see her. She expected, almost from day to day, that he would tire of her, and when she saw him coming in the door wanting that same thing of her, she was always happy for a moment.

Then, in March, things changed. Sonny came in one day and repeated a story about Coach Popper, one he had just heard. The week before the coach had taken the track boys to a meet in Fort Worth. Bobby Logan was sharing a room with the coach and in the middle of the night the coach mistook Bobby for Mrs. Popper and kissed him on the ear. All the boys thought that was pretty hilarious, and Sonny repeated the story to Ruth because he thought it might get her to talking about the coach a little. He could not help being curious about their life together. She told him that the coach seldom touched her, but Sonny could hardly believe that. The coach was so hairy and horny looking that the boys all supposed he kept after her all the time. Around the gym and the practice field the coach gave the impression that he was an inveterate woman chaser. "Find 'em, fool 'em, fuck 'em, and forget 'em," he was often heard to say. Sonny had the nagging feeling that the reason Ruth couldn't come with him was because the coach's tool was bigger and better. Time and again the coach had pointed out to one boy or another the ignominy of having an insufficient tool.

"Why hell yes, Joe Bob," he would say. "A feller can get along with false teeth and a glass eye and hearing aids and even a hook or a wooden leg if he has to, but there ain't no known substitute for a big dick. I guess you're just out of luck."

When he told Ruth about the ear-kissing incident he half expected her to be flattered that her husband would miss her so, but instead she looked miserable and forlorn. They had already finished lovemaking and she was so dispirited by the news that she neglected even to cover herself with the flannel shirt.

"I don't care," she said, tears seeping out of her eyes. "I don't care who he likes. If he wants to play around with little boys and they think it's funny why should I care? I just get tired of everybody thinking he's such a mighty man just because he coaches football. I'm the one they think is nothing, just his mousy wife, and they're right, I am mousy. I might not have been if I hadn't been ignored for twenty years. Now I'm forty and I don't have any children and I can't even do . . ." She sniffed. "I can't even do sex."

Sonny was stunned. He had never been so surprised.

"Why did you stay with him?" he asked finally. Then it was Ruth who was dumb. It was a question she had avoided for years.

"I wasn't brought up to leave a husband," she said in a small voice. "I guess that's why. Or maybe I was just scared to."

"But how did you come to marry him?" Sonny asked, still curious.

"Because my mother didn't like him, I guess," Ruth said. "I was fooled too. I was twenty years old and I thought hairy-chested football coaches were about it. I've paid for my own bad judgment."

There the conversation stalled—Ruth was too depressed to talk, and Sonny was confused. It seemed to him that Ruth must think the coach was queer or something, and the coach was the last man that anyone would accuse of such a thing. A few of the boys thought Mr. Cecil must be—they knew he got some kind of a kick out of watching them all swimming and horsing around naked at the irrigation ditch—but Mr. Cecil was much too much of a gentleman to do anything out of the ordinary, and nobody knew for sure about him. To suspect the coach of being that way was entirely too much—he didn't even mention the conversation to Duane. In fact, he had never told Duane he was sleeping with Mrs. Popper because he was afraid Duane would make fun of him for sleeping with an older woman.

It was that night, after that conversation, that things began to change for Ruth. She dreamed she was having a baby. She had had such dreams for years, but usually they were vague and fragmentary, but this one was vivid. It was not just a baby she had, though; it was Sonny. He was removed from between her legs, and afterward lay at her breast.

The next day Sonny came, and while they were spreading the blue quilt on the bedroom floor Ruth remembered the dream. It was very vivid in her mind as she undressed. She lay quietly, her eyes closed, as Sonny began, but almost before she knew it she became excited, so much so that she could not be still. She thought of the dream again, hoping the excitement would die before she became completely possessed by it, but instead of dying it became keener. Because of the dream, pleasure took her over: with her eyes shut she could pretend she was giving birth. Sonny was inside her but in truth she was bringing him out—it was that which excited her. She grabbed his hands and put them on her thighs, so that he would force them wider. She was filled with a strength that she had not suspected and held him with her thighs, just at the entrance, just connected, both of them struggling, until she was finally seized, rent by what she felt. Then she took Sonny back to her, her heart was pounding, her eyelids fluttering; she almost fainted with the relief of delivery. For half an hour she slept, not moving, and Sonny lay on top of her, not knowing if he dared move. He had no doubt that Ruth had broken through, but her success was as strange and almost as frightening as her failures. The strength she had called up amazed him: for minutes she had held him with just her thighs, his arms pinned to his sides so tightly he could not get one free. Yet, sleeping beneath him, she might have been a girl, so still and at peace she seemed.

When Ruth awakened she did not want Sonny to leave. She felt entirely comfortable, and she wanted to touch him, play with him, have his hand on her. After that, she never used the dream again, but she kept it in her mind as a safeguard, and even though she still sometimes missed, having the dream was a great reassurance.

In the weeks after Ruth's breakthrough the two of them became very close and comfortable. Once Sonny quit worrying about her response or lack of response, he found her much more pleasant to be with, and there were even afternoons when he visited her, not to make love but just to talk, hold hands, or watch television.

Only one problem arose, and that was one they had been expecting: the town knew about them. A couple of the housewives who lived along the alley compared notes, and in a few days the town knew. Sonny worried about it a lot, Ruth hardly at all.

"What do you think the coach would do if he found us?" Sonny asked one day. Ruth was sitting on the quilt combing her brown hair. She had decided to let her hair grow longer.

"Probably shoot us both," she said lightly. "He's always glad to have an excuse to use his deer rifle."

Sonny mused on that and decided she was right. "What do you think we ought to do about it?" he asked.

"I don't know," Ruth said, puckering her mouth at him happily. "Why don't we buy a new quilt? This one's about had it."

The next day she got one, for sentimental reasons also blue.

CHAPTER XII

One night in mid-March Sonny woke up too early —around 3:30 A.M. The first thing that occurred to him was that Sam the Lion would be asleep. Sam the Lion had made his decree of banishment stick, and, though Sonny had endured it as best he could, he had about reached the point where he could endure it no longer. It occurred to him that if he got dressed and went down to the café Genevieve might let him sit and talk awhile. A cold March norther was blowing and the warm blankets were hard to leave, but the chances were he would have to leave them in an hour or so anyway, to make an early butane run.

Genevieve was sitting in one of the booths, reading an old issue of the *Ladies Home Journal*. To his immense relief she looked delighted to see him.

"Come on in here," she said. "I'm not going to throw any bottles at you."

"Could I have a cheeseburger?" he asked quickly. One of the worst parts of the penalty had been eating at the drive-in, where the cheeseburgers were half raw and the tomatoes soggy.

"You can have two if you want them," she said, and she made him two while he sat nervously in the booth. When she brought them in he swallowed the first one in only five or six bites.

"Quit eating so fast," Genevieve said. "You've lost weight. Even if it was a terrible thing to do to Billy, I'm on your side."

Sonny was grateful. "I couldn't talk them out of it," he said. "It was Leroy's idea."

"Where was Duane?" she asked.

It was a ticklish question. Duane had gone right on using the café and the poolhall, just as if he hadn't been along. It was a sore spot with the other boys, and a few of them wanted to tell Sam the Lion about Duane's part in it. Thinking about it made Sonny uneasy.

"He was there," he admitted. "Just don't tell Sam."

"I figured he was," Genevieve said quietly. "He just didn't have the decency to own up and take his punishment. He probably got just as big a kick out of it as Leroy did."

Sonny was embarrassed and kept eating the cheeseburger. Nobody had ever criticized Duane in front of him before—for no reason that he could think of life was becoming more complicated.

"Well, I won't say no more about it," she said. "That's between you and him. But you've got to make up with Sam, that's for sure. I won't have you eating at that drive-in anymore. He misses you and he'll make it up if you do it right. He knows you too well to think you really went out of your way to upset Billy."

"How's Dan?" Sonny asked.

"Coming along. He's well enough to be contrary."

Sonny began to relax. The café was just the same:

the jukebox, the booths, the high-school football schedule pinned on the wall. Genevieve cradled the coffee cup in her hand and stared at the frost-smoked windows.

"I've gotten into something else," Sonny said tentatively. She was the only person he could think of that he might be able to talk to.

"Got a new girl friend?" She grinned, and then she suddenly remembered the gossip. Until that moment she had not taken it at all seriously.

"I guess I have," Sonny said. "Not a girl friend, a lady friend. It's Mrs. Popper." He didn't know whether he was glad to have the secret out, and Genevieve was not sure at all that she was glad to have received it.

"Ruth Popper?" she said, amazed. "How do you mean, Sonny? Have you been flirtin' with her like you do with me, or is it different?"

"It's different," he said. "It's . . . like in a movie."

She saw that he was watching her face, dreadfully anxious to know what she thought about the news.

"I don't know what to think about you," she said. "Quit lookin' at me that way. This is an awful small town for that kind of carrying on, I can tell you that. You can't sneeze in this town without somebody offerin' you a handkerchief."

"Coach Popper don't care nothin' about her," Sonny said. "I don't see why he should care."

"He cares about himself, though—and about what people think of him. He owns a lot of guns, too."

Sonny looked so young and solemn and confused that after a moment it all amused her and she chuckled. He looked far too confused to be into anything wicked.

"All right," she said. "I won't say no more about it.

You're a man of experience now, you don't need my advice anyway."

Sonny didn't know about advice, but he was glad to have her approval, however he could get it. He had some pie and chatted about lesser things until the streets outside were gray with a cold dawn. Genevieve got up to tend to the coffee maker.

"I better go on," Sonny said. "Sam's going to be coming any time."

"You stay," Genevieve said, not even turning around.

Sonny didn't like the idea, but he didn't have long to worry about it. In a few minutes the café door opened and Sam the Lion and Billy stepped inside. Sam had on his old plaid mackinaw, his khakis, and his house shoes. When he saw Sonny he opened his mouth to say something but Genevieve cut him off.

"Don't say a word," she said. "I won't have him eating at that drive-in no more. He can apologize like a civilized person and you can listen to him."

When Billy saw Sonny his face brightened and he went right over and sat down by him. He had forgotten all about the bad night, and didn't remember anything bad that Sonny had done. Sonny turned his baseball cap around backward for him.

"I'm sorry," Sonny said, when Sam the Lion came to the booth.

"Scoot over," Sam said, a little embarrassed. "If Billy can stand you I can too." He sat down by Sonny and ordered his sausage and eggs. Sonny was so relieved that he couldn't think of anything to say, and Sam the Lion was so relieved that he couldn't keep quiet. There was the basketball team to talk about, a disgraceful, hapless basketball team that hadn't come within thirty points of winning a game. Sam the Lion gave it hell, and continued giving it hell as the café filled, as the cowboys and the truckers came in, blowing on their cold hands. Soon smoke was rising from a dozen or more cups of Genevieve's coffee. Sam the Lion poured his in a saucer and went on talking while the two boys, not listening, happily ate their breakfasts.

CHAPTER XIII

It was in the early spring, when Sonny was really beginning to get in touch with Ruth, that Duane really began to get out of touch with Jacy. He forgave her for going to the nude swimming party in Wichita, but somehow they were never as comfortable with one another as they had been before that happened. The thing that bothered Duane most was that, instead of going to Wichita less and less, Jacy was going more and more. It got so he was lucky if he spent one Saturday night a month with her. Time after time she drove off to Wichita with Lester Marlow, always, she said, because her mother insisted. Duane raged and stormed, but he never quite got up the guts to have it out with Lois. Instead, he decided to concentrate on getting Jacy to marry him as soon as they graduated. He knew she had her application in to several fancy girls' schools, and he realized that if she got away to college he would have seen the last of her. His only chance was to marry her sometime during the summer, while she was still at home.

Jacy, however, had put aside all thought of marrying Duane. She had convinced herself that that would be a very selfish thing to do. Her parents, particularly her father, would never stand for it: he would have it annulled, Duane would lose his job and would probably be in the army before the summer was out. It would clearly be unfair of her to put Duane in such a position. If she sacrificed what she felt for him, he could keep his job and stay out of the army several months longer. It was the sort of thing he would thank her for someday.

The truth was, Jacy had been very strongly affected by the nude swimming party. Unknown to anyone but herself and Lester she had been back several times to exactly the same type of party. All the Saturday night trips were of her own arranging, but she told Duane they were her mother's doings. Duane was too naïve to understand her wanting to mix with kids like herself, kids who had money and lived recklessly. It would save everyone misery to let him think it was her mother's fault.

Jacy had begun to be very attracted to Bobby Sheen, the leader of the wild set. He was not especially handsome, but he combed his hair in a rakish fashion and he was always merry and lustful. It was rumored that he and Annie-Annie made love four times a week, sometimes in curious ways. He had an air of absolute confidence, as if he were ready for anything and could do anything that might be demanded of him. At first Jacy didn't give herself much of a chance with him, supposing that he and Annie-Annie would soon get married; but then she danced with him one night and took hope. He got erections while dancing with her, just like other boys did.

A week or so after that she thought it was really going to happen between Bobby and herself. After one of the naked swimming parties the boys and girls paired off and went to bed in various bedrooms of the huge Sheen house. Jacy had to share a bed with Lester Marlow, but that was all right; the first time it had happened she made it quite clear to Lester that sharing the bed was all she intended to do. Anything more intimate was out of the question. Lester had red pubic hair, which seemed to her ridiculous. After this particular party Lester and Jacy both went to sleep, as usual, but somebody woke Jacy up by kissing her. It was Bobby Sheen, and he didn't have any clothes on. When he saw she was wide awake he quietly motioned for her to follow him, and she did, trembling a little. Fortunately she had on some green pajamas, so it was not too immodest.

Bobby led her down the carpeted hall to an empty bedroom and the minute he got her through the door he unbuttoned her pajama top and began to play with her breasts. He was merry and confident about it all and it didn't occur to Jacy to stop him. There was a huge double bed in the room and once they got on it Bobby undressed her completely. Jacy was excited and decided to cast caution to the winds. She let him get between her legs and was prepared to let him go all the way, but he stopped wanting to. He started to and did something that hurt a little before he stopped, looking at her with disbelief.

"Are you a virgin?" he asked.

"I guess so," Jacy admitted miserably. "But I don't want to be."

Bobby made a face of mock-horror, as if he had discovered a leper in his bed.

152

"What a letdown," he said, but with his usual good cheer. "I'm sorry I woke you up. Why don't I give you the name of a gynecologist? There's no point in being messy on Momma and Daddy's bed."

"Okay," Jacy said, eager to be agreeable. She was not sure what having the name of such a person committed her to, but she was willing to try anything Bobby recommended. The look on his face made her realize that it was absolutely ridiculous for her to be a virgin: she was probably the only one in the whole house. That thought was so mortifying that she sat up and reached for her pajamas, prepared to go ignominiously back to bed. Bobby, however, was not all that discouraged.

"Don't run off," he said cheerfully. "I was just surprised. If you're not sleepy we can still play around a while."

Jacy was not sure what that involved either, but she dutifully lay back down. "What about Annie-Annie?" she asked.

"That bitch sleeps like a horse," Bobby said.

Jacy was quite shocked to discover all that "playing around" involved. Bobby Sheen knew amazing things to do, things she would not have put up with one second if it had been anyone other than him. As it was, she was determined not to show her ignorance and just let him do whatever he pleased. Him doing things was okay, but when he wanted her to do things to him she was so nervous and shaky that she got goose bumps all over. Bobby couldn't help giggling.

"Don't boys have cocks in that town you live in?" he asked, laughing.

Jacy was at a loss for an answer. For days she could not get the evening off her mind. It seemed to her she

153

had come off very badly with Bobby. He didn't call her for any dates afterward, and every other boy who had ever been near her had promptly called her for dates. The only conclusion possible was that Bobby found her backward and country, and if there was anything she hated and loathed it was to be thought backward and country. It was clear that she was going to have to get rid of her virginity. She gave the matter much thought and came up with a plan that seemed to have multiple advantages. The week after graduation the senior class was going on what was called their senior trip. For four years the class had saved up money for it, and had given bake sales, conducted scrap iron drives, and done all sorts of other chores to make the money. They were going all the way to San Francisco and back on the bus and it would take every bit of the money they had made. She and Duane would thus be together practically all the time for a whole week, and it occurred to her that if she let Duane sleep with her sometime during the trip it would solve all kinds of problems. For one thing, it would *make* the senior trip. She and Duane would be regarded as extraordinarily daring, and all the kids would talk about them all the way home. Also, if she slept with Duane a time or two it would make it that much easier for her to break up with him after the senior trip was over. Duane would have something beautiful to remember, and he wouldn't be able to say she had promised him anything she hadn't delivered.

Then when she got back from the trip she would no longer be a virgin and could set about taking Bobby Sheen away from Annie-Annie. If she could get him in love with her before the summer was over she might forget about the girls' school and go to S.M.U., where

Bobby was going. They might even pledge related fraternities.

The one flaw in the whole plan was Duane. It occurred to her that he might not want to break up with her even if she let him sleep with her before breaking the news. He was dead set on their getting married in the summer, and he was a very stubborn boy. She decided that the best thing to do would be to make an ally of Sonny—she knew Sonny would do anything she wanted him to if she played up to him the least little bit. If Duane got ugly and wouldn't quit trying to go with her she could then date Sonny a few times. Duane would never in his life excuse that.

The senior play was rehearsing at that time and Sonny and Jacy both had parts. In order to strengthen her hold over him Jacy started giving Sonny a ride home every night; often, at her suggestion, they would ride out to the lake and sit and talk a while before going home. Jacy mostly wanted to talk about Duane, about how much she wanted to marry him but how frightened she was that it would never work out, her parents being set against it like they were. Sonny tried to listen, but mostly he just looked. Jacy had a way of leaning forward so she could hook a finger inside her blouse and straighten her bra strap, a movement that always made him ache with desire. Even the flash of her white teeth as she popped her chewing gum— even that could cause discomfort. Once in a moment of emotion she reached out and they held hands for a little while. "I tell you I don't know what I would do if I didn't have you to talk to, Sonny," she said affectionately.

At such times Sonny could hardly keep from wishing that Duane and perhaps Ruth too were out of the picture. Jacy was everything he wanted. She had always seemed infinitely more desirable than Charlene or the other girls, but she had also begun to seem cool and simple and lovely in contrast to Ruth, who had begun to disturb him a good deal. Once Ruth found pleasure her need for him rapidly increased and her sensual appetite had become, if anything, stronger than his own. At first he had found it delightful—he had never imagined that he would ever in his life have as much sex as he wanted. By the time he had visited Ruth almost daily for a month he was forced to admit to himself that it might even be possible to have more than he wanted. Ruth lost all caution, all concern for what the townspeople might think. All she wanted was Sonny, and he began to feel strangely washed out and restless. He ceased to eat particularly much, or to sleep particularly well. Despite almost daily sex he had erotic dreams at night and would often wake up to find himself painfully engorged.

As he grew more tired and less certain of himself, Ruth seemed to grow fresher, more self-possessed, and more lovely, though it was only at odd, oblique moments, lying beside her or coming into her room, that he noticed that she was lovely. Instead of drooping about the house as she had once done she acquired grace and animation and moved about as active and lithe as a girl. She even repapered the bedroom, much to the coach's disgust.

Sonny found he could not keep a consistent feeling about her two days or even two hours in a row. At one moment, during lovemaking, seeing her become avid, sweaty, almost frenzied, he felt as he had the first day with her in the car, as if he were being pulled by some force stronger than his own. A few moments later, an hour later, he would see her, her face calmed, lit from within, her eyes wide and soft, and feel completely happy with her. He simply could not understand what had happened to her. When she touched him, drew him into her, it was not that she was trying to have him exactly—she was insisting that he have her. She was not saying "You're mine," she was saying "I'm yours," and that was almost more troubling. She was completely focused on him; the rest of her life had ceased to matter.

Her hair had grown longer, and he loved to smooth tendrils of it back behind her ears. But he wasn't sure that he wanted any person to be his: it made him too responsible.

"You're my love, I can't help it," she would say, if he brought the matter up. And she would go on brushing her hair, completely at peace with herself because of him.

One night he almost gave way to an impulse and spoke of Ruth to Jacy, but he didn't because he realized just in time that it would mean the end of his talks with Jacy. She wanted to talk about her problems, not his. Because of their talks she began to fill his fantasies again, and the fantasies made a fitful background to his afternoons with Ruth. Somehow he was sure that passion with Jacy would be more intense and yet less strained than it sometimes was with Ruth. With Jacy things would be sharper and better timed, and would never be blunted by anxiety or bad balance or anything.

To Ruth, that period of her life later seemed a little insane, but insane in a good way. She remembered little about it, just Sonny's person. Occasionally it occurred to her that people were probably talking, or that she ought to go to the store or somewhere, but none of those things seemed immediate. Sonny was the only thing immediate.

Later, when time was passing much more slowly, she told herself that she had not planned well—she had not thought to save anything. She had held nothing back for the morrow, but it was because she did not suppose she could afford to think about the morrow.

It was not until an evening in early May that the fact of a future was brought home to her. Sonny had come that afternoon, and all had gone well. Three hours later, while Herman was finishing his supper, Ruth went out into the backyard and began to take some clothes off the line. It was just dusk, a soft spring dusk, and as she was unpinning Herman's stiff, unironed khakis a car went by on the street. Idly curious, she glanced around to see who was passing and saw Sonny and Jacy, on their way to play practice in Jacy's convertible.

She only glimpsed them as the car passed between her house and the next, and all she saw really was the glint of spring sunset on Jacy's gold hair. She did not even see Sonny's face, did not know whether he looked happy or glum to be with Jacy, but the glimpse ruined her content. For a moment or two she had to hold onto the clothesline—it was as if she had been struck a numbing blow across her thighs. Her legs felt so unsteady that she could hardly move down the line to the next stiff pair of pants. Sonny had never mentioned Jacy to her: she had glimpsed the very beginning of something. Duane and Jacy might have broken up. As she dragged the sheets off the line she felt a sudden panic, silly but nonetheless terrifying.

She was sure that Sonny was in love with Jacy and would never come to her house again. She would have wept, but the dread that seized her was too dry. It was as if she had suddenly been faced with her own end, an end too dry and commonplace to cry about. When all the clothes were piled in the basket she stood in the yard a minute, under the empty lines, her only comfort the soft evening air. She could not stand the thought of going into the tight, hot kitchen, where Herman was eating black-eyed peas, but the next moment a thought came to her and she grabbed the clothes basket and hurried in. Herman had finished the peas and was eating a bowlful of yellow canned peaches, one of his favorite desserts.

"Herman," she asked, "have Duane and Jacy broken up? I thought I saw her go by just now with someone else in the car."

The coach looked up with mild interest. "Hope so," he said. "Nothin' I'd like better than to see them two bust up. I might get a couple of good baseball games out of Duane if they would."

Ruth took heart and took out the ironing board and sprinkler bottle. Life came back into her legs; she decided the spasm of dread had been irrational. Even so, considering it calmly, it was clear that in time she was bound to be hurt, and badly so. She was twenty years older than him, and he would not keep wanting her forever. Sooner or later he would leave and she would have to get over him, but she was so relieved to know that it was going to be later—not for a week, at least, and perhaps not for a month or even a year— that she resolved not to care. As she ironed she indulged herself in the pleasant fantasy that she was in Sonny's room, doing the ironing for him. She nursed a

159

strong secret wish to go to his room sometime, to be with him where he lived rather than where Herman lived.

The coach finished his peaches and lay on the couch for a couple of hours, watching television while Ruth finished ironing. When the late news came on he turned the set off: news bored him. He straggled lazily into the bedroom to undress, and found that Ruth was there ahead of him, sitting on the edge of the bed rubbing hand lotion into her hands. She had her shoes off and was barefooted. It seemed to the coach that she looked younger than a woman her age ought to look: her ankles were slim, and even her face looked young. He didn't know it, but she had managed to sustain her favorite fantasy all the way to the bedroom and was pretending to herself that she was undressing in Sonny's room. All the coach knew was that she irritated him. She went to the closet to hang up her dress and even the lightness of her walk irritated him. He sat down in the rocker to pull off his sweaty socks, remembering that she had mentioned Jacy and Duane.

"Who was it you seen with Jacy?" he asked, stirred by his dislike of the girl.

"I didn't get a good look at the boy," Ruth said, a little surprised. "It was Sonny Crawford I think."

The coach grunted. He stood up, emptied his pockets onto the dresser, and pitched his pants through the bathroom door in the general direction of the dirty-clothes hamper. It was a warm night and the room seemed a little close to him. He threw up a window and stood in front of it a minute, idly scratching his testicles and enjoying the nice south breeze.

After a minute he stretched out on the bed, but for some reason he couldn't get Jacy Farrow off his mind. It was little twats like her that ruined young athletes, so far as he was concerned. If it hadn't been for her, Duane would have come out for track and they might have won a track championship. As he lay on his back, still scratching himself, he thought how nice it would be to hump a little rich girl like her until she got so sick of it she would never want to see another boy, much less bother one. That would be a smart piece of coaching, but hard to bring off.

While his thoughts were running in that direction he happened to glance over and notice Ruth—or at least he noticed half of her. She was undressing behind the closet door, but the strong breeze had blown the door open a bit wider than usual and Ruth was half exposed, the line of the door bisecting her body. The coach saw one leg, one breast, one shoulder and the side of her head as she turned and reached into the closet to take her gown off the hook. Ordinarily the sight of Ruth's body gave him a feeling of mild distaste: his own mother had stood five-eleven and had worked just as hard as men worked nearly every day of her life. Nothing seemed more pathetic to him than a skinny woman, Ruth especially, but when he glanced at the closet he was not thinking of Ruth at all but of Jacy Farrow. He was thinking that if he ever got Jacy into the right corner he would pay back all the little pusses who had kept his boys stirred up over the years. The thought of administering such a lesson had him a little excited—his underwear developed a sizable hump. Ruth stepped out from behind the door, lowering the gown over her body, and the coach looked at her again. Something told him he would

161

never get Jacy into the right corner, but Ruth was right there and she was just like a girl anyway. She had kept *him* stirred up at one time—if she hadn't he would have stayed a bachelor and had the money to take some real hunting trips. He could have gone to Alaska, even. She deserved a prod as much as Jacy; no woman who had done a proper day's work moved as lightly as she moved.

Ruth's mind was still elsewhere—she was unaware of the state her husband was in. It was not a state she had expected him to be in again. She sat down on the bed with her back to him and rubbed her calves a minute before stretching out. While she was sitting there the springs squeaked and Herman got out of bed; she supposed he had forgotten to go to the bathroom.

"Turn off the light in there, please, when you're done," she said. Light from the bathroom made a bright patch on the floor of the darkened bedroom.

Then she turned to lie down and noticed with a start that Herman was not headed for the bathroom at all. He was at the dresser, his underwear bulging out ludicrously. The sight stunned her, as it always had: all their married life Herman had announced his arousal by going to the dresser and rummaging in the sock drawer until he found the prophylactics. While she watched he found a package and strode into the bathroom to make himself ready.

She knew that she was supposed to use the time while he was in the bathroom to prepare herself for wifely service, but she suddenly felt as if her whole body had become stiff as a plank. She had been thinking how nice it would be to spend a whole night in Sonny's room, but when confronted with Herman's intention all thought seemed to leave her. She merely lay on the bed, not thinking at all.

When Herman came out he switched off the bathroom light, so that the bedroom was dark. He lay down heavily and without hesitation rolled himself onto Ruth, only to roll back a moment later, chagrined.

"What the hell?" he said. "You done asleep?"

In her paralysis Ruth had forgotten to do what she was supposed to do on such occasions: lift her nightgown and spread her legs. Those two actions were all that Herman required of her in the way of sexual cooperation. She raised her hips off the bed and pulled up the gown, and when he was satisfied that the obstruction had been removed the coach rolled back onto her and after a couple of badly aimed thrusts, made connection. Once he struck the place he went at it athletically.

Ruth clenched her fists at her sides. Her chest and abdomen felt crushed, but it crossed her mind that she had crushed herself. What was crushing her was the weight of all the food she had fed Herman through the years, all the steaks, all the black-eyed peas, all the canned peaches. It was particularly the canned peaches: she had never until that moment realized how much she hated them. It seemed to her that pyramids of cans of slimy peaches piled on her abdomen. After a moment the weight became intolerable and she moved a little, to try and ease it. She moved from side to side and stretched her legs, to try and escape it. Herman sweated easily and his sweat was already dripping down her ribs, but what bothered her was the weight of the cans. As she kept moving, trying to lighten the weight, she became

aware of a distant pleasure. She began to writhe a
little, in order to adjust the weight of the pyramid and
intensify the pleasure—she flexed her legs and raised
the lower part of her body a little, trying to get the
weight right on the throbbing nerve.

Her movements annoyed the coach a great deal.
When he started he had not even been thinking of her,
but of Jacy, and thinking of Jacy had been very
enjoyable. At first Ruth had acted perfectly decent,
but just when it was getting nicest she began to writhe
and wiggle and even started going up and down
against him. The coach was too surprised and out-
raged to speak, and anyway he had got to the point
where he needed to hold onto Jacy in his mind. He
tried to beat Ruth down with his body, so she would
be still again, but his efforts had the opposite effect:
the harder he tried the more she moved. He couldn't
slow her down at all, and he couldn't stop himself.

For a minute, with pounding heartbeats, they were
running a hundred-yard dash with each other on equal
terms. Neither knew how close the tape was, neither
was sure of victory, but the coach crossed first. He
recaptured Jacy for a second and desperately burst
across, gasping with exhaustion and pleasure. Ruth
was just at the turn. The weight was terribly sharp for
a moment and then the coach's heavy surge burst the
pyramid and left her gasping, free of all weight.

For his part the coach wanted badly to be gone on
his side of the bed. Quickly he withdrew, but to his
amazement and shame Ruth would not let him. She
grasped him, put him back, would not have him leave,
and he was too tired and surprised to fight. Except for
the working of their lungs the two were still. In time,
when their breath became quieter, the room was

totally silent. The coach did not try again to withdraw, for fear he couldn't. When he did in the natural fashion he quickly rolled onto his side of the bed.

Ruth was away, in a misty, drowsy country, but even there she felt a little worried and a little sad. She had not meant it and could not understand how she had done it, given Herman something she thought was only for Sonny. It was as if her body had betrayed a trust and responded to the very man who had neglected it most. Perhaps she was not safe, not even from Herman. Hearing his exhausted breathing in her ear she had had a moment of sympathy for him as a person. She had felt for him a little bit. Perhaps she was no longer safe from anyone?

The coach knew good and well he wasn't safe. His body wanted to sleep, but his mind was far too agitated. He would never have imagined his own wife would grasp him: it was something worse than shameless. He didn't want to remain in the same bed with her and considered going to the couch. Still, Ruth was the one who had beslimed the bed: she ought to go. The messiness of the female body had never been more offensive to him. If he even moved his leg he touched a wet spot. Disgusted, he got up and went in the bathroom to clean himself. The bright light made him blink.

When he came back to the bed, Ruth was dozing. She knew he was offended, but it didn't touch her. She felt pleasantly sleepy and had overcome her mild distress at being suddenly accessible. If Herman was going to insist on his connubial rights, then all the better that she could finally enjoy it.

The coach stood over her in the dark, mad, but vaguely uneasy too. He had never dreamed Ruth had such wildness in her, and he was not sure how to get at her.

"Ain't you gonna change them sheets?" he asked sourly.

"Hum? No. Why?" she asked drowsily.

"Well by God," he said, walking distractedly around the bed. "You're a fine one, ain't you. If my mother was alive and knew how you acted she'd have your hide. I've always heard women got nasty in their old age but I never thought it would happen to no wife of mine."

"Didn't you like it, Herman?" Ruth asked, still sleepily. She was near enough asleep that she could be a little mean.

With a grunt the coach lay down and turned his back on her. Like it! It was a fine come-off. What could a man say to a damn woman?

CHAPTER XIV

"Keep an eye on them corks, Billy," Sam the Lion said, getting to his feet. "I've got to go water the grass a little."

The corks bobbed undisturbed in the brown water of a large stock tank, and Billy, also undisturbed, sat by the water's edge, watching them. Sonny was stretched out on his stomach in the Bermuda grass along the base of the tank dam. The May sun on his back was so warm that it made him drowsy, and he was almost asleep, content to leave Billy in full charge of the three fishing poles.

Sam the Lion took a long time to water the grass, but he finally came back, grumbling and buttoning his pants.

"Be nice to be able to piss," he said. "If I last another year I'll be dribblin' it on my shoes. I'd almost be willing to be young again if I could take a real piss. Looks like we ain't gonna catch much today."

"We never do," Sonny said. Once every year or two the pretty spring weather would tempt Sam the Lion to get out and, as he put it, get a little scenery. The rest of the time he was content to get his scenery from the pretty calendars the local foodstore put out.

When the urge for the outdoors came on him he would get Billy and the three fishing poles, enlist Sonny as a driver, and take the boys year after year to the same tank, perhaps the worst stocked fishing tank in the whole county. Once in a while they caught a perch or two, but always such undernourished specimens that old Marston refused to cook them.

"Hell, Sam, you wouldn't have nothing but two ounces of fried bones if I did cook them," he maintained.

Sam the Lion didn't much care, and neither did the boys. Billy loved to sit on the bank and watch the rings in the water or the dragonflies that skimmed along the surface. He was always surprised and a little disconcerted when Sam the Lion grabbed one of the poles and actually pulled up a fish. When he looked into the water he saw no fish, and he was never really sure where they came from.

After a while Sonny got tired of dozing and got up and walked along the tank dam a little way. It was a beautiful afternoon, a good day not to be doing anything—the sky was very blue and the pastures were green with spring grass and mesquite. In a moment he himself had the urge to water the grass in the way that Sam had, and he walked to the edge of the dam to do it. He felt warm and well and was faintly pleased by the spurt of his own water, even stretching himself a little to see if he could send a stream all the way to the foot of the dam. He didn't quite make it, but it was a high sloping dam and he came close enough to be fully content with his own range.

It was only as he turned around and was buttoning

himself that he noticed that Sam the Lion had observed his little game. It embarrassed him just a little, but it did something much stranger to Sam the Lion. Sam began to snort, always a sign that something was affecting him powerfully, and then he began to laugh his loud, solid, rich laugh, something he did so rarely that both boys were startled. He sat by the water laughing, running his hands through his hair. Tears began to run down his face so freely that Sonny was not sure what was happening, whether Sam was laughing or crying. He pulled his handkerchief out of his hip pocket and began to wipe his face but no sooner had he done that than he burst out cussing and got up and stomped around furiously on the Bermuda grass.

"Goddammit! Goddammit!" he cursed. "I don't want to be old. It don't fit me!"

Then, seeing that the boys were scared, he became embarrassed and sat back down, still sniffing and snorting. He looked at the water and blew his nose and for a minute tried to pretend that nothing out of the ordinary had happened. But both boys continued to stare at him and he gave it up and tried to explain.

"I'll tell you what it was, son," he said, looking at Sonny a little ruefully. "Seein' you pissing off the dam reminded me of something. I used to own this land you know. It's been right at fifty years since the first time I watered a horse at this tank. Reason I always drag you all out here probably—I'm just as sentimental as anybody else when it comes to old times. What you reminded me of happened twenty years ago—I brought a young lady swimming here. It was after my boys were already dead, my wife had lost her mind. Me and this young lady were pretty crazy, I guess. She

169

had all the spirit in the world, and we had some times. We come out here swimmin' one day without no bathin' suits and after we got out of the water I walked off up there to piss. She was always on the lookout for something funny and she offered to bet me a silver dollar I couldn't stand on the top of the dam and piss into the water. I took the bet and gave it a try but I never came no closer than you did. The lady's still got the silver dollar."

He was quiet, looking at the water.

Sonny had never known Sam the Lion except as an old man, and he was surprised and a little awed by the story. He wanted to ask who the woman was, but he didn't have the nerve.

"What became of the lady?" he asked.

"Oh, she growed up," Sam the Lion said, a tone of regret in his voice. "She was just a girl then, really."

"How come you never married her?"

"She was done married," Sam said gravely. "She and her husband were young and miserable with one another, but so many young married folks are that way that I figured they'd work out of it in time. I thought they'd get comfortable when they got a little older but it didn't turn out that way."

"Is growin' up always miserable?" Sonny said. "Nobody seems to enjoy it much."

"Oh, it ain't necessarily miserable," Sam replied. "About eighty per cent of the time, I guess."

They were silent again, Sam the Lion thinking of the lovely, spritely girl he had once led into the water, right there, where they were sitting.

"We ought to go to a real fishin' tank next year," Sam said finally. "It don't do to think about things like that too much. If she was here now I'd probably
170

be crazy agin in about five minutes. Ain't that ridiculous?"

A half-hour later, when they had gathered up the gear and were on the way to town, he answered his own question.

"It ain't, really," he said. "Being crazy about a woman like her's always the right thing to do. Being a decrepit old bag of bones is what's ridiculous."

It had rained the week before and there were deep ruts in the dirt road. Sonny drove as carefully as he could, but Sam the Lion scratched his head and watched the speedometer nervously, convinced that they were proceeding at a reckless speed.

"Did you know about me and Mrs. Popper?" Sonny asked suddenly, feeling that if he was ever going to talk about it the time was at hand.

"Yeah, how is Ruth?" Sam asked. "I haven't had a close look at her in years."

"Sometimes she's okay," Sonny said. "Sometimes she doesn't seem to be too happy."

Sam snorted. "That's probably the understatement of the day," he said. "I figured her for a suicide ten years ago—people are always turning out to be tougher than I think they are."

"I don't exactly know what to do about her," Sonny said hopefully.

Sam the Lion laughed almost as loudly as he had on the tank dam.

"Don't look at me for advice," he said. "I never know exactly what to do about anybody, least of all women. You might stay with her and get some good out of her while you're growing up. Somebody ought to get some good out of Ruth."

They pulled onto the highway and in a few minutes

the fenceposts were going by so fast that Sam the Lion could hardly see them. He breathed as little as possible until they hit the city limits sign—then Sonny slowed down and he relaxed.

"Say, was Duane along that night you all got Billy in the mess?" he asked. "I've been wondering about that lately."

Sonny was caught off guard and was completely at a loss to answer. He automatically started to lie, but because it was Sam the Lion the lie wouldn't come out. He decided it wouldn't hurt to tell the truth, but the truth wouldn't come out either. First the lie and then the truth stuck in his throat, and right in the same place.

"I see," Sam said. "Watch out, that's Old Lady Peters backing out of her driveway up there. She thinks it's still 1930 an' she's just as apt to back right in front of you as not."

He gripped the door handle tightly, prepared to leap out if necessary, but Sonny had seen the old lady blocks before he had and calmly, out of habit, swerved wide around her and coasted them safely up to the poolhall door.

CHAPTER XV

Three days after the fishing trip, Duane got so frustrated that he beat up Lester Marlow. Jacy and Lester had gone to Wichita together three Saturday nights in a row, and Duane could stand it no longer.

"I don't care if it ain't Lester's fault," Duane told Sonny. "Maybe if he has a couple of front teeth missin' Mrs. Farrow won't be so anxious to have Jacy go with him."

Sam the Lion overheard the remark and gave a skeptical chuckle. "The only person who'll profit by that sort of reasonin' is Lester's dentist," he said. "Maybe Jacy likes to go with Lester."

That was an incredible thing to suggest. Duane and Sonny were both flabbergasted.

"You don't think she *wants* to go with that fart, do you?" Duane asked indignantly.

"Well, Lester ain't entirely unlikable," Sam replied, not at all flustered. "I don't know Jacy well enough to know what she wants, but you've been blaming her mother all this time for something that might not be her mother's fault. If I was you I'd investigate."

Duane stormed out of the poolhall, mad as he could be. He didn't want to investigate, he just wanted to whip Lester, and about midnight that night, as Lester was passing the courthouse, Duane waved him down. Sonny was the only other person to see it.

"I know you're mad," Lester said, as soon as he got out of the car, "but you needn't be. All I've done is take her to dances. I've never even kissed her."

It was a shameful admission, but true: Jacy gave Lester absolutely nothing in the way of intimacies. She didn't have to.

"You took her to a naked swimming party," Duane said. "Don't tell me you didn't kiss her."

"I didn't," Lester said, but at that point Duane hit him on the mouth. Lester swung a half-hearted blow in return and found himself sitting down—at least he found himself getting up, and he could only assume he had been knocked down first. The fight was well started and things were easier for him: he couldn't feel himself being hit, and after three or four more licks Duane bloodied his nose and stopped fighting.

"That's just a taste," he said. "Don't you take her anywhere else!"

Lester said nothing, and Duane and Sonny walked away. Not saying anything was something of a triumph, Lester thought. He had made no promises. He went across the street to the filling station and ran some water on his nose, thinking that in a way he had been ganged up on. Sonny had been there. It could even have been that he was not knocked down fairly —Sonny could have tripped him. On the way back to Wichita he concluded that Sonny probably did trip him, and instead of going to his home he drove out to a place on Holiday Creek where some of the wilder
174

boys often gathered on Saturday nights. A lot of boys were there, sitting on the fenders of their cars drinking beer, and when they saw how bloody Lester was they were briefly impressed. What happened? they wanted to know.

"Couple of roughnecks beat me up," Lester said stoically. "You know, Crawford and Moore, over in Thalia. It was about Jacy Farrow. I would have done okay if one of them hadn't tripped me."

"Those motherfuckers," one of the boys said. "We ought to go over there and pile their asses."

"No," Lester said gallantly. "I don't want anybody fighting my fights."

"Aw, hell, it'd be somethin' to do," a boy said. "Besides we can get the Bunne brothers to do the fighting." The Bunne brothers were local Golden Gloves champions, a welterweight and a light-heavy. They enjoyed fighting, in the ring or out.

Lester didn't try again to discourage them, but for himself he decided it would be best not to go back to Thalia. The boys took that in stride—they didn't really like Lester much and were just as glad he stayed in Wichita. The nice thing about his getting beat up was that it gave them an excuse to drive to Thalia and watch a fight.

The Bunne brothers were located at a Pioneer drive-in, trying to make some girls in a green Pontiac. The welterweight was named Mickey, the light-heavy, Jack. They were glad to get a chance to go fighting: the girls were just a bunch of pimply virgins who had run off from a slumber party in Burkburnett. A couple of boys elected to stay and work on them, but that still left seven raring to go. They piled in a second-hand Mercury and headed for Thalia, driving about eighty-

175

five and laughing and talking. Saturday night had taken a turn for the better.

After the fight with Lester, Sonny and Duane walked over to the café to have a cheeseburger. Duane really wanted sympathy, but Genevieve was not inclined to give him any.

"No sir," she said. "There wasn't any point in your bullyin' Lester—it ain't his fault you can't make your girl friend behave."

"You're as bad as Sam," Duane said bitterly. "Why Jacy would marry me tonight, if she had the chance."

Sonny got up and put a couple of nickels in the jukebox, hoping a little music would ease the tension. It didn't seem to help much, so after a few minutes the boys left and drove out to the Y, a fork in the road about five miles from town. The fork was on top of a hill, and when they got there they sat and looked across the flat at the cluster of lights that was Thalia. In the deep spring darkness the lights shone very clear. The windows of the pickup were down and they could smell the fresh smell of the pastures.

They only sat a few minutes, and then drove back to town. When they pulled up at the rooming house the Wichita boys were there, sitting on the fenders of the Mercury.

"There's the Bunne brothers," Duane said. "That damn Lester must have sent 'em."

Both of them were badly scared, but they didn't want the Wichita boys to know that so they got out as if nothing were wrong. For a moment no one said anything. Sonny nervously scraped his sole on the pavement and the sound was very loud in the still night.

Mickey Bunne came cockily over and broke the silence.

"Hear you men beat the piss out of Lester," he said.

"I beat the piss out of him," Duane said quickly. "Sonny wasn't involved."

"That ain't the way Lester tells it."

The other boys got off the fenders and began to edge around.

"He probably lied about it," Duane said. "I didn't hit him over five times, anyway. I told him to stop going with my girl."

Mickey moved a step closer. "He said you both whipped him."

"You don't really think it would take two of us to whip Lester, do you?" Sonny asked. "All he had was a bloody nose and a busted lip. If we'd both fought he wouldn't have been able to drive home, much less tell lies about it."

The Wichita boys were momentarily silent, even Mickey. What Sonny said was obviously true: it didn't take two people to whip Lester Marlow, and he hadn't been damaged much, anyway. Most of the boys didn't feel particularly unfriendly to Duane and Sonny, but that didn't matter. There had to be a fight. The Bunne brothers wouldn't go home without a fight. Fortunately Mickey Bunne was quick-witted and saw right away what tack to take.

"Who whipped him don't matter," he said. "We don't like you country boys tellin' us who to go with and who to leave alone. We like to screw country girls once in a while."

Duane was getting a little nervous. "I didn't tell him not to screw country girls," he said. "I told him not to

177

bother Jacy. He can fuck the whole rest of this town for all I care—I'm just tired of him botherin' Jacy."

Mickey grinned. "Lester don't bother her," he said. "She laps it up. I seen her naked one time myself, out at Bobby Sheen's. She ain't bad lookin'. Who she really likes is Bobby Sheen—him and her played around all one night. I guess she's about as much ours as she is yours. I may want to go with her myself some time, you can't tell."

That was too much for Duane: he hit at Mickey, and the fight was on. It was not too bad for Duane, although Mickey beat him handily and knocked him down once. Duane was so mad he didn't really feel the pounding he took. He was fighting for his girl, after all. Sonny was the one who suffered most. He wasn't mad at all, and he wasn't fighting for anyone in particular. Besides that, he didn't like to fight and didn't know how, whereas Jack Bunne liked it and knew how very well. It made for a painful beating.

Fortunately the Bunne brothers knew when to quit. They were not looking for trouble, just for excitement. Sonny and Duane were both standing when they quit, although Sonny wanted very much to sit down. He had a pain in his ribs.

"Well let's go, men," one of the boys said. "The deputy sheriff's liable to come drivin' by."

"We ain't broke no laws," Jack Bunne said, not even winded, but the boys all went on and piled in the Mercury. They whooped and laughed as the car pulled away.

"Motherfuckers," Duane said wearily.

Sonny walked over and sat down on the curb. One of his ears was paining him severely, and he had caught at least a couple of hard licks in the rib cage.

Duane came and sat down too. They were both too winded and depressed to say anything. It was enough just to sit. The town was very quiet. From the west, far out in the pastures, they heard some hounds, so far away that their braying sounded as thin as the yapping of puppies.

"Why don't we just take off an' go someplace," Duane said. "I'm sick of this town. You're the only friend I got here, except Jacy."

"You mean go and stay gone?" Sonny asked.

"No, just for a day or two. We could go to Mexico and get back by sometime Monday."

"Reckon the pickup would make it?" Sonny asked, welcoming the prospect.

They got out their billfolds and counted their money. Saturday had been payday, and between them they had almost a hundred dollars.

"We can make it on that," Duane said. "Let's go clean up."

A few minutes later Sonny vomited all over the bathroom, but once he got the mess cleaned up he felt much better. His ear was not throbbing so badly. They put on clean Levi's and shirts and doctored themselves with aspirin, convinced they would both survive. The pickup didn't have much gas in it and they had to stop in town and wake up Andy Fanner, who had a key to one of the gas stations.

"Why you boys or-tant to go all that way," Andy said cheerfully. "The water's buggy in Mexico."

"We'll just drink beer and tequila," Duane said.

"You need-ernt to tell me," Andy said sagely. "I been there. You get the clap you'll wish you hadn't drunk nothin'. Where you goin', Laredo?"

The boys looked at one another. They hadn't

179

planned that far ahead; they were just going to Mexico.

"Which is the best place?" Sonny asked.

Andy wasn't positive and he didn't have a map, so they went back to the café and got one out of the glove compartment of Genevieve's old Dodge. They took it inside to read it.

"Good lord," Genevieve said, when she saw their skinned-up faces. They explained, and she sat down in a booth with them. "You all can just have the map," she said. "I ain't going far enough away that I need to worry about getting lost, I don't guess."

"Let's go all the way to Matamoros, since we're goin'," Duane suggested. "I've heard it's about the wildest."

"Matamoros suits me," Sonny said, gulping his coffee. They could hardly believe such an adventure was before them, and they wanted to get away before something happened to stop it.

Genevieve, however, was a little dubious. She followed them out to the pickup to see them off. The streets were empty, the streetlights shining palely. The stoplight blinked red and green all to itself.

"This pickup don't look so good," she said. The boys were so eager that it made her strangely sad. "Have either of you ever been that far away before?"

"Austin's the farthest I've been," Sonny said. It was the same with Duane, and Matamoros was almost twice as far as Austin. It made them all the more eager, but to their amazement Genevieve suddenly began to cry about something, right there on the street. Sonny had been just about to start the motor when she put her elbows on the pickup window and wiped away the tears with her hand. Both boys were stricken, afraid they were going to miss the trip after all.

"Why don't you boys take my car?" Genevieve sniffed. "You'll never make it in this old pickup."

They were astonished. It was an unprecedented offer. Women were clearly beyond all understanding.

"Naw, we better go in this one," Sonny told her softly. She was looking off down the street—he had never noticed before, but she seemed lonesome.

"We might wreck yours, an' then where would we be?" he added.

"Okay," Genevieve said, hardly paying attention. Something made her breasts ache. "Wait just a minute."

She went in the café and got a ten-dollar bill out of her purse. After she had wiped her eyes with a Kleenex she took the money outside and handed it to Sonny.

"Hide that somewhere," she said. "Use it when you don't have anything else to use. I'd like for you to get back in time for your graduation."

Both boys assured her that the money was quite unnecessary, but she pressed it on them anyway. "Sam's up there sitting on the curb," she said. "Guess he can't sleep. You might go say good-bye to him."

The boys were glad of anything that would prolong the ecstasy of departure a few more minutes. Sonny backed solemnly into the empty street and turned toward the poolhall. Sam the Lion was sitting on the curb, scratching his ankles. Sonny drove right up in front of him and leaned out the window.

"Better come go with us," he said. "We're headed for the Valley."

Astonished, Sam got up from the curb and came over to the pickup. He peered at the boys curiously.

"Going to the Valley tonight," he said. "My God." He was touched by the folly of youth and stood with his foot on the running board a moment.

"I guess the town can get along without us till Monday," Sonny said.

"I reckon," Sam said lightly. "If I was young enough to bounce that far I'd go with you. Need any money?"

"No. We got plenty."

"You can't tell," Sam said, fishing out his billfold. "Better take ten dollars for insurance. They say money kinda melts when you take it across a border."

The boys were too embarrassed to tell Sam that Genevieve had given them some already. They took the bill guiltily, anxious to be off. Sam stepped back to the curb and the boys waved and made a wide U-turn in the empty street. Genevieve was still outside the café and they waved at her too as they went by. She watched them, hugging her breasts. When they got to the stoplight it was red and they stopped, even though there wasn't another moving car within fifteen miles of them. The light winked green and the pickup turned the corner and sped out of sight.

Genevieve went over and kicked lightly at the front tire of her Dodge—to her the tire always looked low. The boys had made her remember what it was to be young. Once, before they had any kids, she and her husband Dan took off one weekend and drove to Raton, New Mexico. They stayed in a motel, lost twenty dollars at the horse races, made love six times in two days, and had dinner in the coffee shop of a fancy restaurant. She had even worn eye shadow. Romance might not last, but it was something while it

182

did. She looked up the street and waved at Sam the Lion, but he was looking the other way and didn't notice her and she went back into the empty café, wishing for a few minutes that she was young again and free and could go rattling off across Texas toward the Rio Grande.

CHAPTER XVI

All day the boys alternated, one driving, the other sleeping, and by late evening they were in the Valley, driving between the green orange groves. It was amazing how different the world was, once the plains were left behind. In the Valley there were even palm trees. The sky was violet, and dusk lingered until they were almost to Matamoros. Every few miles they passed roadside groceries, lit with yellow light bulbs and crowded with tables piled high with corn and squash, cabbages and tomatoes.

"This is a crazy place," Duane said. "Who you reckon eats all that squash?"

They drove straight on through Brownsville and paid a fat, bored tollhouse keeper twenty cents so they could drive across the bridge. Below them was the Rio Grande, a river they had heard about all their lives. Its waters were mostly dark, touched only here and there by the yellow bridge lights. Several Mexican boys in ragged shirts were sitting on one of the guardrails, spitting into the water and chattering to one another.

A few blocks from the bridge they came to a stoplight on a pole, with four or five boys squatting by it. Apparently someone had run into the light pole because it was leaning away from the street at a forty-five-degree angle. As soon as Sonny stopped one of the boys ran out and jumped lightly onto the running board.

"Girl?" he said. "Boy's Town? Dirty movie?"

"Well, I guess," Sonny said. "I guess that's what we came for."

The boy quickly got in the cab and began to chatter directions in Tex-Mex—Sonny followed them as best he could. They soon left the boulevard and got into some of the narrowest streets the boys had ever seen. Barefooted kids and cats and dogs were playing in the street, night or no night, and they moved aside for the pickup very reluctantly. A smell of onions seemed to pervade the whole town, and the streets went every which direction. There were lots of intersections but no stop signs—apparently the right of way belonged to the driver with the most nerve. Sonny kept stopping at the intersections, but that was a reversal of local custom: most drivers beeped their horns and speeded up, hoping to dart through before anyone could hit them.

Mexico was more different from Thalia than either of the boys would have believed. The number of people who went about at night was amazing to them. In Thalia three or four boys on the courthouse square constituted a lively crowd, but the streets of Matamoros teemed with people. Groups of men stood on what, in Thalia, would have been sidewalks, children rushed about in the dust, and old men sat against buildings.

Their guide finally ordered them to stop in front of a dark lump that was apparently some sort of dwelling.

"This couldn't be no whorehouse," Duane said. "It ain't big enough to have a whore in it."

Not knowing what else to do, they got out and followed their guide to the door. A paunchy Mexican in his undershirt and khakis opened it and grunted at the guide. "Ees got movies," the boy said.

They all went inside, into a bedroom. Through an open doorway the boys could see an old woman stirring something in a pot, onions and tomatoes it smelled like. An old man with no shirt on and white hair on his chest sat at a table staring at some dominoes. Neither the old man nor old woman so much as glanced at the boys. There were two beds in the bedroom and on one of them three little Mexican boys were curled up, asleep. Sonny felt strange when he saw them. They looked very helpless, and he could not feel it was very polite for Duane and him to barge into their room. The paunchy man immediately brought up the subject of movies. "Ten dollars," he said. "Got all kinds."

He knelt and drew a tiny little projector out from under the bed and took several rolls of eight-millimeter film out of a little bureau. The boys looked uncomfortably at one another. They either had to pay and watch the movies or else refuse and leave, and since they had driven five hundred miles to see some wickedness it was pointless to refuse. Duane handed over a ten-dollar bill and the man stuffed it in his pocket and calmly began to clear one of the beds. He picked the sleeping boys up one at a time, carried them into the kitchen, and deposited them under the table where the old man sat. The little boys moaned a little and stirred in their sleep, but they didn't wake up. The paunchy man then put the projector on their bed and prepared to show the movies on a sheet hung against the opposite wall.

"I don't like this," Sonny said, appalled. "I never come all this way just to get some kids out of bed. If he ain't got a better place than this to show them I'd just as soon go on."

Duane was of the same mind, but when they tried to explain themselves, the guide and the projectionist both seemed puzzled.

"Ees okay," the guide said. "Sleepin' away." He gestured at the three little boys, all of whom were sound asleep on the dirt floor.

Sonny and Duane were stubborn. Even though the little boys were asleep, it wouldn't do: they couldn't enjoy a dirty movie so long as they were in sight of the displaced kids. Finally the projectionist shrugged, picked up the projector, and led them back through the hot kitchen and across an alley. The guide followed, carrying the film. Above them the sky was dark and the stars very bright.

They came to what seemed to be a sort of long outhouse, and when the guide knocked a thin, middle-aged man opened the door. He had only one leg, but no crutch, the room being so small that he could easily hop from one resting place to the next. As soon as they were all inside the guide informed the boys that it would cost them five dollars more because of the change of rooms: the one-legged man could not be put to the trouble of sitting through a pornographic movie for nothing. Sonny paid it and the projectionist plugged the projector into a light socket. An old

American calendar hung on the door, a picture of a girl in mechanic's overalls on the front of it. The one-legged man simply turned the calendar around and they had a screen.

"You mean they're going to show it on the back of a calendar," Duane said. "For fifteen dollars?"

The light was turned off and the projector began to buzz—the title of the picture was *Man's Best Friend.* It was clearly an old picture, because the lady who came on the screen was dressed like ladies in Laurel and Hardy movies. The similarity was so strong that for a moment the boys expected Laurel and Hardy to come on the screen and do dirty things to her. As the plot unfolded the print became more and more scratchy and more and more faded; soon it was barely possible to tell that the figures on the screen were human. The boys leaned forward to get a better look and were amazed to discover that the figures on the screen *weren't* all human. One of the actors was a German shepherd dog.

"My God," Duane said.

They both immediately felt the trip was worthwhile, if only for the gossip value. Nobody in Thalia had ever seen a dog and a lady behaving that way: clearly it was the ultimate depravity, even more depraved than having congress with Negro whores. They were speechless. A man came on and replaced the dog, and then the dog came back on and he and the man teamed up. The projectionist and the guide chuckled with delight at this development, but the boys were too surprised to do anything but watch. The ugliness of it all held them spellbound. When it was over they walked to the pickup in silence, followed by the guide and the projectionist. The latter was making a sales pitch.

"Lots more reels," he said. "Got French, Gypsy, Chinese lesbians, all kinds. Five dollars a reel from now on."

The boys shook their heads. They wanted to get away and think. The guide shrugged and climbed in beside them and they drove away, leaving the fat man in the middle of the road.

"I hope he puts them kids back in bed," Sonny commented.

"Boy's Town now," the guide said happily. "Five hundred girls there. Clean, too."

They soon left the downtown area and bumped off toward the outskirts of Matamoros. A red Chevrolet with Texas license plates was just in front of them, throwing the white dust of the dirt road up into their headlights. Soon they saw Boy's Town, the neon lights from the larger cabarets winking red and green against the night. At first it looked like there were a hundred clubs, but after they drove around a while they saw that there were only fifteen or twenty big places, one on every corner. Between the corners were dark, unlit rows of cribs. The guide gestured contemptuously at the cribs and took them to a place called the Cabaret ZeeZee. When the boys parked, a fat policeman in khakis walked up and offered to open the door for them, but the guide chattered insultingly to him and he shrugged lazily and turned away.

The boys entered the cabaret timidly, expecting to be mobbed at once by whores or else slugged by Mexican gangsters, but neither thing happened. They were simply ignored. There was a large jukebox and a

189

few couples dancing, but most of the people in the club were American boys, sitting around tables.

"The competition's gonna be worse here than it is in Thalia," Duane said. "We might as well get some beer."

They sat down at one of the tile-topped tables and waited several minutes before a waitress came over and got their order. She brought them the first Mexican beer they had ever tasted, and they drank the first bottles thirstily. In their tired, excited state the beer quickly took effect—before they knew it they had had five bottles apiece, and the fatigue of the trip seemed to be dropping away. A fat-faced girl in a green blouse came over, introduced herself as Juanita, and with no further preamble squeezed Sonny intimately through his blue jeans. He was amazed. Though responsive, he felt the evening would bring better things than Juanita, so he politely demurred. Juanita went around and squeezed Duane the same way, but got the same reply.

"Texas ees full of queers," she said, swishing her buttocks derogatorily as she walked away. The boys contemplated themselves over the beer bottles, wondering if they had been seriously insulted.

As the night wore on Sonny gradually set his mind on a slim, black-headed girl who spent most of her time on the dance floor, dancing with boys from Texas A & M. There were a good many boys from Texas A & M in the cabaret.

"I thought Aggies was all irresistible cocksmen," Duane said. "What's so many of them doing in a whorehouse?"

In time Sonny approached the girl, whose name was Maria. She cheerfully came to the table with him and
190

downed three whiskeys while he was having a final beer. Between drinks she blew her warm, slightly sticky breath in his ear and squeezed him the way Juanita had.

"All night party?" she asked. "Jus' tweenty-five dollars. We can leef right now."

It seemed ungallant to haggle with such a confident girl, so Sonny agreed. It turned out he owed eight dollars for the drinks, but it didn't seem gallant to haggle about that either. He paid, and Maria led him out the back door of the Cabaret ZeeZee into a very dark alley, where the only light was from the bright stars far above. The place she took him didn't even have a door, just a blue curtain with a light behind it. The room was extremely tiny. The one light bulb was in a socket on the wall and the bed was an old iron cot with a small mattress and a thin green bedspread.

In the room, Maria seemed less perky than she had in the club. She looked younger than she had inside. Sonny watched her unzip her dress—her back was brown and smooth, but when she turned to face him he was really surprised. Her breasts were heavy, her nipples large and purplish, and she was clearly pregnant. He had never seen a pregnant woman naked before, but he knew from the heavy bulge of her abdomen that she must be carrying a child. She tried to look at him with whorish gaiety, but somehow it didn't work: the smile was without life, and showed her gums. When he was undressed she splashed him with coolish water from a brown pitcher, and scrutinized him with such care that an old worry popped into his mind. Perhaps his equipment was too small? He had worried about that when he first began to go with Ruth, and had even tried to find out how large

191

one's equipment was supposed to be, but the only two reference works in the high-school library were the *World Book* and the *Texas Almanac,* neither of which had anything helpful on penises. Gradually it had ceased to worry him, but with Maria he had begun to feel generally hesitant.

"But aren't you going to have a baby?" he asked, not sure that the question was proper.

Maria nodded. "Two already," she said, meaning to reassure him. Her heavy breasts and large grape-colored nipples were not at all congruous with her thin calves and girlish shoulders.

Sonny lay down with her on the cot, but he knew even before he began that somehow twenty-five dollars had been lost. He didn't want to stay in the room all night, or even very much of it.

Two minutes later it came home to him why Ruth had insisted they make love on the floor: the cot springs wailed and screamed, and the sound made him feel as though every move he made was sinful. He had driven five hundred miles to get away from Thalia, and the springs took him right back, made him feel exposed. Everyone in town would know that he had done it with a pregnant whore. Suddenly he ceased to care about the twenty-five dollars, or about anything; the fatigues of the long trip, down from the plains, through the hill country and the brush country, through Austin and San Antone, five hundred miles of it all pressed against the backs of his legs and up his body, too heavy to support. To Maria's amazement he simply stopped and went to sleep.

When he awoke, he was very hot. The green counterpane was soaked with his sweat. It was not until he had been awake a minute or two that he realized the sun was shining in his face. He was still in the room where Maria had brought him, but the room had no roof—the night before he had not even noticed. It was just an open crib.

He hurriedly got up and put on his clothes, his head aching. While he was tying his shoes he suddenly had to vomit, and barely made it past the blue curtain into the street. When he had finished vomiting and was kneeling in the white dust waiting for his strength to come back he heard a slow clop-clop and looked up to see a strange wagon rounding the corner into his part of the street. It was a water wagon, drawn by a decrepit brown mule and driven by an old man. The wagon was entirely filled by a large rubber water tank wrapped in ragged canvas; as the wagon moved the water sloshed out of the open tank and dripped down the sides of the wagon into the white dust. The old man wore a straw hat so old that it had turned brown. His grizzled whiskers were as white as Sam the Lion's hair. As he stopped the mule, three or four whores stepped out of their cribs with water pitchers in their hands. One passed right by Sonny, a heavy woman with a relaxed face and large white breasts that almost spilled out of her green robe. The whores were barefooted and seemed much happier than they had seemed the night before. They chattered like highschool girls and came lightly to the wagon to get their water. The old man spoke to them cheerfully, and when the first group had filled their pitchers he popped the mule lightly with the rein and proceeded up the street, the slow clop-clop of the mule's feet very loud in the still morning. When he passed where Sonny was kneeling the old man nodded to him

193

kindly and gestured with a tin dipper he had in his hand. Sonny gratefully took a dipper of water from him, using it to wash the sour taste out of his mouth. The old man smiled at him sympathetically and said something in a philosophic tone, something which Sonny took to mean that life was a matter of ups and downs. He stayed where he was and watched the wagon until it rounded the next corner. As it moved slowly up the street the whores of Matamoros came out of their cribs, some of them combing their black hair, some with white bosoms uncovered, all with brown pitchers in their hands and coins for the old waterman.

Sonny found Duane asleep in the front seat of the pickup, his legs sticking out the window. Three little boys were playing in the road, trying to lead a dusty white goat across into a pasture of scraggly mesquite. The goat apparently wanted to go into the Cabaret ZeeZee. A depressed-looking spotted dog followed behind the boys and occasionally yapped discouragedly at the goat.

Duane was too bleary and sick to do more than grunt. His hair was plastered to his temples with sweat. "You drive," he said.

By some miracle Sonny managed to wind his way through Matamoros to the Rio Grande—in daylight the water in the river was green. The boys stood groggily under the customs shed for a few minutes, wondering why in the world they had been so foolish as to come all the way to Mexico. Thalia seemed an impossible distance away.

"I don't know if I can make it," Sonny said. "How much money we got?"

They found, to their dismay, that their money had

somehow evaporated. They had four dollars between them. There was the money that Sam and Genevieve had given them, hidden in the seat springs, but they had not planned to use that.

"I guess we can pay them back in a week or two," Sonny said. "We'll have to use it."

When the customs men were through the boys got back in the pickup and drove slowly out of Brownsville, along the Valley highway. Heat waves shimmered above the green cabbage fields. Despite the sun and heat Duane soon went to sleep again and slept heavily, wallowing in his own sweat. Sonny drove automatically; he was depressed, but not exactly sleepy, and he paced himself from town to town, not daring to think any farther ahead than the next city limits sign.

Soon the thought of Ruth began to bother him. In retrospect it seemed incredibly foolish that he should drive a thousand miles to go to sleep on a pregnant girl's stomach, when any afternoon he could have a much better time with Ruth. The thought of her slim, familiar body and cool hands suddenly made him very horny and even more depressed with himself. It occurred to him that he might even be diseased, and he stopped in a filling station in Alice to inspect himself. Duane woke up and exhibited similar anxieties. For the rest of the day they stopped and peed every fifty miles, just to be sure they could.

There was money enough for gas, but not much for food, so they managed on Cokes, peanuts, and a couple of candy bars. Evening finally came, coolness with it, and the boys got a second wind. The trip ceased to seem like such a fiasco: after all, they had been to Mexico, visited whorehouses, seen dirty movies. In Thalia it would be regarded as a great adventure, and they could hardly wait to tell about it. The country around Thalia had never looked so good to them as it did when they came back into it, at four in the morning. The dark pastures, the farmhouses, the oil derricks and even the jackrabbits that went dashing across the road in front of them, all seemed comfortable, familiar, private even, part of what was theirs and no one else's. After the strangeness of Matamoros the lights of Thalia were especially reassuring.

Duane was driving when they pulled in. He whipped through the red light and turned toward the café. Genevieve would be glad to see they were safely back.

To their astonishment, the café was dark. No one at all was there. The café had never been closed, not even on Christmas, and the boys were stunned. Inside, one little light behind the counter shone on the aspirin, the coughdrops, the chewing gum, and cheap cigars.

"It ain't a holiday, is it?" Sonny said.

There was nothing to do but go over to the courthouse and wake up Andy Fanner—he would know what had happened.

Andy woke up hard, but they kept at him and he finally got out of the car and rubbed his stubbly jaw, trying to figure out what the boys wanted.

"Oh yeah, you all been gone, ain't you," he said. "Gone to Mexico. You don't know about it. Sam the Lion died yesterday mornin'."

"Died?" Sonny said. After a moment he walked over to the curb in front of the courthouse and sat down. The traffic light blinked red and green over the empty street. Andy came over to the curb too, yawning and rubbing the back of his neck.

"Yep," he said. "Quite a blow. Keeled over on one of the snooker tables. Had a stroke."

Soon it was dawn, a cool, dewy spring dawn that wet the courthouse grass and left a low white mist on the pastures for the sun to burn away. Andy sat on the fender of his Nash and told all about the death and how everybody had taken it, who had cried and who hadn't. "Good thing you all got back today, you'd 'a missed the funeral," he said. "How'd you find Mexico?" Sonny could not have told him; he had lost track of things and just wanted to sit on the curb and watch the traffic light change.

CHAPTER XVII

Sonny was embarrassed that he didn't have a suit to wear to the funeral—all he had was a pair of slacks and a blue sports coat that was too short at the wrists. No one seemed to notice, though. The graveyard was on a rough, gravelly hill, where the wind was always blowing. Sonny was able to quit being embarrassed because of Mrs. Farrow, who cried all through the graveyard ceremonies. She stood at the edge of the crowd, the wind blowing her long hair, and her cheeks wet; when she walked back to her Cadillac to drive away she was still crying and wiping her eyes with her gloves.

It was because of her crying so much that Sonny learned she had been the woman who watched Sam the Lion piss off the tank dam. That night at the café Sonny asked Genevieve about it and she didn't hold back.

"Sam's gone and Lois never cared who knew," she said. "Everybody knew but Gene. She and Sam carried on for quite a while. Lois was just crazy about him. She would have married him, old as he was, but he wouldn't let her leave Gene."

A few weeks before Sonny would not have believed it, but the world had become so strange that he could believe anything. Genevieve was wiping the counter with a gray washrag.

"Sam was quite a man, you know," she said. "And Lois was just beautiful when she was young—I always envied her her looks. She was prettier than her daughter ever will be, and nine times as wild. She had more life than just about anybody in this town."

Sonny didn't tell her about the bet at the tank dam, but he thought about it a lot, just as he thought about many of the things Sam the Lion had done. Some of them were very strange things—the will he left, for instance. He left the poolhall to Sonny and Billy; he left the picture show to Old Lady Mosey and her nephew Junior Mosey, who was the projectionist; he left the café to Genevieve, five thousand dollars to the county swimming-pool fund, and strangest of all, a thousand dollars to Joe Bob Blanton. No one knew what to make of it, not even Joe Bob. People thought it was a damned outrage, but that was what the will said.

Two weeks after the funeral the seniors left for San Francisco, on their senior trip. Sonny was glad to go. It seemed to him he had jumped up and gone to Mexico on the spur of the moment and had never quite managed to get back to Thalia, really. The town had become strange to him, and he thought it might be easier to return to it from San Francisco.

The bus left Thalia at midnight and when dawn came was crossing the Pecos River, a dry winding rut cutting through the naked flats of West Texas. Most of the seniors had cut up all night and worn themselves out, but Sonny was awake, and just tired enough that his memory could do what it pleased. The sky was completely cloudless, a round white moon hanging in it. He had not thought of Sam the Lion much since the funeral—in Thalia it was no good thinking about him—but for some reason the bitter flats of the Pecos brought him to mind and Sonny remembered the way he used to slop around the poolhall in his house shoes, complaining about the ingrown toenail that had pained him for years. A bronc had stomped on his foot once, and the toenail had never recovered. Sam the Lion, the horsebreaker, pissing off the tank dam while Lois Farrow watched—it was too much to be thinking about on the way to San Francisco, and his eyes kept leaking tears all the way to Van Horn.

They got to San Francisco in the middle of the night and checked into an expensive cheap motel on Van Ness Avenue, not far from the bay. Duane and Jacy were full of secret plans about the Thing they were going to do, and all the boys were itching to go bowling or find whores. The first day there the room mothers kept them all herded together and saw to it that they rode a cable car, visited the Top of the Mark, and went across the Golden Gate bridge. All the Californians looked at them as if they were freaks, whereas it seemed to the kids it was the other way around. The room mothers were scandalized by the number of bars in the city and kept everyone in a tight group to protect them against lurking perverts.

The second day was unscheduled and most of the boys spent it on Market Street, looking at dirty magazines and talking to girls and sailors in the cheap sidewalk lunch counters. Sonny and three other boys wandered into a bar between Market and Mission and were met by a tall black-headed girl named Gloria who offered to let them take pictures of her naked. The bar itself was plastered with pictures of Gloria naked, a great inducement to photography. Unfortunately her fee for the privilege was twenty dollars and none of the boys could afford it.

The major event of the trip occurred on the afternoon of the second day in San Francisco when Jacy finally allowed Duane to seduce her. The girls were all supposed to accompany the room mothers to the De Young Museum that afternoon, but Jacy cleverly got out of it. She was rooming with an obliging little girl named Winnie Snips, and she got Winnie to tell the room mothers that she had taken to her bed with menstrual cramps. No one ever doubted the word of Winnie Snips. She was valedictorian, and just unpopular enough that she was glad to do anything anyone wanted of her.

After the girls and the room mothers left, Sonny stationed himself in the lobby of the motel so he could give the alarm if the party got back early. It was an ugly lobby full of postcard racks and it depressed him a little to sit in it. The only senior who bothered with postcards was Charlene Duggs who sent about a dozen a day to an airman boy friend of hers in Wichita Falls. She wanted everyone to know how much in love she was, but she didn't have much to say and just wrote "Gee, I miss you, Love and kisses, Charlene" on every card. When Sonny thought about Jacy he got even more depressed, but Duane was his friend and a scheme of such daring had to be supported.

As it turned out, Sonny's depression was nothing at all compared to the one Duane had to cope with in the seduction chamber upstairs. The glorious moment

201

had arrived, and was going to be just perfect: they could even see the bay and a part of Alcatraz through the window. "I love you," Duane said, as soon as they had kissed a few times. "I love you too," Jacy said, breathing heavily. It was the way things were done. Then she let Duane take absolutely all her clothes off, something she had never done before. For some reason, being naked with him was different than being naked around a bunch of Wichita kids. She caught him looking right at the place between her legs, and that seemed rather discourteous. Still, there was no backing out, so she stretched out on the bed while Duane undressed. He had been in a state of anticipatory erection for at least half of the 1,800-mile drive, and could hardly wait to get his socks off. They kissed again for a moment, but both supposed speed to be of the essence and Duane soon rolled on top. Jacy sucked in her breath, preparing to be painfully devirginized. For a moment or two she did feel something that was hard and slightly painful, but it wasn't nearly as painful as she had expected it to be and in a moment it ceased to be hard at all and became flexible and rather wiggly. It certainly wasn't hurting her, but it wasn't going in, either. It sort of tickled, and kept sliding off into her pubic hair. Curiosity got the better of her and she opened her eyes. Duane had a very strange look on his face. He was horrified at himself, unable to believe his member should betray him—not then, of all times.

"What's wrong, honey?" Jacy asked, wiggling slightly. She couldn't stand to be tickled.

"Um," Duane said, a little choked. "I don't know."

He held himself above her, embarrassed to death but hoping beyond hope that his body would come to its senses and enable him to go on. He hoped for two or three long minutes, while Jacy offered her intimate of intimates, but his body continued to register complete indifference. Duane didn't have the faintest idea what to do: no emergency had ever been more unlooked for.

After a time Jacy felt a rising sense of exasperation.

"Well get off a minute," she said. "You might get tired and fall on me."

Duane complied, too disgraced to venture speech. He sat hopelessly on the edge of the bed, looking out at the bay. Jacy sat up and shrugged her hair back across her shoulders. Obviously they were faced with a crisis. The situation had to be salvaged or they would be the laughing stock of the class. Suddenly she felt furious with Duane. She looked with vexation at the offending organ.

"It was Mexico," she said. "I hate you. No tellin' what you got down there. I don't know why I ever went with you."

"I don't know what happened," Duane said glumly. He got up and crept reluctantly back into his clothes, but Jacy stalked about the room, indignantly naked and not giving a damn.

"What'll we say?" she said. "The whole class knows what we were going to do. I just want to cry. I think you're the meanest boy I ever saw and my mother was so right about you."

"I don't know what happened," Duane said again. He really didn't. He started for the door but Jacy stopped him.

"Don't go out there yet," she said. "We haven't had time to do it—Sonny would know. I don't want one soul to know."

Duane sat back down on the bed and Jacy went into the bathroom and cried a few real tears of anger. It seemed to her Duane had been a monster of thoughtlessness to put her in such a position. She didn't want to touch him again, ever, and it angered her to think she would have to go on pretending to be his sweetheart for the rest of the trip. It would never do to let the class think they had broken up over sex. In fact, she would have to be even more loving with him in public, so everyone would think they were having a warm, meaningful affair.

When she thought they had been in the room long enough she went out and told Duane to leave.

"You better not tell one soul, either," she said. "You just pretend it was wonderful. And wear your slacks when we go to supper tonight—I think we're going someplace nice."

She stood naked, hands on hips, conscious that her nudity embarrassed Duane a little, and thoroughly pleased that it did.

"Well, I'm sorry," he said again. "I don't know what happened."

"If you say that one more time I'll bite you," Jacy said.

When Winnie Snips and the other girls piled into the room an hour later, pale with curiosity, Jacy was sitting in a well-rumpled bed with only her pajama tops on, staring out at the bay. The evening fog was coming in.

"Oh gee," Winnie said. "Tell us about it, Jacy. What happened?"

Jacy looked languorously around at them, calm, replete, a little wasted even.

"I just can't describe it," she said. "I just can't describe it in words."

The very next day, to Duane's immense relief, the seduction happened after all. Jacy insisted he take her for a walk to show everyone how much they wanted to be alone, and while they were walking down Geary Street, holding hands in case anyone from the class should see them, Duane suddenly felt himself return. They were just outside a cheap hotel, and without hesitation he seized his chance.

"Come on," he said. He had Jacy in the lobby of the hotel before she even knew what he meant. An old lady in a blue-flowered silk bathrobe registered them without comment and took five dollars from Duane. In the creaky cage of an elevator he kissed Jacy hungrily and fondled her breast, conscious that all was still well below. Jacy was skeptical and didn't return the kiss, but there *was* something rather adventurous about being fondled in an elevator—Winnie Snips would faint if she heard of such a thing.

Their room was tiny, with green walls, an old-fashioned bed, and a narrow window that looked across Geary Street to a one-story nightclub with a dead neon sign outside. Duane wasted absolutely no time—he was taking no chances with himself. He was out of his clothes by the time the door closed, and he tugged Jacy toward the bed, pulling rudely at her skirt. She shrugged loose and went to the window to undress at her own pace.

"If you can't wait you can jump out this window," she said. "I don't think it will work anyway."

Duane was not certain it would either, and waited nervously. The room was chilly and Jacy had goose bumps on her breasts. As she lay down she looked at Duane casually—men were certainly strange. All she really expected was something tickly, but Duane surprised her horribly. He didn't tickle a bit, but instead he did something really painful. At first she was too startled to move, and then she yelled out loud. Someone in an adjoining room kicked the wall indignantly. "Quit, quit," she said—it was intolerable. Duane was much too thrilled to quit, but fortunately he didn't take long. Jacy was at her wit's end as it was.

She got gingerly out of bed, meaning to take a hot bath, and discovered that the little room didn't even have a bathroom in it, just a lavatory. "There must be one down the hall someplace," Duane said, but she wouldn't let him go look for it. She felt strange and wanted to leave. All the way back to the motel she kept glancing over her shoulder, expecting to see a trail of blood on the sidewalk behind her. Duane was walking happily along, infuriatingly proud of himself.

"Oh, quit prissing," Jacy said. "You needn't think I'm going to take you back just because of that. I don't think you did it right, anyway."

"Sure I did," Duane said, but he wasn't really positive, and he brooded about it during the remainder of the trip. They did it twice more, once in the motel in San Francisco and once in Flagstaff, Arizona, on the way home. Duane was confident he was doing it right, but for some reason Jacy didn't swoon with bliss. She only allowed it twice more because she thought Bobby Sheen would like it if she had a little more experience. The whole business was far from delightful, but she supposed that was probably because Duane was a roughneck. In Flagstaff it went on much too long and she got exasperated and told him off once and for all.

"You never will learn," she said. "I don't know why I went with you so long. I guess we have to keep on being sweethearts until we get home, but that's gonna be the end of it. We'll just have to think of something big to break up over."

Duane just couldn't understand it: he was more dejected and more in love than he ever had been. Jacy was bending over to slip her small breasts back into their brassiere cups; she had never looked more lovely, and he could not believe she was serious about breaking up. He tried to talk her out of it, but she went over to the motel dressing table and combed her hair thoroughly, looking at herself in the mirror and paying absolutely no attention to him.

The rest of the way home, across Arizona, New Mexico, Texas, he tried to think of ways to make her realize that they had to stay together. He was sure her disaffection would only be temporary. Jacy was thinking how glad she would be to get home. She had even decided there was no point in making a big production of breaking up: she was sick and tired of the seniors. As an audience they were not worth bothering about. When the bus finally pulled into Thalia late one June afternoon she didn't so much as tell Duane good-bye. She was tired and went right over to her parents' Cadillac while her father got her bags. Lois was watching her shrewdly.

"I see you got enough of him," she said quietly. "That's that."

"I'm just not interested in saying one word about it, if you don't mind," Jacy said.

Watching them drive away, Duane felt a little sick at his stomach. He realized Jacy had meant what she said: she was really done with him. It was very confusing to him because he had always thought you were supposed to get whoever you really loved. That was the way it worked in movies. It was all he could do to carry his suitcase to the pickup.

Sonny had merely endured the return trip, sitting in the back of the bus watching the desert go by. He had paid Duane and Jacy as little attention as possible, and it was not until he and Duane got in the pickup in Thalia that he noticed his friend was depressed.

"What's the matter?" he asked, surprised.

"Nothin'," Duane said.

Sonny knew better. "Well what is it?" he persisted. "You feel bad?"

For a moment Duane considered telling the truth, but then he decided not to.

"I'm worn to a frazzle," he said. "That California's hard on a person."

They were living over the poolhall, Billy with them, though Genevieve had kept him while the seniors were gone. Returning to the poolhall was a little strange, particularly since Sam the Lion wasn't there. If he had been there they would have shot some pool and had a great time telling him all about the trip. It would have picked everyone's spirits up. As it was, the poolhall was quiet and empty, and there was not a great deal to do.

CHAPTER XVIII

While the seniors were in California a great scandal rocked Thalia. All the mothers were agreed that it was the very worst thing that had ever happened in the town: John Cecil was fired from his teaching job for being a homosexual.

The scariest thing of all, the mothers thought, was that it was just by a happenstance that he was found out. If it hadn't been for Coach Popper's vigilance and his interest in the welfare of the children, nobody would have known about Mr. Cecil, and a whole generation of young innocents would have been exposed to corruption.

The gist of the matter was that Mr. Cecil had persuaded Bobby Logan to take a summer-school course in trigonometry, in Wichita Falls high school. Mr. Cecil was going to summer school himself, at the college there, so he drove Bobby over to his class every day. That seemingly innocent arrangement was enough to arouse the coach's suspicions. He had been planning to have Bobby work out in the gym every day during the summer, so he would be in good shape

209

when football season came. It was a pleasure to work with a fine young athlete like Bobby, and when Bobby told him about the trigonometry class he was angered.

"Why goddamn," he said. "You mean you're gonna sit in a damn schoolhouse all summer when you could be workin' out? What kinda shit is that?"

Bobby was a little embarrassed. "I'll have to have trig to get in a good college," he said.

"Trig my ass," the coach said. "I can get you a scholarship anywhere and you won't need to know a fuckin' thing."

He raged on, but Bobby was determined, and that night, thinking it over, it came to the coach in a flash: Cecil was a queer.

He didn't say anything to Ruth about it because it wasn't a thing to talk to women about. The next morning he happened to be standing around the filling station and he mentioned his suspicion to some of the men. They were sitting on piles of old tires, chewing tobacco and discussing masculine matters, and all of them agreed with the coach right down the line.

"Hell yes," one said. "Whoever heard of a man teachin' English. That's a woman's job."

"Oughta see the school board about it," the coach said sternly. The idea got quick support.

"By God, if you don't I will," Andy Fanner said. "I got two boys in that school."

"Well, I tell you, men," the coach said, squaring his shoulders with purpose. "I hate to cost a man his job, but if there's anything I hate it's to see a goddamn homasexyul messing around with a bunch of young kids. I got too much respect for the teachin' profession to put up with that."

210

It turned out the coach didn't have to say a word to the school board. Some of the men went home and told their wives and the wives called the school board president even before they began to call one another. The school board president was a Pontiac salesman named Tom Todd. When Tom was fourteen years old he had been seduced one night at a family reunion by a male cousin from Jonesboro, Arkansas, and he had felt guilty about it ever since. He went right into action and that very night they got John Cecil before the board and fired him.

All Mr. Cecil could say was that he hadn't done anything to Bobby, or to anyone else. He was stunned and guilty looking though, and the board knew they had their man. They didn't question Bobby Logan because his father didn't want him to know what homosexuality was yet. If it had already happened to him his father preferred that he didn't realize it.

Mr. Cecil went home and tried to explain to his wife what a terrible mistake had been made. "Why I've never even touched one of my students," he said.

"Oh, they wouldn't have fired you if you hadn't," she said. Then she screamed and ran across to the neighbor's house and then screamed again and ran back and got the two girls. She didn't return that night, but the next morning she got some of her stuff and headed for Odessa in Mr. Cecil's car. Her sisters lived in Odessa.

Ruth Popper found out about it the night Mr. Cecil was fired. The coach was in an unusually good mood that night and was propped up in bed reading an old issue of *Sports Afield*—there was a fishing story in it he had read at least fifty times.

211

Ruth could not sleep with the light on, and was reading the *Reader's Digest*. She lay flat on her back, and Herman noticed.

"Prop up if you're gonna read," he said. "It ain't good for your eyes to read laying down."

She obediently tucked a pillow under her head, and as she did, noticed that Herman was looking at her in a very satisfied way. Suddenly, to her complete surprise, he reached under the cover and rubbed her in rough, husbandly fashion.

"I guess tonight there's a lot of women in this town glad they ain't in Irene Cecil's shoes," he said. "I feel awful sorry for Irene."

"Why?" Ruth asked. "I've always felt a little sorry for John."

"You would," the coach said, abruptly removing his hand. "I guess you'd like to be married to a queer. The school board fired him tonight. Me and some other fellers found out about him an' took some action. He'll never teach in this part of the country again."

Ruth didn't credit her hearing. "What did you say?" she asked.

"Why, didn't you know it, honey?" he said, gruffly condescending. "I could tell that feller was queer as a three-dollar bill—been thinking it for years. Reason I never spoke up sooner was because I never noticed him actually botherin' with any of the kids. When I saw he was after Bobby, I knew it was time to put a stop to it. That's one boy I don't intend to see messed up."

He farted gently into the sheets and went contentedly back to his fishing story.

Ruth wanted not to be there; not to be anywhere. She wanted to hug her knees with shame. Then gradually the shame was replaced by a dull, hot feeling inside her that soon filled her completely. Before she even recognized it as anger it had taken possession of her, and with no warning she swung her feet around in the bed and began to kick Herman furiously and as hard as she could. She kicked the magazine he held clear across the room and her bare heels caught him in the ribs and groin. The coach was so surprised he didn't know what to do. He tried to catch her ankles but he couldn't seem to and she continued to flail at him with her feet until he hastily got out and stood uncertainly by the bed, not sure what was happening to his wife.

"Here, now, here," he said. "You gone crazy? What's the matter with you?"

"You!" Ruth yelled, sitting up in bed. She was beside herself and meant to pursue him out of the house. "You're the matter," she said, her voice shaking. "You fat . . . you fat . . ." she didn't know what to call him. Looking around wildly, she saw the open bathroom door. "You fat turd!" she finished, a little lamely.

The two of them were both stunned. Quiet fell on the room. Ruth was panting, but since the coach had got beyond the range of her heels she had lost the urge to chase him. He would have liked to sit back down on the bed, but Ruth looked too strange and dangerous for him to risk it. He knew it would mean a fight if he got near her, so he stood where he was and scratched himself nervously. He would never have believed his own wife could look so dangerous.

"I never done nothin'," he said finally. "What if I did fart?" It was the only thing he could think of that might have made her mad.

"Oh, Herman," Ruth said. Her legs were trembling and all the strength had gone out of her.

"You got John Cecil fired."

"But he's a goddamn queer," the coach said righteously. "He needed it."

"Then how about you?" she said. "Who roomed with Bobby in Fort Worth, John or you? You think I don't know about things like that? Now you've ruined John's life."

The coach's mouth fell open. He felt tired and went over and sat down on the couch, fumbling with his undershirt.

"Why Ruth, you don't think nothin' like that," he said. "Nobody in this town would believe that. I'm the *football coach!*"

"Don't yell at me," she said. "I know what you are."

Herman looked at her solemnly. "I sure don't know what to think about a wife like you," he said, not at all belligerent.

"We're even," she said. "I don't know what to think about a husband like you, either. Marriage is a bad joke, isn't it."

She saw that she could rip him wide open if she said the right mean things, but she didn't really have the energy and it didn't seem worth doing.

"What are we going to do?" he asked.

'You're going to sleep on that couch from now on," she said, throwing his pillow across the room.

"Hell I am," the coach said, getting up. "Hell I am." But he picked up the pillow and stood holding it.

"You are," Ruth said, switching off the bedside light. "There's some sheets in the bathroom."

"Goddammit, I ain't gonna sleep on this couch,"

Herman said. "It's gonna take more than your kicking to keep me out of my own bed."

"I'll do whatever it takes," Ruth said. "Maybe I'll call the school board and get a few things off my chest."

Her calm voice infuriated the coach, but it frightened him, too. She was clearly an unstable woman. He felt like kicking hell out of her, but instead he went and got some sheets and made a bed on the couch, feeling like a martyr. She didn't deserve it, but the manly thing to do would be to give her a night to cool off. It seemed to him that his mother must have been the last good woman who had ever lived.

The next day Ruth went to see John Cecil, hoping to comfort him. It occurred to her that he might be hungry, so she took what was left of a banana-nut cake she had baked the day before and walked over to the Cecils' house. The porch was dusty and the morning paper lay in the flower bed where the newspaper boy had thrown it. John took a long time to answer her knock.

"Hello, John," she said. "Can I come in?"

He looked tired and a little sick, and she felt silly for bringing the rich cake. He had on a long-sleeved shirt with the sleeves rolled up unevenly.

"I'll just put this on the cabinet," she said awkwardly, moving past him with the cake. She got to the kitchen just in time to see a little pot of asparagus boil over—John had put too much water in the pot. "Oh, goodness," he said. She turned the burner off and he sponged off the stove. Curiously, the event seemed to lift his spirits a little.

"That's exactly the kind of bachelor I make," he said.

He pulled up a kitchen chair for Ruth to sit in and they looked at one another directly for the first time since she had entered.

"What are you going to do, John?" she asked. He seemed such a kind man, and she realized at that moment that they had lived three blocks apart for fifteen years without really becoming friends.

He shook his head, rubbing the back of his neck with both hands. "I'll just have to do what I can for Irene and the girls," he said. "I've got a friend who runs an Indian reservation in New Mexico—maybe he'll let me teach out there. If that don't work out I guess I can go back to Plainview and work in my brother's grocery store. When you've messed up your life the way I've messed up mine it doesn't much matter."

"But *you* didn't mess it up," Ruth said. "My husband messed it up. I'll never forgive him for it. If anybody needed to be fired for . . . what they fired you for, it was him."

John Cecil looked at her with astonishment. "Oh, you don't mean that, Ruth," he said, after a moment. "Why Herman's the football coach."

She saw that he didn't believe her, and knew that Herman had been right. Nobody, not even John Cecil, would believe her, and in truth she didn't even know for sure herself what Herman was. She just felt sad and uncertain and wanted to cry.

"But you've even got two kids," she said. "We don't have any kids, and we never will."

John chuckled. "It's kind of amazing to me that me and Irene had the girls," he said. "I guess it just don't take much enthusiasm for people to have two kids."

Suddenly Ruth wanted to be home, away from John Cecil. His sadness was so heavy that just being with him made her feel the weight, made her own limbs seem heavier. She made an excuse and left quickly, glad to be outside.

The next day John Cecil left Thalia for good, to go back to Plainview to his brother's grocery store. The job on the Indian reservation hadn't worked out.

When Sonny returned from the senior trip, Ruth and he discovered that they were famished for one another. The first afternoon he stayed so long that, while they were dressing, the coach's pickup drove into the driveway. It was something they had dreaded and been frightened of for months, but just then they felt so calm and comfortable with one another that they were not even scared. Besides, the coach customarily spent ten or fifteen minutes carefully putting away his fishing equipment. Sonny quietly finished dressing and went in the living room, so he could go out the front door as the coach came in the back. Ruth, wearing only her panties, folded the quilt and took it to the cedar chest in the hall closet, where it was kept. She was still a little excited, still a little warm. She picked up her dress and went into the living room—the late sun was filtering through the Venetian blinds and Sonny was peeping out of one window, watching the garage. Ruth came up behind him, slipped her arm around his waist and rubbed his stomach. When he realized she was still almost naked he turned with a smile and lifted her breasts. She put the dress on and Sonny buttoned it in back.

"I love you," she said. "You must treat me right from now on."

He didn't reply, but when they heard the back door open he kissed her lightly and walked blithely away, down the front sidewalk.

Herman was in the kitchen, poking around in the cabinet trying to find some Mercurochrome to put on a skinned hand. He could never find things like that when he needed them. Ruth stood in the door a moment, watching him fumble in the cabinet, and her mood was so good that she felt a moment of fondness for him. All he really needed of her was an occasional small kindness.

"I'll find that," she said. "How was fishing?"

For three weeks she continued to make his bed on the couch, and he accepted it, bewildered. Every night he thought he would think up a way to get his supremacy back, but every night the task proved too much for him and he decided it wouldn't hurt Ruth to have one more night to cool off.

In fact, he needed only to wait. Ruth found that she didn't like to sleep alone. She slept better with a body next to hers, even if it was Herman's. For a night or two she fought with herself, determined to keep the advantage she had gained, but she just felt more and more restless and decided finally that it was a silly way to keep an advantage. The next evening, when she was changing the pillowcases, she put Herman's pillow back on the bed. Without a word being said, he came too.

CHAPTER XIX

Summer shaped up very well for Sonny, but very badly for Duane. The first thing Sonny did was quit his job with Frank Fartley. He then hired on as a roughneck with Gene Farrow. He liked driving the butane truck better, but doing it full time gave him no chance to be with Ruth, whereas if he roughnecked at night he could count on spending the whole afternoon with her. Coach Popper was away fishing almost every day. Ruth was becoming happier every day, and was a lot more fun to visit than she had been. She and Sonny both lived for the afternoons.

Duane, unfortunately, had no one to make his days worthwhile. True to her word, Jacy had cut him off cold. Once in a while he saw her driving through town, her sunglasses on, the top of her convertible down, her bare arms tanned from all the hours she spent lying around the country club pool in Wichita. Such glimpses made him ache with desire, but ache was about all he could do. He spent most of June futilely trying to get her to talk to him on the phone—usually

219

she just hung up, but the few times she didn't hang up were even worse.

"Why don't you go back to Mexico," she said once. "I guess girls are just easier to please down there."

"Just go with me once more," he kept saying. "Just one more time. You can at least see me."

He was convinced that if he were actually in her presence for a few minutes all her craziness would go away and they could be in love again.

Jacy knew how he felt, and repeatedly refused to see him. The whole town knew he was desperate to get her back, which suited her fine. After a month had gone by she put a stop to the calls.

"You find somebody else to pester," she said. "I've got a new boy friend now and I can't be talking to you."

"Who?" Duane asked, confused. The blow was unexpected.

"Lester Marlow," Jacy said. "I guess I've just been wanting to go with Lester all along and didn't realize it."

Duane hung up, went downstairs, and threw three pool balls against the back wall of the building as hard as he could, knocking out three big hunks of plaster and scaring Old Man Parsons almost to death. Old Man Parsons was a retired hardware salesman who looked after the poolhall during the day.

That night Duane told Sonny that he was leaving town—he had already packed his suitcase.

"There's not a goddamn thing to stay for," he said. "I'm goin' to Midland. All the roughnecks say you can get a job out there anytime. Jacy's goin' with Lester, why not leave?"

Sonny had no answer. Late that night he and Duane

and Genevieve had coffee and pie together and Duane caught the three o'clock bus out. The prospect of setting out into the world had already taken Duane's mind off his problem. He was speculating about what sort of wages he could draw in Midland. Sonny felt okay about it, figuring to see Duane back in Thalia as soon as Jacy got off to college. When they walked Duane to the bus in the warm summer night they all felt good. Sonny and Genevieve stood on the curb in front of the café and watched the bus pull out. Soon all they could see of it were the red taillights, far out beyond the city limits sign.

"Wouldn't mind goin' someplace myself," Sonny said.

"Well, Uncle Sam will see you get your chance," Genevieve said, stretching her arms.

Abilene's Mercury was parked in front of the poolhall. Sonny was ready to go home, but he hated to go through the poolhall while Abilene was practicing. Finally he went in and had another cup of coffee with Genevieve, waiting to hear the Mercury roar away.

When Jacy heard about Duane leaving town she was a little bit upset. His calls had not been all that annoying—sometimes when she was bored the calls picked her up a little. It was true that she had started going with Lester more or less officially, but it was certainly no deep love affair. She was getting ready to be deeply in love with Bobby Sheen, and she regarded Lester as a necessary stepping-stone. Only by going with someone in Bobby's circle could she keep herself constantly before his eyes, and she knew that if she kept herself constantly before his eyes he would soon realize that she was more beautiful than Annie-Annie. Jacy knew quite well that she was prettier than

Annie-Annie, but at the same time it worried her a little than Annie-Annie always managed to look extremely sexy. The only thing Jacy could figure was that the sexy look was something Annie-Annie had acquired with experience, and there was certainly no reason why she couldn't get just as much experience as Annie-Annie had. Lester Marlow was exactly suitable for such a purpose: he adored Jacy and was completely manageable. She still thought red pubic hair was a little ridiculous, but some things had to be accepted if one was to become a woman of the world.

The Wichita kids called sexual intercourse "screwing," so Jacy took to calling it that too. Lester's parents were in Colorado for the summer, so she and Lester could screw whenever they wanted to—Lester was always willing and usually more or less able. In a week or so Jacy managed to become completely unshy about the whole business, and even worked out a sort of routine. She slept until noon, got up, ate some peanut butter, called Lester to see if he was home, put on shorts, sandals, a blouse, and her new sunglasses and drove to Wichita. The drive always made her sweat a little and it was pleasant to walk into Lester's big cool house. Lester would always be there looking slightly nervous.

"Hi," Jacy would say. "Want to screw?" That was the favored approach among the Bobby Sheen set. Lester wouldn't have dared not to want to, so Jacy would go up to his parents' bedroom, the room with the biggest, most comfortable bed. There she would peel off her clothes and wait for Lester to peel off his. The screwing itself was pretty athletic—Jacy had never been very big on athletics, but she knew good and well she could learn to screw if she put her mind

222

to it. Fortunately, Lester had a good attitude: he would do exactly as directed. When they were finished they usually drove over to the country club and lay around the pool with Bobby Sheen and Annie-Annie and all the other kids, most of whom had been screwing too. One day Bobby Sheen offered to rub suntan oil on Jacy's back and legs and she knew she was making progress. He rubbed the oil on in a very sexy way, she thought.

From time to time it occurred to her that she had really run Duane off too soon. He wasn't quite as manageable as Lester, but he was really a good bit sexier, and she discovered that some of the girls thought there was something pretty romantic about sleeping with roughnecks. She could probably have got another month or so of good out of Duane, but that she hadn't didn't really worry her: Bobby Sheen was the main objective, and if for prestige reasons it became necessary to have a roughneck in love with her there was always Sonny. He was very available, and just as nice as Duane.

Once, just to show that she wasn't snobbish, she called Sonny up and invited him to have a hamburger with her. It was a pleasant summer evening in early July and they decided to drive to Wichita and eat. Jacy drove, her hair blowing across her face. She had on a white silk blouse with the ends tied together in a knot across her stomach—an inch or two of her midriff showed between blouse and shorts.

"Do you ever hear from Duane?" she asked, sighing. "I really feel bad about that."

"I had a postcard," Sonny said. "He's makin' three-twenty a month. Said he bought a car."

"Well, I guess I'll always be a little bit in love with

Duane," Jacy said. "We just had too much against us. It wasn't easy having to be the one to break up."

Talking about it made Sonny uneasy. In fact, just riding with Jacy made him feel a little disloyal. He still thought of her as Duane's girl.

They ate hamburgers, drank milk shakes, and rode slowly back to Thalia, looking at the millions of summer stars. Jacy let Sonny out at the poolhall and went on home, realizing only after she got there that she had enjoyed the evening. Dating no one but Lester Marlow was really tiresome. Except for not being rich, Sonny was more her type of boy. The thought of screwing Lester one more time was utterly boring, but she didn't really feel like she could push things with Bobby Sheen. She decided that in a day or two she would call Sonny again and perhaps go to the lake with him to find out if she liked to kiss him. It would be nice once more to go with somebody she liked to kiss.

The very next day, Bobby Sheen seduced her. Annie-Annie had gone to Dallas to buy her college wardrobe, and Jacy had skipped Lester and gone straight to the club to swim. Bobby asked her if she wanted to go to his house to play some records and that was it. They spread towels over the seats of his MG and wore their wet bathing suits to the house. As soon as they were inside Bobby slipped her straps down so he could play with her breasts. Jacy tried to concentrate and do everything right but it was actually pretty arousing, screwing Bobby Sheen, and she couldn't keep her head clear. He was about five times as athletic as Lester and when she thought it over later she was pretty sure she came, which was what one was supposed to do. At any rate, she went to sleep and

224

didn't wake up until six o'clock. She found Bobby downstairs. He had on Bermuda shorts and was eating a peanut butter sandwich while he watched the news on TV.

"Peanut butter?" he asked absently, when he noticed Jacy. She didn't want to eat, she wanted to sit in his lap, but she saw he was really watching the news and made herself refrain. They had come home in his car, she had no way to leave. During the commercial Bobby got up to fix himself another sandwich. "Oh, you're afoot, aren't you," he said. "As soon as the news is over I'll run you back to the club."

He was quite cheerful and relaxed, but Jacy was a little surprised that he didn't take on over her more than he did. For the next four or five days she hung around the club pool almost constantly, expecting to hear that Bobby and Annie-Annie had broken up; she was sure that as soon as that happened Bobby would call her for another date.

The next Sunday morning Jacy was in the kitchen peeling an orange when her mother came in from the bedroom to get more coffee. On Sunday mornings Lois always lay in bed and drank coffee until the coffee pot was empty. Gene was gone—he always spent Sunday morning inspecting his leases.

"Honey," Lois asked, "don't you know that Sheen boy in Wichita? Bobby Sheen?"

"I sure do," Jacy said. "Why?"

"He got married yesterday to some girl named Annie Martin," Lois said. "It's in the paper this morning. I knew I'd seen them around the club. They got married in Oklahoma a couple of days ago and it just now made the paper. You know her?"

Jacy walked into the bedroom and found the article.

It was just a tiny article with no picture, the kind the paper always ran when kids of prominent families ran off and got married without their parents' consent.

When Lois came into the bedroom with her coffee, Jacy was sitting on the bed crying bitterly.

"He's the luh-ast one," she said. "I'll just be an ol' maid."

Lois set her coffee down and got her daughter a box of Kleenex. She had seldom seen Jacy so upset, and least of all over a boy. Her tears were ruining the newspaper, and since she hadn't finished reading it Lois gently pulled it away.

"Oh, honey," she said. "Don't cry like that. That's the way it is, you know. Win a few, lose a few. That's really the way it goes, all through life."

CHAPTER XX

About a week after Bobby Sheen got married, something totally unexpected happened to Jacy, and it was led up to by an event so startling that everyone in Thalia almost went mad with surprise. Joe Bob Blanton was arrested for rape!

It was one of those days when it seemed to Christian people that the Lord must have lost all patience with the town. It was a wonder he hadn't simply destroyed it by fire, like he had Sodom, and since the heat at midafternoon that day was 109 degrees He could easily have done so simply by making the sun a little hotter. A few degrees more and the grass would have flamed, the buildings begun to smoke, and the asphalt streets to melt and bubble.

Joe Bob didn't rape Jacy, of course, but the general confusion that followed his arrest made possible what did happen to her. Joe Bob didn't actually rape anybody, but very few would have believed that at the time.

"That poor kid's downfall started the day old man Blanton got the call to preach," Lois Farrow said, but she was the only one who took that view. No one else thought of blaming Brother Blanton for his son's disgrace, and still less did they think of blaming Coach Popper or the school board president or San Francisco or Esther Williams, the movie star. They were all quite willing to put the blame squarely on Joe Bob himself.

Joe Bob was a seventeen-year-old virgin. For years he had been tormented by lustful thoughts. When he was only fourteen Brother Blanton slipped into his room one night and caught him masturbating by flashlight over a picture of Esther Williams. Joe Bob had torn the picture out of a movie magazine one of their neighbors had thrown away. Of course Brother Blanton whipped him severely and disposed of the picture; he also told Joe Bob in no uncertain terms what the sequel of such actions would be.

"Joe Bob," he said, "have you ever been through the State Hospital in Wichita? The insane asylum?"

"No sir," Joe Bob said.

"Well, sometime I'll take you," Brother Blanton promised. "There are three or four hundred men over there, pitiful creatures, rotting away, no good to their families or to the Lord or anybody. I don't know about all of them, some of them may have come from broken homes or been alcoholics, but I'm sure most of those men are there because they did just what you were doing today. They abused themselves until their minds were destroyed. I don't want to scare you now. You're young, you haven't hurt yourself much, and the Lord will forgive you. I just want you to know what will happen if you keep on with this kind of filthiness. You understand, don't you?"

"Yes sir," Joe Bob said.

He understood, but he soon discovered he was just too weak to stop. He kept right on playing with himself, all through high school, in the face of certain insanity. His father hadn't told him how long it took for a mind to be destroyed, but he never doubted that his would be, sooner or later.

In the summer of his junior year, when he got the call to preach, he thought there still might be hope. If he preached, girls might like him, and if they did he might be able to overcome his vices and lead a normal life. The hope was very short-lived. The very night he preached his first sermon he succumbed to the vice again. Besides that, he found he did not really like to preach. He didn't have anything to say, and he soon decided he must have heard a false call: he could always get the Lord off his mind, but the only way he could get girls off his mind was by jacking off. In San Francisco he had been with the boys who wandered into the bar where Gloria was, and the thought of Gloria haunted him for weeks. By the time he got back home he had decided to resign himself to eventual insanity, and he ceased to make any effort to curb his self-abuse. If the Lord spared him until he got through college that would be enough to ask.

Joe Bob might have got through the summer all right if it had not been for the scandal caused by Mr. Cecil's dismissal. That set the town on its ear so that it made things hard for all sinners. The church ladies decided the time had come for some widespread soul-saving. If a homosexual was teaching English in high school, there was no telling what state of degeneracy the ordinary populace had fallen into. Ruth Popper herself was known to be sleeping with a high-school boy. They decided to have an All City

229

Revival, and they didn't waste any money bringing in a slick traveling evangelist who would have charged them three hundred dollars. There were six active preachers in the town, plus Joe Bob and a few old ones that were retired, so the ladies decided to put aside denominational differences and make do with the native preaching stock.

Everybody but Joe Bob thought it was a fine idea. He didn't because it meant he would have to preach two sermons.

"Yes sir," Brother Blanton told him. "We've all got to get out there and preach our hearts out if we're going to get this town back on the right track."

Joe Bob agreed, but he was afraid he could preach his own heart completely out in just a minute or two. During the winter his ministerial flame had burned very low—he was not even confident that he himself was saved. He knew that he harbored hatred in his heart for about three-quarters of the boys of the town, and that was surely not a Christian attitude. He had no idea what he could say that might prompt anyone in the congregation to rededicate their life to Christ, and so far as he knew, getting people to rededicate their lives was the only point of a revival.

He worried about it for two weeks, and it turned out his worries were fully justified. Joe Bob had to preach the last sermon in the first go-round of preachers, which meant that he had to preach on a Thursday night, the worst possible night to preach. The first wave of revival spirit had had time to ebb, and the second wave had not yet begun to gather. The revival was held in the local baseball park under the lights, and when Joe Bob got up to preach there was just a sprinkle of a crowd, old faithfuls from all the churches in town, people so habituated to churchgoing that they never missed a sermon, no matter how dull. Joe Bob was dressed in his black wool suit, the only suit his father would let him preach in. The night was sweltering. For days Joe Bob had racked his brain, trying to come up with a sermon, but the only moral advice he could think of was that people ought to read the Bible more. That was his theme, and he sweated and stammered away at it for twenty minutes.

"When I say back to the Bible I don't mean just a chapter here and there," he tried. "I mean the *full* Gospel, the *whole* Bible, *all* of it! Ever bit!"

He kept working that point over desperately, hoping somebody, at least one person, would come down and rededicate his life. Finally, to his great relief, the Pender family got down out of the stands and came. It was not much of a triumph, because the Pender family rededicated their lives regularly, several times a year, but it was better than nothing. The Penders lived in a cabin down on Onion Creek where they shot squirrels and farmed sweet potatoes. Every two or three months, when things got boring, they came to church and rededicated their lives, hoping thereby to move the community to charity. They were a generally scruffy lot—in fact old man Elmer Pender spat tobacco juice right on home plate as Joe Bob was calling for the closing hymn.

Because of the Penders, the first sermon was not a total disgrace, but Joe Bob still had the second one to preach. That one was scheduled for a Saturday night, only one night before the revival was due to end. Hysteria would be at its height, and Joe Bob knew he would need something more potent than the Full Gospel to exhort on that night. On the next-to-last

231

night of a revival it would be a black disgrace not to get twenty or thirty rededications.

All week he brooded about the final sermon. He knew good and well there was no way he could get out of it, and as the week wore on the only way he could get it off his mind was by abusing himself. By Saturday morning he was in a serious state. He stayed in his room until noon and abused himself twice. Then he talked his father into letting him use the family Plymouth, on the grounds that he needed to go off and commune with nature in order to get inspiration for his sermon. Nature that day was about as hot as the place Joe Bob was supposed to be saving people from. He drove out to the lake and sat staring at the water for a couple of hours, thinking how much he didn't want to preach that night. Finally he tired of staring at the bright sun-whitened water and drove into town to get a Coke. That move turned out to be his downfall.

The facts of it almost passed belief. Nobody in Thalia would have supposed that Joe Bob could get in so much trouble in Thalia, Texas, right in the middle of a hot Saturday afternoon. Sonny heard about it almost as soon as the news got out. The sheriff happened to be in the poolhall shooting a quiet game of snooker when Monroe, his skinny deputy, came bursting in, white as a sheet.

"Sheriff, Johnny Clarg's little girl has kinda been kidnapped," he said. "They seen the preacher's boy putting her in his car about an hour and a half ago, in front of the drugstore."

"What the hell?" the sheriff said, taking aim at a red ball. "Maybe Joe Bob gave her a ride home—be doing her a favor, hot as it is. Why should Joe Bob want to kidnap Molly Clarg?"

232

"Don't ask me," Monroe said. "She ain't at home, though. Miz Clarg's all upset—she's done looked everywhere for 'em. They was seen drivin' out of town toward Olney. Miz Clarg's afraid Joe Bob might be goin' to mo-lest her or something."

At that the sheriff quickly slapped his cue into a rack. He was getting beat anyway, and a sex crime called for immediate action.

"Some of you boys might come with us," he said. "If that's the way it is, no tellin' what we'll find."

In all, three cars set out on the search. Brother Blanton was in one, with his wife and some good church deacons. Mrs. Clarg was in another, with a deputy and some of her friends, and the sheriff and several men were in the lead car. Sonny was with the sheriff.

Fortunately, no particular searching was required. It was clear to everybody that Joe Bob had taken Molly out to an old lovers' lane, three or four miles south of town.

"Boys, I don't know what to think, but I fear the worst," the sheriff said, wiping his sweaty face on his shirt sleeve. He drove like sixty, roaring over the rattly cattle guards as if they weren't there. If they hadn't been lucky and encountered Joe Bob on an open stretch of dirt road the sheriff might well have plowed right into him and killed Molly and several other people. When they spotted him Joe Bob was on his way back to town, but he was coming reluctantly, at a speed of five miles an hour. He stopped instantly when he saw the three cars coming toward him.

The sheriff quickly got out of his car and rolled down the cuffs of his shirt sleeves, while Joe Bob sat in the Plymouth, looking miserable. Everyone but

Brother Blanton and his wife got out of the cars and stood looking indecisively at the Plymouth. After a moment Mrs. Clarg became hysterical and ran over to the Plymouth and yanked Molly out. Molly was five, and had been sitting quietly in the front seat eating a lemon all-day sucker Joe Bob had given her. When her mother yanked her out everybody noticed that she didn't have her panties on.

"Get him, ain't you goin' to?" Mrs. Clarg cried. "He's the one done it, here's my little girl, why don't you get him. If my husband was here he'd kill him dead."

At that the sheriff and Monroe leaped in and pulled Joe Bob out of the car.

"What'd you do to that child?" the sheriff said. "We all know you done somethin'."

Joe Bob started to say something but he was too scared and nervous to get it out. Instead he collapsed, and they carried him to the sheriff's car and rushed him back to Thalia.

Sonny volunteered to drive the Blantons' Plymouth into town. Seeing Joe Bob so scared depressed him and he drove slowly. Molly Clarg's panties were lying in the car seat—no one had noticed them, but Sonny supposed they were evidence so he left them there. By the time he got back to town the poolhall was full of men, all of them talking about the crime. It was generally agreed that Johnny Clarg would go to the jailhouse and kill Joe Bob as soon as he came in off his rig.

Then Monroe came in with news that the doctor had said Joe Bob hadn't actually done anything to Molly. Apparently he had just given her the lemon all-day sucker as a bribe to get her to take her panties off, and that was all he had done. It was kind of a letdown.

"Never had the guts," Andy Fanner said. "Preacher's boy."

"Well, the sheriff figures he might have mo-lested her a little bit," Monroe said. "It stands to reason."

"I've thought for years the boy was that kind," Coach Popper said, when he found out about it.

At any rate, Joe Bob had found the one method available to him for getting out of his second revival sermon. He spent that night and many others in jail, but in a way, what *did* happen at the revival that night was his triumph. His disgrace made possible the greatest upsurge of religious feeling the town had ever known. Brother Blanton insisted on preaching his son's sermon, and what he said did it. He rose above calamity and got right out there on home plate to lay matters on the line.

"Good people," he said, "I guess today I've suffered about the worst shock that can come to a man of God. My own son sits in jail tonight, sick with corruption. This very afternoon he was caught in an act of carnal trespass, a thing so foul it's almost unspeakable. How that tears my heartstrings I can't say, but what I want you to know tonight is that I've come through. The Lord has held me up. I've not lost one bit of faith. As for Joe Bob, I've given him up to the Lord. I've prayed to the good Lord this very night that they'll send my boy to prison. Yes, to prison! Sometimes in this life things just don't work out, and I believe it is God's merciful will that Joe Bob go to suffer with the murderer and the thief. It will be a hard thing but a just thing, and I know Joe can count on God's help."

At that Brother Blanton broke down, stretched his

235

arms to the crowd, and began to cry. "Oh, my friends," he said. "If only you would take heed from my trouble. If only you would listen and realize that Jesus Christ is the only answer. If only you would come down tonight, just come down and pray with me and let all of us rededicate our lives right now to the pure way, the righteous way. . . ."

The crowd was overcome by Brother Blanton's self-sacrifice. They flocked down, weeping and hugging one another, the women all slapping at their faces with damp powder puffs, trying to keep their makeup from running completely off. The Penders even came again, Elmer, Lee Harvey, and Mag, the three of them swept away by the general fervor.

There was one strange moment though, right at the start of the sermon: Lois Farrow walked out. As soon as Brother Blanton said he hoped Joe Bob would go to jail, Lois left the stands, got in the Cadillac, and drove away. A lot of tongues clicked—most people thought Lois needed saving worse than anyone in town. Even Brother Blanton felt a momentary irritation when he saw her leaving. Saving a soul as far gone as hers would have really gained him some heavenly credit.

What Lois did after she left was even more unusual: she went down to the jail and made Monroe let her play checkers with Joe Bob. It almost passed belief, but she sat right in the cell and played Joe Bob three games, two of which Joe Bob won. He was not feeling too bad, really. Getting out of the sermon had taken a big load off his mind.

Jacy stayed home from the revival and spent the evening watching television. While *Gunsmoke* was on, her Daddy and Abilene came in. She could hear them in the kitchen, drinking and talking about some drilling problem. After a while Abilene came into the room with a whiskey glass in his hand and stood looking at her.

"Hi," she said. "Where's Daddy?"

"Gone to bed."

"Want me to turn the TV off?" she asked. She was never quite sure what Abilene expected of her.

"Naw, I'm going to the poolhall soon as I finish this drink," he said, leaning against the doorjamb. She was in shorts and her legs were stretched out on Gene's footstool.

"Wish I could go to a poolhall," she said, with a small pout. "I've always wanted to. It's terrible the things girls aren't allowed to do."

"Why hell, come on," Abilene said. "No problem there. I'll show you the poolhall. I got my own key."

He had always thought of her as a prissy kid, but her legs convinced him he hadn't been watching close enough.

"Aren't there people there?" she asked.

"If there are they'll be upstairs asleep," he said. "They won't bother us."

"Okay, I will go then." She felt a little nervous, but she knew he would be irritated if she backed out. She stepped out into the night in front of him. Just getting in the Mercury was exciting: it was the most famous car in that part of the country, and the seat covers smelled of tobacco and beer. Abilene kept it very neat. There was nothing vulgar in it, no dice hanging from the rearview mirror, but there *was* something on the dashboard that fascinated Jacy. It was a tiny, expensive-looking statue of a naked woman. A magnet held it to the dashboard, and as the car moved the statue wiggled provocatively. The woman had a gold stomach and tiny little bloodstones for nipples. Jacy tried not to stare at her.

When they stopped in front of the poolhall Abilene took a comb from behind the sun visor and slicked his hair back a little. The building itself was very dark. Abilene went in first and turned on a little light behind the cash register; he looked at her so inscrutably that Jacy began to be nervous. After he locked the door he got his special cue out of its drawer.

He pulled the light string above one of the snooker tables and the fluorescent tubes blinked on and spread bright light over the green felt and the neat triangle of red balls. As Jacy watched, Abilene put the jointed cue together and glanced appreciatively down its polished length. The cue had an ivory band just below the tip. Jacy was fascinated. She had never been in such a male place before, and it was thrilling.

After he had carefully chalked his cue, Abilene took a white cue ball out of one of the pockets and rolled it slowly across the table. Then he nudged the ball gently with his cue and it went across the table and came back, right to the end of the cue. Abilene smiled, and Jacy came over and stood beside him, so that she could see better. He handled the cue as lovingly as if it were a part of his body.

"Can I see it a minute?" she asked.

Abilene held it out to her a little reluctantly, clearly unwilling to let it leave his hand. Jacy held it awkwardly, trying to sight along it as expertly as he had. When she leaned over the table and playfully attempted to shoot the cue ball Abilene stepped in and took the cue away.

"I don't let nobody shoot with this one," he said.

"There's plenty of others to shoot with, if you just want to practice."

Jacy pouted a little, not really interested in the other cues. She sat down on a bench and watched Abilene as he got ready to shoot. She had never seen a man who was so absolutely sure of himself. He put the white cue ball in the center of the table, sighted quickly, and then with a quick hard thrust of his hips sent the white ball ramming into the tight triangle of red balls. There was a sharp crack, and the red balls scattered and rolled all over the table, a few of them bumping together with soft little clicks. Abilene began to shoot them into pockets, moving lightly and purposefully around the table. The cue was never still. Sometimes he held it up and rubbed a little more chalk onto the tip, or propped it briefly against his hip as he contemplated a shot, but most of the time he didn't contemplate, he just moved rapidly and smoothly from shot to shot.

Jacy began to bite a hangnail on her thumb. She had never seen anything like what she was seeing. Sometimes Abilene seemed to be teasing the red balls across the table, nudging the white ball softly and gently and barely easing the red ball into the pocket. Sometimes he was quick with one stroke and slow with the next, and sometimes, as if excited or annoyed, he suddenly shot a ball very hard, ramming it into a pocket with a quick disdainful thrust of the cue. The balls made a solid thonk when they were whammed into the pockets. Abilene was totally absorbed in the table full of balls, and Jacy became almost as absorbed in the lovely movements of the cue. When all the balls were gone Abilene racked them and quickly broke again.

The hard crack of the cue ball affected Jacy strangely. She felt a trickle of sweat roll out of her armpit and down her ribs. She was vaguely aware that she wanted something, but she couldn't take her eyes off Abilene long enough to think what. He took his time with the second rack, moving around the table more slowly, now lifting the cue and dropping it, withdrawing it and shoving it forward, drawing out every stroke. Jacy was almost annoyed that he had forgotten her—she squirmed a little on the bench, feeling sweaty. She wanted to run and grab the cue away from him, so he would realize she was there. But she merely sat, and he kept shooting until only the cue ball and one red ball were left. That one he shot terribly hard, without caution, thonking it into one of the corner pockets. The sound made something happen in Jacy, something like what used to happen when she and Duane courted on the basketball trips.

Abilene must have known it happened. He laid the cue gently on the green felt and the next minute was kissing her, one hand rubbing her shorts. Jacy found she had no muscles left—she was limp, leaning back against the wall. But when he stepped back a little her hand followed and caught his wrist. Abilene shook her hand off and went and got an old pair of overalls that were hanging on a nail near the door of the poolhall. He turned off the light by the cash register and then carefully spread the overalls on the snooker table before he switched that light off too. When he came back to Jacy the hall was dark except for the rows of light coming through the south windows from the lampposts along the street.

"Come on, stand up," he said. When she did, he urged her out of her clothes, waiting impatiently, and when the clothes were strewn at her feet, he ran his hands down her sides, grinning a little, not at the thought of her but at the thought of her mother. "Be sure you got them overalls under you," he said, when he helped her up on the table.

In a moment he was above her and Jacy pressed her hands against the hard muscles of his arms, not sure of anything. Then he moved and she was sure again, sure it was hurting, sure he was too much. She stretched her arms above her head and caught her fingers in the corner pockets, sucking in her breath. She wanted to tell him to quit but he was ignoring her, and before she could tell him it changed; she was no longer hurting but she was still ignored. He was just going on, absorbed in himself, moving, nudging, thrusting— she was no more than an object. She wanted to protest that, but before she could she began to lose sight of herself, lose hold of herself. She was rolled this way and that, into feelings she hadn't known, hadn't expected, couldn't avoid. She lost all thought of doing anything, she was completely lost to herself. He played her out as recklessly as he had played the final ball, and when he did she scattered as the red balls had scattered when the white one struck them so hard. She spread out, diffused, almost unconscious. Abilene said nothing. Jacy didn't know anything until she realized he had left the table and was not touching her anymore.

In a minute she got up too and tried to find something of herself. It was all new, and it was going to be wonderful. Abilene was going to be in love with her, and he counted for more than Bobby Sheen or any of the boys at the club. The only thing that worried her was that he kept ignoring her. He didn't even help her find her clothes. But it was such a romantic situation, screwing in a poolhall, that surely being in love would follow. When they got back in the Mercury she tried to make him say something to her.

"What a night," she said. "I never thought anything like this would happen."

"Yeah," Abilene said. They pulled into the Farrow driveway and he glanced at her. She leaned over and kissed him but he turned his face away. Jacy got out, very puzzled, and walked across the yard. When she was halfway across, Abilene raced his motor and made his mufflers roar, so that anyone in the neighborhood who was awake would know what car was in the driveway. Then he backed out and left.

It was not until she stepped in the back door that Jacy realized her mother was home and would have heard the mufflers.

Lois did hear them—she was in the den in her bathrobe and slip, having a light drink and watching a Spencer Tracy movie on the Late Show. When she heard Abilene's car she got up and went to the kitchen, wondering what he wanted at that time of night. She had not even realized that Jacy was out until they met in the kitchen. Jacy's hair was tangled and she was barefooted, her slippers in her hand. She looked scared and very confused, and in a moment a couple of tears leaked out of her eyes—she had just realized that Abilene wasn't going to be in love with her at all. It was a terrible disappointment. She was too upset to keep quiet.

"Oh, he's awful," she said. "Why do you fool with him, Mama? Daddy's a nicer man than him, isn't he?"

Lois could only shake her head. She sat her glass down and with a Kleenex ruefully wiped Jacy's wet face. "He sure is, honey," she said. "Your daddy's a very nice man. I ought to have given Abilene hell, instead of him."

At that moment she didn't feel capable of giving anyone hell, or anything else, either. What Abilene had done hit hard, and her legs felt weak. She freshened her drink and went back to the den to sit down, but the movie was just a blur. For a minute she felt like crying, but she felt too insignificant to cry, too valueless. When she went back in to get another drink, Jacy was sitting morosely at the cabinet reading an article on lipsticks in an old fashion magazine.

"Go to bed, honey," Lois said. "Or come and watch television with me. Brooding's no good."

Jacy didn't feel like going to bed, so she obediently followed her mother into the den and they looked at Spencer Tracy for a while. In a few minutes Jacy began to cry again. She was sitting on the floor and she moved back against Lois' legs and put her face in her mother's lap. Lois stroked her hair.

"I don't know what I'm going to do," Jacy said, looking up. "What do *you* do about it, Mama? Life just isn't the way it's supposed to be at all."

"You're right," Lois said, smoothing back the hair on her daughter's temples. "It isn't the way it's supposed to be at all, but what I've done about it hasn't worked very well. Maybe we better work out something different for you."

CHAPTER XXI

Her disappointment with Abilene left Jacy very depressed. It was only the middle of July and she couldn't leave for college for six weeks, but she just couldn't stand the idea of staying in Thalia that much longer. She had slept with two of the most interesting men in the whole area, and neither one of them had fallen in love with her or even shown any particular interest in sleeping with her again. Screwing in the poolhall had been wild while it lasted, but it was hardly going to keep her from rotting with boredom for the rest of the summer. It would have helped if she could have told somebody about it—if the story got out that she had slept with Abilene on a snooker table she would have been a legend in Thalia forever, but she couldn't think of any way to publicize it. Neither Abilene nor her mother were going to, that was for sure, so the whole thing was just wasted. It was disgusting.

The more she thought about matters the more annoyed she was at Duane for leaving town so soon. Things would not have looked quite so dull if he had stayed around. She was not about to start up again with Lester.

One morning while she and Lois were eating a listless breakfast, Jacy gave vent to her irritation.

"I'll be so glad to get to Dallas," she said, "I don't see how people keep livin' in this town. There's not one thing to do."

"Well, there is *one* thing to do," Lois said, chewing a section of orange. "The problem is finding a man to do it with who isn't either dull or obnoxious. Right now I guess Ruth Popper's got about as good a setup as anybody."

Jacy was amazed. "Ruth Popper," she said. "You mean you would like to do that with the coach, Mama? Why I think he's the most horrible man around here. He's even worse than Abilene."

"I didn't say anything about him," Lois said spitting the orange seeds into her hand. "I wouldn't let that tub of guts come within fifteen feet of me. Ruth's been sleeping with Sonny Crawford for about six months now, didn't you know? I don't know Sonny very well but he's reasonably good looking and he's young. If I didn't have anything better than Herman Popper, Sonny would look awfully good."

"What?" Jacy said. "Are you kidding me? Sonny sleeping with Mrs. Popper? Why that's the silliest thing I ever heard of. She's forty years old."

"So am I, honey," Lois said. "It's kind of an itchy age. You want the rest of this orange?"

Jacy was just flabbergasted—life was crazy. She didn't want the orange, and she didn't like the idea of Sonny sleeping with Mrs. Popper. That wouldn't do at all. She had always considered Mrs. Popper mousy, and besides Sonny had always wanted to go with her, not with someone forty years old. It was unflattering of him to sleep with Mrs. Popper.

It did end her boredom, though. She decided then and there that she would stop that romance and stop it good. She would go with Sonny for the rest of the summer, and he would never give Mrs. Popper another thought. He was reasonably good looking, like her mother said, and going with him wouldn't be too unpleasant. It would make August pass a lot quicker. Necking with him might even be fun, but she made up her mind right away that she wasn't going to let him screw her. She had had quite enough of that for one summer—it didn't really work out. She was nostalgic for the days when boys necked with her and wanted her desperately and didn't get her. That was better than actually screwing, somehow. When she got to college she could start screwing again and there it would probably be altogether great. Fraternity boys were gentlemen and would fall right in love with her when she let them screw her.

That very evening Jacy called Sonny and told him she was bored and lonesome; why didn't they go to Wichita and eat Mexican food? Sonny was eager, and the very thought of someone eager perked Jacy up. She took a long bath, shaved her legs and armpits, perfumed herself, and did her hair in an Italian way that made it look casually disarrayed. She wore a sleeveless dress and a sexy bra that left the tops of her breasts uncovered.

When Sonny went to pick her up he was not sure exactly what might happen. Jacy was relaxed and at ease and chattered away about one thing and another. They left Sonny's pickup in the Farrows' driveway and went in the convertible. One of Jacy's arms was stretched out on the top of the seat, almost touching Sonny's shoulder. Before they got to Wichita she scooted over next to him, close enough that he could smell her perfume. The wind whipped a few strands of her hair against his neck. On the way back, after the meal, she rested her arm lightly against his shoulder.

Sonny was in a quandary. He didn't know if he was still honor-bound to treat Jacy as Duane's girl, or if he could treat her as if she were free. Duane might decide to come back any time, but of course there was no guarantee that Jacy would go with him if he did. It was confusing, and having her so close to him made Sonny feel a little bit disloyal.

"Let's go to the lake," Jacy suggested, when they were back in Thalia. "I haven't been there in a long time."

It was exactly what Sonny wanted to do, but as he drove there his uneasiness increased. The thought of Ruth popped into his mind—they had seen each other that very afternoon, and had had an ardent, sweaty, good time. It was more sweaty than was usual because the Poppers' air conditioner had broken down and the coach had gone off fishing without fixing it. After their lovemaking Ruth and he had showered together, to cool off. He had stood behind her and watched the streams of water sluice off her shoulders, her back, her small hips. Driving to the lake, it occurred to him that in a way he was bound to Ruth, but with Jacy sitting close beside him, light-voiced, her hair fragrant, her arm cool, it was hard to keep Ruth in mind. He had wanted Jacy for years, and had fantasized just the sort of situation he was approaching. The lake was very still, but the crickets were singing and bullfrogs croaked loudly in the south channel, where the water was shallow.

For a moment, after stopping, Sonny sat still. Any move would put Jacy in his arms and involve him in two disloyalties, but Jacy was very close to him, so close that he could hear her breath, and soon he was unable to think about anything but her. When he turned, Jacy closed her eyes and they kissed for a long time. She was delighted. It was thrilling to bestow oneself upon someone young and worshipful. It made her feel like a generous, experienced, worldly woman, and feeling that way did something for her that Abilene and Bobby couldn't do. It was the way life was supposed to be, and because it was so nice she rewarded Sonny with all the little amorous flourishes she could think of, nibbling his lower lip and now and then slipping her tongue into his mouth. She could not really believe all those stories about Mrs. Popper—he seemed too hesitant and inexperienced. She would be the one to teach him about love and passion. That thought excited her even more, and when his hand touched her bare throat she sat back and with a wanton shrug undid the front of her dress. She rested her head against the back of the seat and smiled at him when he lifted her breasts out of the shallow cups of the bra. To Sonny it seemed a little incredible that he was holding those particular soft breasts in his hands at last. He held them and fondled them for quite some time, and not only that night but almost every night for the following two weeks. Jacy's breasts were his, her mouth was his, indeed almost all of her was his. She shivered, smiled, kissed his fingers, nibbled at his throat, even let him touch her panties on occasion, but when he grew bold and began to want to go all the way, she diverted him with her mouth or her breasts and told him it wouldn't do.

"Not here," she said huskily. "I'm too old for screwing in cars. I like beds."

Sonny was surprised at her language, but encouraged. He suggested they go to Wichita and get a motel room, but Jacy quickly thought her way out of that.

"I would, but I'm afraid to right now," she said. "I think my folks are watchin' us. They know I don't want to go to college and they think we're goin' to run off and get married." Sonny was surprised, but not entirely persuaded and Jacy nuzzled at his ear. "We'll do it when it's safe," she said. "I don't like to be in a hurry."

Until that night it had never occurred to Sonny that he could marry Jacy, but the idea was not long in taking hold of him. He began to think about it practically all the time.

Nothing at all was said about Ruth. Jacy never let on that she knew anything about him and Ruth, and Sonny didn't mention it. After the first date with Jacy he did not once go back to Ruth's. He could not have faced her. At times he missed her, and he often missed making love to her, but he did not go back. Sometimes in the middle of the night he would wake up and feel nervous and ashamed. Late at night he could not help facing the fact that he had treated Ruth shamefully and probably hurt her very much. He didn't understand it, but he knew Ruth loved him. It was unreasonable, but she did; she had put herself at his disposal, and he had left her. It wasn't right and it made him feel terrible, but at the same time he knew

249

he wasn't going to quit going with Jacy. He was being unfair to Ruth, but what he felt for Jacy was beyond fairness. He had a chance to have something he had always wanted, and he wasn't going to pass the chance up.

He and Ruth would soon have had to quit anyway, he told himself. She was old. Her brown hair was not free of gray. Seeing Jacy at close range had made him realize how old Ruth really was. Ruth's thighs were a little thin, and when she sat up her breasts sagged, not much but some, enough to notice. It didn't make much difference, and yet it did. Jacy's body was fresher and smoother, and it even smelled a little better.

All the same, he hated being the cause of Ruth's suffering. The only way he knew how to handle it was just not to go near her, or to say anything to her, or to try to justify what he had done.

To Ruth, his absence spoke very clearly. She knew at once what it meant. Three days after he quit coming a neighbor of hers named Fanny Franklin mentioned that she had seen Sonny with Jacy Farrow. "They better get that girl off to school before she marries one of these roughnecks," Fanny said happily. She knew all about Ruth and Sonny, though she had never mentioned it, and it gave her a good bit of satisfaction to break such news to Ruth.

For a day or two Ruth spent much of her time sitting listlessly in front of the television set, not crying, just sitting. She didn't despair. Sonny had always wanted the Farrow girl—it was natural he would go with her if he got the chance. Still, she thought he might continue to come and see her once in a while, if only for sex. Even if he only did that it would be okay. She just needed to be with him a little while, from time to time.

When he had not come for two weeks, Ruth was forced to conclude that sex with her did not mean that much to him, and then she did despair. She knew he would never come, not ever again. If she saw him at all it would be on the street, and he would do his best to avoid her. She looked in the mirror often, and it told her more plainly than ever that she was old. She hated being old and despised Jacy Farrow for being young. Before long she began to despise Sonny too. The afternoons were long and hot and unrelieved and she would have forgiven him in a minute if he had come through the door. She could not do anything in the afternoons for wondering if he would come, and she could barely handle her disappointment when he didn't. At first she didn't cry, but later she cried a great deal and it only made her look older and uglier.

All the neighborhood women began to come to see her, friendly and smug, but she herself scarcely ever went out—she only went to the grocery store. At times she felt dizzy and almost feverish. She discovered that she missed Sonny sexually, as well as in other ways. From time to time she tried playing with herself, but it didn't work very well. One night in a moment of bitterness she grasped Herman and tried to get him to play with her, but he jerked himself angrily away and she didn't try again. If Sonny was not coming back, there was no point in her wanting sex anymore. It was a door she might just as well close.

The nadir came one day in the grocery store, when she bumped into Jacy. Ruth was in an old dress, her hair was dry, and she had not bothered to put on makeup. Jacy was in shorts, tight at the thighs. Her

251

legs were tanned and her hair shone. They passed one another in front of the pork and beans. Jacy had on sunglasses, but she took them off when she met Ruth.

"Why hello, Mrs. Popper," she said, grinning with delight. "Haven't seen you in the longest time. I thought you must have left town for the summer."

When Ruth got home she began to tremble. She carried the blue quilt across the hot yard and stuffed it in the garbage can. She could think of no reason why anyone should desire her or want to know her or touch her, and she did not expect to touch or make love to anyone she cared about as long as she lived. It was a terrible feeling, knowing she would never really touch anyone again. She lay on the bed all afternoon staring dully at the wallpaper and wishing there were some simple way to die. She tried to remember herself when she was young, tried to recall one time in her life when she had been as attractive as Jacy, but she couldn't think of one. It seemed to her she had always been old. There was no relief in blaming Sonny, because what was there to blame him for? Jacy was exactly the type of girl with whom boys were supposed to fall in love. She herself was just the football coach's wife.

CHAPTER XXII

One Saturday morning Sonny came in from his tower and found Duane in the apartment, asleep on the couch. While Sonny was taking a shower he woke up and came groggily into the bathroom.

"How you doin', buddy?" he said. "It's a real drive from here to Odessa, especially if you don't start till after you get off work."

"Where's your car?" Sonny asked.

Duane took him downstairs and proudly showed him the car—it was a second-hand Mercury, nice and clean. "Thirty-eight thousand miles on her," Duane said. "Runs like new. I like to drive it so much I thought I'd run home for the weekend."

Sonny was a little relieved. For a few minutes he had been worried that Duane's trip home might have something to do with his relationship with Jacy. Fortunately she was in Dallas that weekend, buying her college clothes.

Duane looked almost the same, except that he was browner. He wore shirts with the sleeves cut completely out, and his shoulders and upper arms were tanned almost black.

"You don't know what sun is till you live out on that desert," he said. "Them folks in Odessa don't even know it's a desert; they think it's God's country." He smoked a lot more than he had, but he was out of school and not in training, and it was natural.

The poolhall was always full of people on Saturdays. It was almost football season and football was what everybody wanted to talk about. The men were glad to see Duane and asked him what kind of football teams they had way out in West Texas.

"Wish you was back here, Duane," several said. "We could use a good fullback this year."

Such talk made Duane feel fine. He had always been very proud of being in the backfield.

When it began to get dark Sonny and he decided to drive to Wichita and drink some beer. They put on fresh Levi's and clean shirts and drove over in Duane's Mercury. He insisted that Sonny drive it.

"Handles wonderful," Sonny said. "Quite a change from that pickup."

They started the evening at a place called the Panhandle Tavern, out on the Burkburnett highway. It was a good place to drink beer, but then nearly any place was. When they left there they stopped in at the big Pioneer drive-in and watched a steady stream of teen-age boys and girls circling around one another in their cars. Finally they went on to Ohio Street and drank in a big roomy bar the size of a barn. There were a lot of airmen there, dancing, playing shuffleboard, guzzling beer. Duane and Sonny drank and idly watched the dancing.

It was pleasant for a while, and then for some reason it began to go wrong. An edge came into the evening. Sonny felt it long before anything was said. He kept drinking beer, but he didn't get high, the way he should have. He should have been comfortable with Duane, too—after all, they were best buddies—but somehow he wasn't comfortable with him at all. The pretty girls on the dance floor reminded both of them of things they didn't really want to remember.

"Still screwin' that old lady?" Duane asked casually.

"Yeah, ever now and then," Sonny said. It seemed to him the best thing to say. Duane hadn't mentioned Jacy all day, but Sonny knew he must have been thinking about her.

"Seen old Jerry Framingham last week," he said. "He came through going to Carlsbad with a load of goats. Said he thought you and Jacy had been going together a little."

"Yeah, we have," Sonny admitted quickly. "Once in a while we come over here and eat Mexican food or something. She's been kinda bored, waitin' for school to start."

He didn't look at Duane but he could tell that something was wrong. Instead of looking at Duane he looked around the room. There were jars of pigs' feet on the bar. Bunches of glum airmen stood around with beer glasses in their hands. There was a jukebox, a Schlitz sign, and a clock that said Lone Star Beer underneath it.

"Way I heard it what you probably been eatin' is pussy," Duane said, his voice shaky and strained. "Not old lady Popper's, either."

"It ain't true," Sonny said. "Whoever told you that didn't know what he was talkin' about. Sure, I been goin' with Jacy, why not?"

He couldn't keep down a pulse of irritation with Duane for having kept so quiet about the matter all day. He had kept quiet about it too, but then it wasn't his place to bring it up.

"I never said I blamed you for it," Duane said. "I don't blame you much. I just never thought I'd see the day when you'd do me that way. I thought we was still best friends."

"We are," Sonny said. "What are you so mad for? I never done nothin' to you."

"I guess screwin' my girl ain't nothin' to you," Duane said stiffly.

"I haven't screwed her, but she ain't your girl anymore, anyway. Hell, you don't even live here anymore."

"Don't make no difference," Duane insisted. He was beginning to seem drunk. "She's my girl and I don't care if we did break up. I'm gonna get her back, I'm tellin' you right now. She's gonna marry me one of these days, when I get a little more money."

Sonny was astonished that Duane could be so wrong. He knew Duane must be drunk.

"Why she won't marry you," he said. "She's goin' off to school. I doubt I'll ever get to go with her agin myself, once she gets off. I never saw what it could hurt to go with her this summer, though. She's never gonna marry you."

"She is, by God," Duane said. "Don't tell me she ain't. She'll never let you screw her, that's for sure. Hell, I was just seein' how honest you was. I knew Jacy
256

wouldn't let you screw her. You ain't that good a cocksman. You never even screwed Charlene Duggs, all the time you went with her."

Sonny didn't know what to say. He was amazed that Duane would bring up such a matter. It was unfair, and the more he thought about it the madder he felt.

"Course I didn't," he said. "You know why? Because you and Jacy had the pickup all the time on Saturday night. Nobody could have screwed her in the time I had left."

"I could have," Duane said smugly. "I could have screwed her in five minutes."

Sonny knew that was true, but because it was true it seemed even more unfair of Duane to bring it up. Suddenly, for the first time in his life, he felt like hitting Duane.

"You know why you could," he said, almost choking. "The only reason you could have was because you was in the backfield. I was in the fuckin' line. That's the only reason Jacy went with you as long as she did, because you was in the backfield."

"That's a lie, you chickenshit," Duane said. "What are you talkin' about? Me an' her was in love."

"You was, she wasn't," Sonny said confidently. "Just because you was in the backfield. She likes me as good as she ever liked you. I'll stay all night with her one of these nights, too—she's done promised."

"You won't either," Duane said, furious.

"Why shouldn't I? She's done told me you couldn't even do it that time in San Francisco. What about that?"

Duane couldn't take that. He came out of his chair and slammed Sonny in the face with the beer bottle he

257

had in his hand. It knocked Sonny backward, but he was soon up and at Duane. It was too much to take, saying he couldn't have screwed Charlene, just because he was in the line. Sonny couldn't see too well, but it didn't matter because in a minute they were both rolling on the floor anyway, punching and kicking at one another. The barmaids and the airmen calmly got out of the way and the boys rolled over against the bar, whacking at one another and bonking their heads on the brass footrail. They got up and slugged a minute on their knees but before they could get to their feet the cops were there. The next thing they knew they were out on the curb, each handcuffed to a cop. One of Sonny's eyes was hurting and he had to hold his hand over it, but otherwise he didn't feel too bad. He and Duane stood beside one another at the police desk, and to their surprise were no longer particularly mad.

"Don't know what happened," Duane said. "Never meant to hit you with that bottle. Reckon we got enough money to pay our fines?"

They did have, barely, and in a few more minutes, without knowing exactly what had taken place, they were on the sidewalk again, walking back up Ohio Street. They walked past the bar where they had had the fight and one of the barmaids waved at them, tolerant, jolly, and apparently amused. It deflated the boys a little bit. Theirs must not have been much of a fight, as fights went on Ohio Street.

"My damn eye sure hurts," Sonny said. "Run me up by the General Hospital—maybe they can give me a shot or something. It's a wonder we didn't tear up that bar."

258

"I guess they get worse fights than us in there ever night," Duane said unhappily. "When it comes to Jacy I guess I'm just crazy."

By the time they got to the hospital Sonny's eye had swollen shut and was paining him terribly. The momentary good feeling that he had had at the police station was entirely gone, and he was a little scared. It was nice that he and Duane were not going to be enemies for life, but he was still scared. When a doctor finally took a look at his eye he immediately ordered Sonny a hospital room.

"You're not leavin' here tonight," he said.

"You could lose the sight in that eye if we aren't careful, and you might lose it even if we are. In the morning we'll have to have a good look at it."

"Damn," Duane said nervously. "Why'd I have to have that bottle in my hand?"

"Aw, they're always tryin' to scare you," Sonny said. "It feels like it's just swole up."

Duane was really worried, and it made him so nervous and stiff that Sonny was almost glad when he left. He had a shot that made him sleep, and the next day the eye was hurting so badly that he had several more shots and was just in a sort of daze all day. He knew his father was there some of the time. The day after that he had some kind of operation, and when he woke up his father was there, shaking a little but not too badly. It was the first time they had seen one another since graduation night, when Sonny had reluctantly accepted fifty dollars as a graduation present.

"Son, must have been some fight," Frank said.

"Oh, just me and Duane. He gone back to Odessa?"

"Yeah, he had to. Tried to see you yesterday, but they wouldn't let him. He said to tell you he was awful sorry."

"Well, it's over now," Sonny said. "I might have done it to him if I'd been holding a bottle. What'd they say about my eye?"

"They don't know yet," Frank said. "You didn't lose all your sight in it, but I guess you might lose some."

Sonny found it was not so bad having his father around. Frank didn't say much, just sat in the room. He seemed comfortable and Sonny was too. There was only one awkward moment in the three days Frank stayed. It came one night when Sonny was eating supper.

"Son," Frank said, "reckon it would work out if we put the poolhall and the domino hall together? The building's big enough, ain't it?"

It was, but the whole idea made Sonny nervous. "I don't think it would do too well," he said. "The men who play dominos wouldn't want a lot of kids in there shooting pool and making racket."

Frank said that might be so, and didn't mention it again.

Sonny was in the hospital eight days. He got lonesome, but it was just about as bad when visitors came. Genevieve came one afternoon and brought Billy, who was scared of the hospital and didn't know whether to sit down or stand up. Sonny was so used to seeing Genevieve in her waitress uniform that she looked strange to him in her regular clothes. She came right out and asked about his eye.

"How is it, really?" she said.

"I don't know," Sonny said honestly. "It wouldn't surprise me if I was one-eyed when they take the bandages off. Duane caught me a good hard lick."

"Well, it was awful of you two to fight. You knew he joined the army, didn't you? His mother told me two or three days ago."

Sonny hadn't known it, and was very surprised. For the first time he really wondered about his eye. He had always planned to go to the army too, and it occurred to him that if he was one-eyed the army wouldn't take him. He had never supposed he would be unable to make the army.

The next afternoon the nurse brought in a note.

"A lady's down in the waiting room," she said.

The note just said: "May I come in and see you a little while? Ruth."

Sonny looked at the nurse, who was young and friendly.

"Could you tell her I'm asleep?" he asked.

"Sure I could. But you're not asleep."

"If I go to sleep right now will you tell her I'm asleep?"

The nurse did as he asked, but Sonny was blue anyway. He would not have minded seeing Ruth, but he felt bad whenever he thought about her and he was afraid that if she came up something bad might happen. In a way he wanted to see her—indeed, the more he thought about her the more lonesome he became for her—but it seemed like seeing her would only make everything worse.

The next to last day he was there, Jacy came to see him. She wore a sleeveless green dress and looked a little sad. As soon as the nurse left the room she came to the bed and kissed Sonny for a long time. It surprised him and he embarrassed himself a little by getting a hard-on.

"Oh, I was so worried," Jacy said. "I just had to see you. When do you get out?"

"Tomorrow," Sonny said. "Why?"

"I want us to get married," Jacy said, her dewy mouth close to his. "I really do. Whenever you get out, just as soon as you want to."

Sonny was stunned. "Get married?" he said. He thought he must be having a dream.

"Do you want to?" she asked.

"Oh yeah, yeah," he said. "But ain't you goin' to college?"

"No. I don't care about that. I love you and that's more important. My folks won't like it, but we can run off."

It was an inspiration she had had as soon as she heard about the fight. Sonny was so dear, to fight for her. Running off with him would make her whole summer, and the fact that she did it even though he only had one eye would knock everyone in Thalia for a loop. It would be a lot wilder than Bobby Sheen and Annie-Annie—they were both rich and healthy. She would be running off with someone poor and sort of mutilated. Of course her folks would catch them and have it annulled, but at least she could show Sonny how much she was willing to sacrifice for him.

Jacy sat on the hospital bed and they kissed some more and talked about how wild it would be being married. Life seemed almost too crazy to be true.

The next day they unbandaged Sonny's eye. It wasn't that he couldn't see anything out of it, it was just that all he could see was fog. It was like being inside a cloud. He could tell when people moved around, but he couldn't tell who they were until they spoke.

"Could be a lot worse," the doctor said. "We'll see how it responds before we do anything else."

They gave him a black patch to wear over his eye and told him to come back weekly for checkups, but Sonny hardly listened. Marrying Jacy was all he could think of, and he thought about it on the ride back to Thalia, while his father drove.

As soon as they got home Sonny took the extra eye patch the doctor had given him and showed Billy how to wear it. Billy was tickled to death. Because Sonny did it, he thought seeing out of only one eye was a great way to see, and from then on he wore the spare eye patch whenever he went out to sweep the town.

CHAPTER **XXIII**

Jacy was dead serious about getting married: the day after Sonny left the hospital they drove to Wichita and got the license. They had to wait three days, so to be doing something Sonny quit his roughnecking job and arranged for a new job pumping leases, something he could do with one eye. The rest of the time he just stayed around the poolhall thinking about sleeping with Jacy. The prospect helped take his mind off his eye.

Jacy spent the three days imagining the effect her marriage would have on her parents and on the town. Everybody was curious about Sonny's eye, which made it absolutely the ideal time to run off with him. Her folks would simply have a fit. Probably they would call the police and have them arrested and torn out of one another's arms, but at least they would have been married and everyone would know it.

Friday afternoon, when it actually became time for them to run away, she wrote her parents a quick note:

Dear Mama and Daddy—

I know this is going to be a shock to you but I guess it can't be helped. Sonny and I have gone to Oklahoma to get married—I guess it will be in Altus. Even if he is poor we are in love. I don't know what to say about college, I guess we'll just have to talk about that when we get back. We are going to Lake Texoma on our honeymoon and will be home Monday. I guess I will live at the poolhall until we find someplace else to live. Even if you don't like Sonny now I know you will love him someday.

Jacy

She left the note on the cabinet, propped up against a box of crackers. Gene found it when he came in from work three hours later. Lois was in Wichita that day and returned late. When she came in, Gene was pacing the kitchen floor, obviously distressed. He handed her the note.

"Oh, goddamn her," Lois said. "I can't believe it."

"Well, we got to get going," Gene said. "I want to catch 'em. Even if we can't get 'em before they marry we can sure as hell get 'em before they go to bed. That way we can get it annulled with no trouble."

"Why bother?" Lois said. "I suppose we could get it annulled anytime—that's what money's for. Why don't we just let her do the getting out—you know she won't stay with Sonny ten days. I just hate to think of what she'll do to him in that length of time. If we don't get that little bitch off to college she's going to ruin the whole town."

Gene was so upset he couldn't take what Lois said.

He turned and slapped her, but it was a light, indecisive slap.

"You just change your clothes," he said, shoving her in the direction of the bedroom. "I said we're going to get 'em and by God that's all there is to it. What do you mean calling my daughter a bitch? You're her mother, ain't you?"

"I don't see what that has to do with it," Lois said, but she didn't feel like arguing. She felt sorry for Gene, and pity always made her feel wretched. She already had visions of a horrible scene somewhere in Oklahoma. She stood in the doorway and heard Gene call the highway patrol and ask them to stop Jacy's car. When he hung up he seemed to feel better. A man should react to such an event in a certain way, and he was doing what he should.

"I won't have her living over no poolhall, not even for ten days," he said. "Hurry up and get changed, and don't call my daughter a bitch again."

"No promises," Lois said. "You know what she's doing as well as I do, Gene. She doesn't give a damn about Sonny, she just wants to hurt us and get a little attention while she's doing it. What is that but bitchery?"

"Well, she comes by it honest," he said, looking his wife in the eye. "I know right where she gets it."

Lois merely nodded. "I'm sure you do," she said. She obediently went into the bedroom and put on more somber clothes.

Sonny and Jacy, meanwhile, were off on the realest of adventures: running away to get married. Jacy had an expensive suitcase and enough clothes to last her a week, while Sonny, who owned no suitcase, had a canvas overnight bag and an extra pair of slacks hung on a hanger in the back seat. They were in the convertible, and Jacy drove. Sonny didn't yet trust himself to drive on the highway with one eye.

Jacy was wearing a lovely white dress she had bought at Neiman's the week before, to wear to fraternity parties. She had some new sunglasses, and drove barefoot. It was great fun to be running away to get married—both of them were delighted with themselves. All Sonny had to do was lean back and watch Jacy and imagine the bliss that was going to be his in only a few hours. It was a bright, hot day and there were drops of sweat on Jacy's upper lip. Neither of them minded the heat, though. They stopped in Lawton and had milk shakes, probably the last milk shakes they would ever have as single people. Both of them were hungry and they sucked up every milky drop.

Then they went on to Altus, a popular place for getting married. It was late afternoon when they arrived—Sonny stopped at a filling station and asked where they might find a justice of the peace. "Why there's one right up the road," the attendant said. "What part of Texas you all from?"

They told him and drove on. It turned out to be absurdly simple to get married. The justice of the peace lived in an old unpainted frame house and came to the door in his khakis and undershirt.

"Been having myself a little snooze," he said. "What part of Texas y'all from?"

He surveyed their license casually, got a pencil, licked the point, and filled in what he was supposed to fill in. Sonny would have preferred him to use a fountain pen, since pencil erased so easily, but he didn't say anything.

"I better go get Ma to witness," he said, belching. "I guess I could put a shirt on too, if I can find one."

"Get many marriages up here?" Sonny asked, to be polite.

"Not as many as I'd like," the J.P. said. "Not like I used to when we was a Christian country. Used to be people feared God, but not no more. I don't marry half as many kids as I used to—fornication don't mean nothing anymore. Kids nowadays fornicate like frogs, they don't never think of marryin'. What decent ones is left is mostly hifalutin' kids, church weddin's and recepshuns and such as that. Ma! Got some customers."

An old woman wearing a sunbonnet and gray work gloves came in from the backyard. She was a thin little woman and looked tired, but she nodded politely. "Pardon this getup," she said. "I was out gettin' the last of my black-eyes. Garden's just about gone for this year. What part of Texas you all from?"

The old man had wandered out, but he came back into the living room buttoning a khaki shirt over his belly. He stuffed the shirttail unevenly into his pants and shuffled over to an old pigeonhole desk to find his service.

"Y'all don't mind if I read this, do you?" he asked. "I ain't got a memory worth a damn."

They didn't mind him reading, but Jacy did mind him standing so close to them. He had a body odor that almost made her gag, but he winked at her with mild lechery and seemed to think she found him attractive.

"Wouldn't mind marrying you myself, honey," he said. "You got more meat on you than Ma has."

"Don't be sassing, now," his wife said. "You can wait till I get this sunbonnet off before you start."

He read the service heavily, sometimes stopping to trace his place with a forefinger. When he asked about rings Sonny shook his head. "She's marryin' a cheapskate, Ma," the J.P. said.

When it was over Sonny gave Jacy a quick kiss, but she wanted a long romantic one so they kissed for almost a minute while the old lady wandered off to start shelling her black-eyed peas. As soon as they quit kissing the J.P. came over and placed a wet kiss of his own on Jacy's cheek—it made her furious. Sonny gave him a ten-dollar bill and he stuffed it in his pocket contemptuously.

"Yeah, a cheapskate," he said. As they left he followed them out on the porch. "Hell, you've got a collapsable," he hollered, when they were getting in the car. "Used to be collapsables were twenty-dollar weddin's ever time. Y'all got any fornicatin' friends down in Texas tell 'em to cut it out and come up here to see me. I'll set 'em right with the Lord as cheap as the next man."

"Why he's just awful," Jacy said. "I never dreamed they let people like him do marryin'."

"Anyway, we're man and wife," Sonny said, barely able to believe it. At the first stop sign they kissed again and wiggled their tongues enthusiastically. Jacy was for going to Lake Texoma to spend their wedding night, and Sonny was agreeable to anything.

They left Altus in a high good mood and drove back to Lawton, where they stopped to eat. In Lawton, for some reason, Jacy began to feel a little depressed. A strange thought occurred to her. They were in the parking lot of the restaurant where they were going to eat, so they kissed for a while, as newlyweds should. While they were kissing Sonny got excited and fondled her in a place in which he was very interested. It was all right for him to do it, of course, but a little later, while she was in the rest room of the steak house, it occurred to her that maybe her parents wouldn't have the police arrest them after all. Maybe they would just wash their hands of it and go on watching television. It might even be that they thought she ought to *live* with Sonny, since she had married him.

That was a very sobering thought: to think that they didn't love her enough to want to keep her from living over a poolhall.

Thinking about it took away her appetite, and though she tried to appear gay she really only picked at her fried shrimp. They ordered beer with the meal and drank it self-consciously. It occurred to Jacy that even if her folks sent the cops they might miss them in the dark, or they might even get to the motel before the cops started looking. The thought depressed her more and more.

Sonny noticed that marriage was making Jacy a little nervous, but he supposed it was just worry over her parents. He was sure she would calm down once they got to Lake Texoma. But the strange thing was, the closer they came to the lake, the more nervous she became. He scooted over next to her and patted her leg, but that just seemed to make her more edgy.

When Sonny scooted close to her Jacy really began to feel funny. She realized suddenly that she just didn't want a wedding night with him at all—she had been wrong to think she did. She didn't know whether she even wanted to kiss him anymore or not. Kissing someone who just had one eye was kind of creepy.

Then, just outside Madill, a cop stopped them and everything changed completely. Jacy ceased to feel the least bit nervous.

"What part of Texas y'all from?" the patrolman asked, holding out his hand for Jacy's license. He flashed a flashlight in their faces.

"Newlyweds, ain't you?" he said, when they told him where they were from.

They admitted it.

"Well, better follow me in," he said. "I think somebody's lookin' for you."

"But we ain't done nothin' wrong," Sonny said. "Ain't we got a right to get married? How can you arrest us, just like that?"

"I ain't arrestin' you," the patrolman said, peeling a stick of chewing gum. "I just want you to come with me, till we find out. I don't have no idea what you've got a right to do."

"I guess we better follow him, honey," Jacy said. She turned to Sonny and kissed him promisingly. "I'll just be heartbroken if my folks have done this," she added, kissing him again lightly as she put the car in gear.

The patrolman led them to a jailhouse in Madill. He didn't put them in a cell or anything, but they had to sit in the jail for almost two hours and that was almost as depressing as being in a cell. Jacy realized she was tragically in love, and clung to Sonny tightly. They even got in some nice kissing, but in a way it was

271

depressing, at least to Sonny. Jacy's folks were in Lawton and were coming after her. He couldn't figure out the justice of it.

"I thought anybody had the right to get married," he said, several times. The patrolman had gone on about his business. There were only two people besides themselves in the whole jail: one was a prisoner and the other was a redheaded jail-keeper named Elmer.

"Well you might have the right and you might not," Elmer said. "I couldn't say. I ain't gonna hold no gun on you, but if you leave you'll just get caught agin. You might as well wait here as anywhere. If you're thirsty we got a Coke machine you're welcome to use."

While they were waiting the sheriff came in, a fat, white-headed man. He took one look at them and concluded they didn't have any right to do anything.

"Kids, we really oughta lock you up," he said. "Running off from home, making your parents chase all the way up here. I don't know what the world's coming to."

Sonny didn't either, but he knew one thing for sure: he was never going to get to sleep with Jacy. They would never be together in an actual bed, not for a whole night or even part of a night. Somehow his whole life had worked out to keep that one thing from happening, and it was the one thing he wanted most of all. He was not at all sure he would ever get to make love to anyone he cared about, much less to Jacy. In the hot little jail lobby, sitting on the one bench, he couldn't even remember why he had ever thought he *would* get to sleep with her.

It disappointed him terribly and made him feel a little sick and very tired. About ten o'clock Elmer let the one prisoner come in and watch the late movie with him on the jail's old Magnavox TV. That was what they were all doing when Lois and Gene arrived. Sonny was so tired by then that he wasn't even scared of Gene, even though Gene started yelling at him the minute he stepped through the jailhouse door.

"You're fired, you whelp!" he said. "What do you mean, runnin' off with my daughter, tellin' her she's gonna live over a poolhall?"

He would have gone on, but Elmer cut him off.

"Just take him out in the yard to bawl him out, Mister," he said. "I can't hear this movie if you bawl him out in here." It was a Randolph Scott movie, and they had all been sort of enjoying it.

As they went out the door Jacy clung to Sonny, crying bitterly. Mrs. Farrow said nothing at all, but Gene was still mad as cats.

"I'll bawl him out all right," he said. "Think I worked like a dog all my life so my daughter could end up over a poolhall?"

"We was gonna get another apartment," Sonny said, though they had not actually given the matter much thought.

"I bet you was," Gene said. He grabbed Jacy by the arm and jerked her away from Sonny. "Where's your car keys, hon?" he asked.

Snuffling, Jacy fished in her purse and handed them to Lois.

"It's a hell of a note," he said.

"Oh shut up and take her home," Lois put in wearily. "I'm tired of this."

"You bet I will. You take her car. So far as I'm concerned Sonny can walk."

He led Jacy to the Cadillac, got in, and spun the big

car off, throwing up dust in the unpaved road that ran by the jailhouse. Lois and Sonny were left standing in the jailyard, by a little cedar bush. It was very quiet all of a sudden, the moon white overhead.

"I would like to apologize for all this, Sonny," Lois said. "It wasn't my doings. So far as I'm concerned you have a perfect right to anything you could get out of Jacy, but I can tell you right now that wouldn't have been much."

Sonny didn't know what to say. He felt awfully tired, and Lois noticed it.

"You're welcome to ride back with me," she said. "In fact I'd enjoy the company. I can understand how you might not want to, though. If you don't just say so and I'll give you some bus money."

Mrs. Farrow didn't seem so bad, and Sonny was much too tired to enjoy the thought of waiting for a bus. "I believe I'll ride with you," he said.

They started back over the same road that Sonny had just driven with Jacy. Mrs. Farrow drove fast, but there was no sign of the Cadillac ahead of them.

"Gene's probably driving ninety," she said. "I bet he's telling Jacy it was all my fault and his, for not loving her more or something."

Sonny didn't know whether he napped or not, but soon they were almost back to Lawton. The wind whipped Mrs. Farrow's hair about her face just as it had Jacy's, when they were driving up. To the west, toward the plains, there were low flashings of lightning and the rumble of thunder. Somewhere over near Frederic it was raining. Sonny noticed that Mrs. Farrow had a little flask that she drank from now and then.

"Here," she said, holding it out to him. "Have a

little bourbon—you can have the rest of it, in fact. I've got to drive. It might pick you up."

Sonny took the flask and sipped from it. The whiskey was very sharp on his tongue, but he kept the flask and continued to sip, and after a time he felt a vagueness spreading through him that was almost comfortable. He was surprised to find Mrs. Farrow so likable.

"Not much of a wedding night, is it?" she said. She grinned at him, but it was not an insulting grin.

"No, not much of one," he said.

"Let me tell you something you won't believe, Sonny. You're lucky we got her away from you as quick as we did. Even if you had got to a motel room she'd have found some way to keep from giving it to you. God knows how, but Jacy would have thought of something. You'd have been a lot better off to stay with Ruth Popper."

Sonny was startled. "Does everybody know about that?" he asked.

"Of course," Lois said. "It sounded like a good thing to me. You shouldn't have let Jacy turn your head."

"She's prettier," Sonny said. "I guess I shouldn't have though. I don't guess I can go see Mrs. Popper any more."

"I shouldn't imagine. I wouldn't have you back if you'd left me for Jacy, but then you never know. I'm not Ruth."

They turned south out of Lawton. The bourbon was going down easier and easier. In the west the lightning flashes were closer together, and in the moments of light they could see heavy clouds low over the plains.

"I hope we don't have to put this damn top up,"

Lois said. She found herself moved by Sonny's youth. He held the bourbon flask very carefully and looked almost comically young. Giving way to an impulse, she reached over and touched his neck. It startled him a great deal.

"Didn't mean to scare you," she said. "I guess I just felt motherly for a second. Or maybe I felt wifely, I don't know. It's strange to have a married daughter who wouldn't go through with her wedding night."

Sonny looked at her curiously and she smiled at him, an honest, attractive smile, as she kept stroking the back of his neck lightly. He drank more bourbon and watched the intermittent lightning yellow the plains. He felt as though life was completely beyond him.

In a little while they crossed Red River, the slap of their tires echoing off the old stone bridge abutments. The water in the channel was shallow and silvery.

"Anyhow, I know why Sam the Lion liked you," Sonny said, and it was Lois' turn to be startled.

"Sam?" she said. "Who told you he liked me? Genevieve?"

Sonny nodded. Lois was silent for a moment. "No, it was more than that," she said. "He loved me, honey."

They were silent almost to Burkburnett, but Sonny noticed that Lois kept wiping her eyes with the backs of her hands.

"I get sad when I think about Sam for long," she said in explanation, her voice unsteady. "I can still remember his hands, you see. Did you know he had beautiful hands?"

They passed by Shepherd Field, with its flickering,

rotating airplane beacons and its rows of dark narrow barracks.

"I think he was the only man in that whole horny town who knew what sex was worth," Lois said, her voice a little hoarse. "I probably never would have learned myself if it hadn't been for Sam. I'd be one of those Amity types who thinks bridge is the best thing life offers womankind. Gene couldn't have taught me, he doesn't know himself."

Then they were coming down on the lights of Wichita.

"Sam the Lion," Lois said, smiling. "Sam the Lion. Nobody knows where he got that name but me. I gave it to him one night—it just came to me. He was so pleased. I was twenty-two then, can you imagine?"

Then suddenly her shoulders began to shake and she did a strange thing. She wheeled the convertible off the highway in a screech of brakes and stopped on the hill across from the auction barn. She scooted across the seat and grabbed Sonny's arms, tears running down her face.

"But you know somethin'," she said, her whole body shaking. "It's terrible to only find one man your whole life who knows what it's worth, Sonny. It's just terrible. I wouldn't be tellin' you if it wasn't. I've looked, too—you wouldn't bu-lieve how I've looked. When Sam, when Sam . . . the Lion was seventy years old he could just walk in . . . I don't know, hug me and call me Lois or something an' do more for me than anybody. *He* really knew what *I* was worth, an' the rest of them haven't, not one man in this whole country. . . ."

She lay against Sonny's chest and cried very hard,

her face hidden. He put his arms around her and waited. He felt so tired that he could be calm through anything. After a while Lois' body quit heaving. She slipped her hand inside his shirt and touched his chest, and when she finally sat up her face was quite calm. In fact there was something almost gay in her face.

"Hey," she said. "I like you. I don't know if you know what I'm worth or not, but I sure like you and I should like you to have a nicer wedding night than Jacy could ever have given you. I'll take you someplace right now and we'll see to that. Okay? You're not scared of me, are you?"

"No," Sonny said, though he was. But he was glad to go with her, scared or not; he would have gone with her anywhere, just to see what she would do next, what crazy thing life would bring next. Lois got back behind the wheel and drove to a big motel on the Henrietta highway, one Sonny had passed many times. He had certainly never dreamed he would be going into it with Jacy's mother, on his wedding night.

Lois paid for a room and got the key. They were right at the back of the court, and she had a little trouble getting the key in the lock. "Gene and Jacy are home now, wondering why we're driving so slow," she said. She went in and Sonny followed her. She turned on a small bed light and raised her hands to her throat to unclip a black necklace she wore.

"We'll let 'em wonder," she said. "I'll tell them we had a flat and had to get it fixed in Lawton. It's amazing how many good excuses there are."

She was undressing, gracefully and without embarrassment, but she stopped a moment to set the bed lamp on the floor. Her breasts were bare—she was the first full-breasted woman Sonny had seen naked.

"I like a little light but I don't like it in my eyes," she said.

With the lamp on the floor the room was mostly in shadow. As Sonny hesitantly undressed, Lois came and stood quietly by him, smiling, occasionally reaching out to stroke his shoulder or arm or chest. "Shy young men are lovely," she said, smiling. He thought her breasts were what was lovely. When they lay on the bed he quickly reached to caress her, but Lois caught his hands and held them for a moment in the valley between her breasts. She raised up on one elbow, her face just above his, and touched him lightly with her lips before she spoke.

"No, no, now," she said. "You're scared to death of me. Your muscles are all tight." She put her hand on his arms, then on his thigh muscles. Sonny knew they were tight.

"You're scared of me because I'm Lois Farrow," she said. "I'm rich and mean, all that. What everybody thinks of me. But that's not true for you. I may be that way with a lot of men because that's what they want and deserve, but it's still not true. Sam . . . the Lion knew I wasn't any of that, and I want you to know it too. See my hand? It's not like that, and hands are what's real. Put yours right here on my throat."

Sonny did—her throat was warm, and she lowered her face and kissed him. After a while she took his hand off her throat and played with his fingers, kissed them. She kissed him and played with him until he began to play too. He relaxed and became as serious and playful as she was. She seemed really glad to be with him, crazy as it was. What surprised him most was the lightness of her movement—her body was heavier than Ruth's, yet she seemed weightless, so light and easy that they might have been floating together. He came right away, without remembering her at all, and it was only a little later, when he did remember, that he wondered if he had come too soon. She seemed secretly pleased, even delighted, and she took his hands again. They played a little more—Lois continued to touch him lightly with her lips or her fingers.

"You've got a big inferiority complex you ought to cure yourself of," she said.

A little later she spoke again. "It's not how much you're worth to the woman," she said quietly. "It's how much you're worth to yourself. It's what you really can feel that makes you nice."

Dressing, she looked at her watch. "God, it's two," she said. "I guess I better tell them we had a flat and had to *walk* to Lawton." She giggled a little and raised her arms to lower her slip over her head. "The excuse never sounds quite so good afterward," she added lightly. She walked over and asked Sonny to button her dress, and then watched him strangely while he put on his shirt.

"Your mother and I sat next to one another in the first grade," she said. "We graduated together. I sure didn't expect to sleep with her son. That's small town life for you." She grinned and stroked his chest again as he buttoned his shirt.

"What will we be?" he asked, when she stopped at the poolhall to let him out.

"Very good friends for a long time," Lois said. "Even I couldn't get away with taking on my daughter's ex-husband on a regular basis. They'd have me committed. Why do you look so sad? You're fine, Sonny."

"I was just thinking of Mrs. Popper," he said. "I guess I treated her terrible."

"I guess you did," Lois said.

He sat in the car a moment longer and then looked at her gratefully. He started to speak but Lois slipped partly across the seat and covered his lips with her palm. When he closed his mouth she took her palm away and kissed him.

"Don't ever say thank you to a woman," she said. "They'll kill you if you do. You let the ladies say thank you."

CHAPTER XXIV

The next morning Sonny woke up feeling in love with Lois Farrow, but by the time a long week had passed he was back to missing Jacy and wishing he had been able to stay married to her. One night at the café Genevieve told him Lois had asked her to tell him they had taken Jacy to Dallas and would stay there with her until school started. The news did not improve his spirits.

"What do you think about it all?" he asked Genevieve.

"I don't know about it *all*," Genevieve said, "but the one thing that stands out nice and clear is that Lois' little girl took you for a nice ride. Boys in this town don't seem to have much sense when it comes to girls like her."

While they were talking all the football boys trooped into the café, laughing and cutting up. They were making a big thing of how sore and bruised they were—the first workout had been that afternoon. They played the jukebox and sat around talking about what a horse's ass the coach was. Sonny felt left out and even more depressed. He had always been on the football team and had done the same things they were doing after workouts, but suddenly he wasn't on the team and the boys didn't even notice him—he might have been out of high school ten years.

After a while he went over to the picture show and watched a funny movie with Dean Martin and Jerry Lewis. The movie took his mind off things, but afterward, when he was buying a bag of popcorn from Old Lady Mosey, he got another disappointment. She told him they were going to have to close the picture show sometime in October.

"We just can't make it, Sonny," she said. "There wasn't fifteen people here tonight, and a good picture like this, Jerry Lewis. It's kid baseball in the summer and school in the winter. Television all the time. Nobody wants to come to shows no more."

Sonny said he would be sorry to see the place go, and it was true. He went outside and sat on the curb, waiting for Billy to get through sweeping out. Since Sam's death Billy had grown nervous and restless, and was only really happy when he was with Sonny. If Sonny wasn't there to meet him after the show, he would go sweeping off somewhere and be lost half the night, so Sonny had got in the habit of being there. He and Billy would go walking together, Billy carrying his broom and occasionally sweeping at a leaf or a paper cup someone had thrown out. Sometimes they walked as far as the lake. Sonny would sit and watch the water while Billy swept the dam.

Once a week Sonny went to Wichita to have the doctor look at his eye, but the doctor seldom told him anything new. "Looks like sometime this fall I'll have to send you to Dallas. Better be saving your money. If the doctor down there decides to operate it'll cost you plenty."

So far as Sonny was concerned the Wichita doctor was costing plenty himself, but for once money was not too big a worry. His pumping job paid him enough to live on and he was able to put what the poolhall brought in in the bank. The pumping job was a lonely kind of job, but that was okay: he was not in the mood for people anyway. He spent his mornings bumping over the country roads in the pickup, going from one lease to the next, checking the rod lines, greasing the pumps and motors. Often he took Billy with him—Billy loved to go. When dove season came around Sonny bought a shotgun, an old L. C. Smith .12 gauge singleshot; occasionally, to Billy's surprise, he would take a shot at a dove or a jackrabbit, but he seldom hit anything.

He thought about Ruth a good deal, always painfully. After football season started he thought about her even more—Coach Popper's name was on every tongue. It looked like Thalia was finally going to win the district, and opinion was divided as to whether the team owed its success to the coach's coaching or to Bobby Logan's quarterbacking. Sonny felt strangely reluctant to go to the games, and stayed home from the first three or four. He felt a little guilty about not going, but somehow he just didn't want to.

Finally, in early October, the game with Chillicothe came up and Sonny broke down and went. It was a game that seemed likely to decide the conference crown—custom demanded that every male in Thalia go. At first Sonny enjoyed himself, and regretted having missed so many games. The night was cool and clear and the grass on the football field looked greener and softer than it ever had when he played. The assistant coach asked him and Jerry Framingham to run the first-down chain, and they accepted. When the band played the Thalia school song it was a little thrilling: it touched something in Sonny and made him feel as though he was part of it again, the high school, football, the really important part of life in the town.

It would have been better if he had never felt that way, because as soon as the game started he realized he was not part of it at all. Bobby Logan was part of it, and Coach Popper was very much part of it. He strode up and down the sidelines, scowling fiercely at the referees—everyone knew the coach was there. Even the linesmen were part of it, even the freshmen and sophomores on the bench—at least they were suited out. But Sonny wasn't part of it, and neither was Jerry, who had been out of school so long that he was used to not being part of it. Sonny couldn't get used to it. He kept wishing he was out on the field playing. Running the chain, measuring first downs, that was nothing: he might have been invisible to everyone but the referees. He was an ex-student—nothing. A feeling came over him sort of like the feelings he used to get in the mornings, only the new feeling was worse. Then he had felt like he was the only one in town, but standing on the sidelines, holding the chain, he felt like he wasn't even *in* town—he felt like he wasn't anywhere.

As the game went on the feeling became worse, even though Thalia was winning. Bobby Logan was quarterbacking beautifully: he got Thalia a seven point lead and they still had it when the fourth quarter began to run out. The whole town began to believe that Thalia had won the conference, and Sonny began to believe that he was not there. The people in the stands were wild, their eyes glazed, they saw nothing but the boys on the field. When the game was over and Thalia had won, it was chaos. The cheerleaders, the band, and a mob of high-school girls rushed out of the end zone to greet the dirty, victorious heroes. The girls hugged the boys and clung to them as they walked off the field. The Quarterback Club, the local gamblers, farmers, lawyers, well-wishers of all sorts crowded around Coach Popper to congratulate him, strewing the green, cleat-torn grass with cigar butts and chewing-gum paper.

Jerry Framingham was as excited as the rest of them: he was going off with some of his truck-driving buddies to get drunk, so Sonny was left to carry the chain back to the football bus. The boys were all crowded around the bus, hugging and kissing the girls who met them on the field. Sonny put the chain with the rest of the equipment and walked back through the crowd to his pickup, feeling like he had been completely erased. People he had known all his life were all around him, but they simply didn't see him. He was out of school.

Back at the poolhall, Billy was gone, sweeping somewhere, probably, and the poolhall was dark and empty. Sonny began to cry. Every minute or two he would think how silly it was and would stop for a little while, but he couldn't stop completely. He was out and could never get back in. He would have got drunk but there was no liquor. The only person who could have made him feel real was Ruth, and he couldn't go to her. Or Lois, but he couldn't go to her either. Or Sam the Lion, but he was dead. Finally he went to hunt for Billy and found him down by the jail. Billy, it turned out, was able to bring Sonny back. They started walking together and Sonny felt okay again. He had started talking to Billy almost as he would have talked to Duane, sometimes even more freely than he would have talked to Duane, and though Billy never answered he was always friendly. Feeling like he wasn't there had made Sonny think about Ruth, and when he really thought about her he felt ashamed of himself. He realized that for years she must have felt like she wasn't there; he was probably the only person who had ever made her feel she *was* there, and he had quit her without a word and left her to feel the old way again. It would have been a bad way to behave even if it had got him Jacy, but it hadn't, and it had probably left Ruth feeling hopeless. He had just begun to realize how hard it was to get from day to day if one felt hopeless.

As they walked, Sonny took off his eye patch and let Billy wear it. They walked north from the jail, past the Masonic lodge and the Jehovah's Witness church. To the south, back toward the drive-in, they could hear horns honking as people celebrated Thalia's victory. Once in a while a dog barked at them as they walked by, but most of the dogs in Thalia knew Sonny and Billy and didn't give them any trouble. They circled past the cemetery and Sonny waited in the road while Billy swept the cattleguard. They didn't often pass the cemetery, because Billy knew that Sam the Lion was

there somewhere and he was always reluctant to leave.
For once Sonny did not particularly mind. Billy swept
the cattleguard and got it very clean—from the pastures to the north they heard the moan of a coyote and
when Billy was satisfied they walked on, past the
rodeo pens and back to the dark poolhall.

CHAPTER XXV

A week before the picture show closed down Duane came home from boot camp. He drove in on Sunday morning and word soon got around that he was leaving for Korea in a week's time. Sonny learned that he was home Sunday night, when he and Billy were having a cheeseburger in the café.

"Wonder where he is?" he asked. "He hasn't been to the poolhall."

"I kinda doubt he'll come," Genevieve said, frowning. "His conscience is hurting him too much about your eye. I think he's gonna stay at the rooming house this week."

"Well, maybe he'll come in," Sonny said. "There ain't much to do in this town. I couldn't live in it a week without going to the poolhall, I know that."

"I think it's all silly," Genevieve said. "Why don't you go see him? Be a shame if he goes to Korea without you all seein' one another."

Sonny thought so too, but he was nervous about going to see Duane. He kept hoping Duane would show up at the poolhall and save him having to make a

289

decision; but Duane didn't. So far as anyone knew, he spent the whole week watching television at his mother's house. A couple of boys saw him out washing his Mercury one afternoon, but he never came to town.

As the week went by, Sonny got more and more nervous. Several times he was on the verge of picking up the phone and calling—once he did pick it up, but his nerve failed him and he put it back down. If Duane didn't want to be bothered there was no point in bothering.

Friday night there was a football game in Henrietta, but Sonny didn't go. He heard the next morning that Duane had been there drunk. All day he considered the problem and finally decided that he would go see Duane at the rooming house and let the chips fall where they may—it couldn't hurt much to try. If Duane didn't want to see him all he had to do was say so.

About five-thirty, as it was beginning to grow dark, Sonny got in the pickup and drove to the rooming house. Duane's red Mercury was parked out front. A norther had struck that afternoon and sheets of cold air rushed through the town, shaking the leafless mesquite and rattling the dry stems of Old Lady Malone's flowers. Sonny rang the doorbell and then stuffed his hands in his pockets to keep them warm.

"H'lo, Mrs. Malone," he said, when the old lady opened the inside door. The screen door was latched, as always. "Duane here?"

"That's his car, ain't it?" she said, edging behind the door so the wind wouldn't hit anything but her nose and her forehead. "He's here if he ain't walked off."

She shut the door and went to get Duane. Sonny

shuffled nervously on the porch. In a minute, Duane opened the door and stepped outside.

"Hi," Sonny said, finding it hard to get his breath because of the wind. "Thought I'd better come by and see you before you got off."

"Glad you did," Duane said. He was nervous, but he did look sort of glad. He was wearing Levi's and a western shirt.

"Want to go eat a bite?" Sonny suggested.

"Yeah, let me get my jacket."

He got his football jacket, the one from the year when the two of them had been cocaptains, they got in the warm pickup, and drove to the café. Conversation was slow in coming until Sonny thought to ask about the army, but then Duane loosened up and told one army story after another while they ate their hamburger steaks. It was pretty much like old times. Penny waited on them—she had had twin girls during the winter, put on twenty-five pounds, and was experimenting that night with purple lipstick. Old Marston had died in February of pneumonia—he had gone to sleep in a bar ditch in the wrong season. Genevieve had hired a friendly young widow woman to do the cooking.

"Guess we ought to take in the picture show," Sonny said. "Tonight's the last night."

"A good thing, too," Penny said, overhearing him. "Picture shows been gettin' more sinful all the time, if you ask me. Them movie stars lettin' their titties hang out—I never seen the like. The last time I went I told my old man he could just take me home, I wasn't sittin' still for that kind of goings on."

"Yeah, we might as well go," Duane said, ignoring her. "Hate to miss the last night."

They went to the poolhall and Sonny got his football jacket too. Then they angled across the square to the picture show and bought their tickets. A few grade-school kids were going in. The picture was an Audie Murphy movie called *The Kid from Texas,* with Gale Storm.

"Why hello, Duane," Miss Mosey said. "I thought you was done overseas. Hope you all like the show."

The boys planned to, but somehow the occasion just didn't work out. Audie Murphy was a scrapper as usual, but it didn't help. It would have taken *Winchester '73* or *Red River* or some big movie like that to have crowded out the memories the boys kept having. They had been at the picture show so often with Jacy that it was hard to keep from thinking of her, lithely stretching herself in the back row after an hour of kissing and cuddling. Such thoughts were dangerous to both of them.

"Hell, this here's a dog," Duane said.

Sonny agreed. "Why don't we run down to Fort Worth, drink a little beer?" he asked.

"My bus leaves at six-thirty in the mornin'," Duane said. "Reckon we could make it to Forth Worth and back by six-thirty?"

"Easy."

Miss Mosey was distressed to see them leaving so soon. She tried to give them their money back, but they wouldn't take it. She was scraping out the popcorn machine, almost in tears. "If Sam had lived, I believe we could have kept it goin'," she said, "but me and Jimmy just didn't have the know-how. Duane, you watch out now, overseas." Outside the wind was so cold it made their eyes water.

Sonny insisted they go in the pickup. He knew

Duane would go to sleep on the way back and he didn't want the responsibility of driving the Mercury. The wind shoved the pickup all over the road, but the road was still a lot better for their spirits than the picture show had been. Rattling out of Thalia reminded them a little of the time—it seemed years before—when they had gone to Matamoros. As soon as they reached a wet county they stopped and bought two six-packs of beer. The cans spewed when they were opened and the smell of beer filled the cab.

By the time they crossed the Lake Worth bridge they had gone through a six-pack and a half and were feeling okay. Soon they came to the Jacksboro highway bars and Sonny pulled off at a place called the Red Dot Tavern. Inside, a lot of tough-looking boys with ducktails were playing shuffleboard, and a couple of women with dyed hair were sitting at the bar with their middle-aged sweethearts. The ducktails looked at the boys belligerently, but no direct challenges were offered.

"All we can do here is get drunk and get whipped," Duane said. "Let's see what the prospects are on South Main."

They drove slowly around the courthouse—the only courthouse they knew that had a neon American flag on top—and parked far down Main Street, where the bars were. The wind whipped around the big granite courthouse and cut right down the street, as cold as it had been in Thalia. The boys went in a hash house and had some chili and crackers to fortify themselves, then let the wind blow them down the street to a bar called the Cozy Inn, where a three-piece hillbilly band was whomping away. One middle-aged couple was dancing, and a few more were sitting in the

293

booths or at the bar. The barmaid, a friendly old woman in her mid-fifties, wiped off their table with the end of her apron and then brought them some beer.

"Where you boys from?" she asked. "Thalia? Ain't it windy up there? I wouldn't live that close to the plains for nothin'. My oldest sister lives out in Floydada."

In a few minutes the band ended its set and the three young musicians straggled off to the rest room to relieve themselves.

"Maggie, you sing us a couple," one of the older customers said.

The barmaid didn't much want to, but the other couples took up the cry and finally she went over and picked up a guitar, shaking her head and deprecating herself.

"I ain't much of a singer," she said, but she strummed a minute or two and sang "Your Cheatin' Heart." Everyone thought she was real good, the boys included. Her voice was rough but strong—it filled the Cozy Inn better than the three sideburned young honky-tonkers had. She sang like she meant every word; it was not hard to believe that she had run afoul of a cheating heart or two somewhere in her life. After that she sang "Making Believe," and would have put the guitar down and gone back to the bar if Duane hadn't gone up and stopped her. He liked her singing.

"I'm goin' off to Korea tomorrow, ain't no tellin' when I'll get to Fort Worth agin," he said. "Sing one more."

"Why sure, if that's the case," the woman said. "Both my boys was in the service. I was right proud of 'em."

294

"These is for the soldier boys," she announced, not wanting the rest of the crowd to think she was singing out of vanity. She sang "Filipino Baby" and everyone applauded loudly; encouraged, she finished with "Peace in the Valley" and went back to the bar to draw someone a Pearl. Sonny felt suddenly depressed. The old barmaid had reminded him that he wasn't in the army. It seemed a fine thing to be going off to Korea and Sonny wished very badly that he could go. When the band came back the boys left and stood on the cold street a minute, both slightly wobbly from the beer.

"We sure ain't findin' no women," Duane said. "Want to look some more or do you want to take the easy out?"

"It's too cold to prowl much," Sonny said.

With no more ado they turned up the street toward the easy out, a whorehouse called The New Deal Hotel. It was about the nicest whorehouse in that part of the country, but a little expensive on that account. Since it was Duane's last night the boys decided to splurge. When they got to the hotel a bunch of high-school boys from Seymour were standing on the sidewalk shivering, trying to get up the nerve to go inside. It was easy to tell they were from Seymour because of their football jackets.

"Yep, it's a whorehouse all right," Duane said. "You boys coming up?"

"How much do they charge?" one boy asked, his teeth chattering. "We're afraid to go up for fear we ain't got the money."

"They start at about ten bucks," Duane said, and the boys' faces fell. They had been hoping for five.

Sonny and Duane went on in and up the green-carpeted stairs, leaving the Seymour boys to count their money. The madame was a quiet, polite woman who looked and dressed like the saleswomen in a Wichita Falls department store. Sonny's girl was a polite, thin-nosed brunette from Corsicana, named Pauline. Everything was splendidly comfortable in the New Deal: the rooms were warm, the beds wide and clean, the carpets good. The girls were pleasant, but so efficient that afterward it seemed to Sonny that he and the girl had barely touched. Before he was even thawed out he and Duane were going back down the green stairs, each ten dollars poorer and neither much less horny.

The Seymour boys were all gone, the streets almost empty. While they were walking back to their pickup the city street-sweeper chugged by and Sonny remembered Billy and hoped Miss Mosey had seen he got home out of the cold.

"Well, I guess the next piece I get will be yellow," Duane said philosophically.

By the time they got back to the Lake Worth bridge, he was asleep. Sonny didn't care—he enjoyed the drive, and was in no hurry. With the wind blowing against him he couldn't make much time, but he didn't need to. North of Jacksboro he stopped the pickup and got out to take a leak, and Duane woke up and followed suit. It was about five o'clock when they pulled into Thalia. The posterboards in front of the picture show were naked. It seemed to Sonny it would have been better to have left *some* posters up, even the posters to *The Kid from Texas.*

"Got about two hours till bus time," he said, when they were at the rooming house. "Want to go down and have some coffee?"

"Yeah," Duane said. "Wait till I go in and get my gear."

In his uniform Duane looked a lot different. When he got back in the pickup he casually handed Sonny the keys to the Mercury. "Here," he said. "Why don't you look after that car for me?"

Sonny took the keys, embarrassed. "Your Ma don't need it?" he asked.

"I wouldn't want her drivin' it, no better than she can drive. You might help her run the groceries home, if you have time."

Sonny didn't know what else to say. In the warm café they both got a little sleepy and ended up playing the jukebox to keep awake. Genevieve wasn't there. Her husband had gone back to work in August and she had hired a girl named Etta May to work the night shift.

When the bus pulled up out front, both boys were glad. Sitting and waiting was hard on the nerves. The bus driver came in to have a cup of coffee and Sonny and Duane walked across the street to the yellow Continental Trailways bus. The wind made their eyes water, and took their breath—they had to turn their backs to it. Duane leaned his dufflebag against the front of the bus.

"Hear anything from Jacy?" he asked suddenly, since there was just two minutes left to talk.

"No, not a thing. She hasn't been back to town since August. I guess she just stays in Dallas all the time."

"I ain't over her yet," Duane said. "It's the damnedest thing. I ain't over her yet. That's the only reason me and you got into it, that night. Reckon she likes it down in Dallas?"

"It's hard to say," Sonny said. "Maybe she does.

Reckon you and her would have got it all straightened out if I hadn't butted in?"

"Aw no," Duane said. "They would have annulled me too, even if we had. You all never even got to the motel?"

"No," Sonny said.

The bus driver came out of the café and hurried across the street, tucking his chin into his shoulder so his face would be out of the wind. Duane picked up the dufflebag and he and Sonny shook hands awkwardly.

"Duane, be careful," Sonny said. "I'll take care of that Mercury."

"Okay," Duane said. "See you in a year or two, if I don't get shot."

He got on and waved quickly from the window as the bus started up. A ragweed skated across the dusty street and the bus ran over it. Sonny put his hands in his pockets and walked back across the street to the pickup, not feeling too good. It was another one of those mornings when no one was there.

CHAPTER XXVI

Of all the people in Thalia, Billy missed the picture show most. He couldn't understand that it was permanently closed. Every night he kept thinking it would open again. For seven years he had gone to the show every single night, always sitting in the balcony, always sweeping out once the show was over; he just couldn't stop expecting it. Every night he took his broom and went over to the picture show, hoping it would be open. When it wasn't, he sat on the curb in front of the courthouse, watching the theater, hoping it would open a little later; then, after a while, in puzzlement, he would sweep listlessly off down the highway toward Wichita Falls. Sonny watched him as closely as he could, but it still worried him. He was afraid Billy might get through a fence or over a cattleguard and sweep right off into the mesquite. He might sweep away down the creeks and gullies and never be found.

Once, on a Friday afternoon, Miss Mosey had to go into the theater to get something she had left and she let Billy in for a minute. The screen was disappointingly dead, but Billy figured that at least he was in, so he went up into the balcony and sat waiting. Miss Mosey thought he had gone back outside and locked him in. It was not until late that night, when Sonny got worried and began asking around, that Miss Mosey thought of the balcony. When they got there, Billy was sitting quietly in the dark with his broom, waiting, perfectly sure that the show would come on sometime.

All through October, then through November, Billy missed the show. Sonny didn't know what to do about it, but it was a bad time in general and he didn't know what to do about himself either. He had taken another lease to pump. He wanted to work harder and tire himself out, so he wouldn't have to lie awake at night and feel alone. Nothing much was happening, and he didn't think much was going to. One day he went to Wichita and bought a television set, thinking it might help Billy, but it didn't at all. Billy would watch it as long as Sonny was around, but the minute Sonny left he left too. He didn't trust the television. He kept going over to the picture show night after night, norther or no norther—he sat on the sidewalk and waited, cold and puzzled. He knew it would open sooner or later, and Sonny could think of no way to make him understand that it wouldn't.

One cold, sandstormy morning in late November Sonny woke up early and went downstairs to light the poolhall fires. Billy was not around, but that was not unusual. Sonny sneezed two or three times, the air was so dry. One of the gas stoves was old and he had to blow on it to get all the burners to light. While he was blowing on the burners he heard a big cattle truck roar past the poolhall, coming in from the south. Suddenly there was a loud shriek, as the driver hit the brakes for all he was worth—the stoplight was always turning red at the wrong time and catching trucks that thought they had it made.

Sonny went back upstairs and dressed to go eat breakfast. He couldn't find either one of his eye patches and supposed Billy must have them. It was the kind of morning when a welding helmet would have been a nice sort of thing to wear. The sky was cloudy and gritty, and the wind cut. When he stepped outside Sonny noticed that the big cattle truck was stopped by the square, with a little knot of men gathered around it. The doctor's car had just pulled up to the knot of men and the old doctor got out, his hair uncombed, his pajamas showing under his bathrobe. Someone had been run over. Sonny started to turn away, but then he saw Billy's broom lying in the street. By the time he got to the men the doctor had returned to his car and was driving away.

Billy was lying face up on the street, near the curb. For some reason he had put both eye patches on—his eyes were completely covered. There were just four or five men there—the sheriff and his deputy, a couple of men from the filling stations, one cowboy, and a pumper who was going out early. They were not paying attention to Billy, but were trying to keep the truck driver from feeling bad. He was a big, square-faced man from Waurika, Oklahoma, who didn't look like he felt too bad. The truck was loaded with Hereford yearlings and they were bumping one another around and shitting, the bright green cowshit dripping off the sideboards and splatting onto the street.

"This sand was blowin'," the trucker said. His name was Hurley. "I never noticed him, never figured nobody would be in the street. Why he had them damn blinders on his eyes, he couldn't even see. What was he doin' out there anyway, carryin' that broom?"

"Aw, nothin', Hurley," the sheriff said. "He was just an ol' simpleminded kid, sort of returded—never had no sense. Wasn't your fault, I can see that. He was just there—he wasn't doin' nothing."

Sonny couldn't stand the way the men looked at the truck driver and had already forgotten Billy.

"He was sweeping, you sons of bitches!" he yelled suddenly, surprising the men and himself. They all looked at him as if he were crazy, and indeed, he didn't know himself why he had yelled. He walked over on the courthouse lawn, not knowing what to do. In a minute he bent over and vomited by one of the dusty, stunted little cedar trees that the Amity club had planted. His father had come by that time.

"Son, it's a bad blow," he said. "You let me take care of things, okay? You don't want to be bothered with any funeral-home stuff, do you?"

Sonny didn't; he was glad to let his father take care of it. He walked out in the street and got Billy's broom and took it over to him.

"Reckon I better go try to sell a little gas," one of the filling-station men said. "Look's like this here's about wound up."

Sonny didn't want to yell at the men again, but he couldn't stand to walk away and leave Billy there by the truck, with the circle of men spitting and farting and shuffling all around him. Before any of them knew what he was up to he got Billy under the arms and started off with him, dragging him and trying to run. The men were so amazed they didn't even try to stop him. The heels of Billy's brogans scraped on the pavement, but Sonny kept on, dragged him across the windy street to the curb in front of the picture show. That was as far as he went. He laid Billy on the sidewalk where at least he would be out of the street, and covered him with his Levi's jacket. He just left the eye patches on.

The men slowly came over. They looked at Sonny as if he were someone very strange. Hurley and the sheriff came together and stood back a little way from the crowd.

"You all got some crazy kids in this town," Hurley said, spitting his tobacco juice carefully down wind.

By the time Sonny got back to the apartment Genevieve was there. She was crying but when she saw Sonny she made herself quit. She stayed for about an hour, made some coffee, and tried to get Sonny to cry or talk or something. He wouldn't. He wandered around the apartment, once in a while looked out at the gritty sky. Genevieve saw it was going to take some time.

"Sonny, I got to go to the café," she said. "People keep eatin', come what may. Come on down when you feel like it. Dan'll be glad to pump your leases for you when he comes in this afternoon."

Sonny didn't know what he would feel like doing that afternoon, so he didn't say anything. When Genevieve left he turned on the television set and watched it all morning: it made a voice in the room, anyway.

About the middle of the afternoon he began to feel like he had to do something. He had the feeling again, the feeling that he was the only person in town. He got his gloves and his football jacket and got in the pickup, meaning to go on out and pump his leases, but no sooner had he started than he got scared. When he passed the city limits signs he stopped a minute. The gray pastures and the distant brown ridges looked too empty. He himself felt too empty. As empty as he felt and as empty as the country looked it was too risky going out into it—he might be blown around for days like a broomweed in the wind.

He turned around and drove back past the sign, but stopped again. From the road the town looked raw, scraped by the wind, as empty as the country. It didn't look like the town it had been when he was in high school, in the days of Sam the Lion.

Scared to death, he drove to Ruth's house. It was broad daylight, mid-afternoon, but he parked right in front of the house. The coach was bound to be in school. Sitting in the driveway was the coach's new car, a shiny red Ford V-8. The Quarterback Club and the people of the town were so proud of his coaching that they had presented him with the car at the homecoming game, two weeks before.

Sonny went slowly up the walk, wondering if Ruth would let him in. He knocked at the screen, and when no one answered opened the screen and knocked on the glass-paneled front door.

In a moment Ruth opened it. She was in her bathrobe—that was about all Sonny saw. He didn't look at her face, except to glance.

"Hi," he said.

Ruth said nothing at all. She was surprised, then after a moment angered, then frightened.

"Could I have a cup of coffee with you?" Sonny asked finally, lifting his face.

"I guess," Ruth said, her tone reluctant. She let him in and he followed her through the dark, dusty-smelling living room to the kitchen. They were awkwardly silent while she made the coffee. Neither knew what to do.

"I'm sorry I'm still in my bathrobe," Ruth said finally. "It gets harder all the time to get around to getting dressed."

But then, as she was pouring the coffee, anger and fright and bitterness began to well up in her. In a moment they filled her past the point where she could contain them, and indeed, she ceased to want to contain them. She wanted to break something, do something terrible. Suddenly she flung Sonny's coffee, cup and all, at the cabinet, then she flung her own, then flung the coffee pot at the wall. It broke and a great brown stain of coffee spread over the wallpaper and dripped down onto the linoleum. Somehow the sight of it was very satisfying.

"What am I doing apologizing to you?" she said, turning to Sonny. "Why am I always apologizing to you, you little . . . little bastard. For three months I've been apologizing to you, without you even being here to hear me. I haven't done anything wrong, why can't I quit apologizing. You're the one who ought to be sorry. I wouldn't be in my bathrobe now if it hadn't been for you—I'd have had my clothes on hours ago. You're the one that made me quit caring whether I got dressed or not. I guess just because your friend got killed you want me to forget what you did and make it all right. I'm not sorry for you! You would have left Billy too, just like you left me. I bet you left him plenty of nights, whenever Jacy whistled. I wouldn't treat a dog that way but that's the way you treated me, and Billy too."

Sonny was very startled. He had never thought of

himself as having deserted Billy. He started to say something, but Ruth didn't stop talking long enough. She sat down at the table and kept talking.

"I guess you thought I was so old and ugly you didn't owe me any explanations," she said. "You didn't need to be careful of me. There wasn't anything I could do about you and her, why should you be careful of me. You didn't love me. Look at me, can't you even look at me!"

Sonny did look. Her hair and lips looked dry, and her face was paler and older than he had remembered it. The bathrobe was light blue.

"You see?" she said. "You shouldn't have come here. I'm around that corner now. You ruined it and it's lost completely. Just your needing me won't bring it back."

Sonny didn't know. Her eyes seemed like they had always seemed, and having her so mad at him was suddenly a great relief. He saw her hands, nervously clasped on the table. The skin on the backs of her hands was a little darker, a little more freckled than the white skin of her fingers. He reached out and took one of her hands. She was startled, and her fingers were stiff, but Sonny held on and in a moment, disconcerted, Ruth let him hold her hand. Their hands knew one another and soon warmed a little.

When Sonny wove his fingers through hers Ruth looked at him cautiously and saw that he was still and numb, resting, not thinking at all. He had probably not even heard the things she said, probably would not remember them—he was beyond her hurting. It was as if he had just come in and they had started holding hands. She would have to decide from that, not from all the things she had said, nor even from the things that had happened, the pain and humiliation of the summer. What if he had valued a silly young girl more than her? It was only stupid, only the sort of thing a boy would do.

She could forgive him that stupidity, but it was not about forgiveness that she had to decide: it was about herself, whether she could stand it again, whether she wanted to. Even if the springs in her would start again it would only be a year or two or three before it would all repeat itself. Something would take him from her and the process of drying up would have to be endured again.

"I'm really not smart," she thought, and with the fingers of her other hand she began to smooth the little black hairs at the back of his wrist. "I'm not smart, and if I take him back again it will all be to go through again."

She didn't know whether she was brave enough to accept it, but she turned his hand over and traced the little lines in his palm, traced them up to the wrist. She pressed the tips of her fingers against the blue veins at his wrist, and followed the vein upward until it went under the sleeve of his shirt. It irritated her that her fingers wanted to go on, to go up the arm to his elbow and over the smooth muscle to the hollow of his shoulder. All at once tears sprang in her eyes and wet her face, her whole body swelled. She knew she was going to have the nerve, after all, and she took Sonny's young hand and pressed it to her throat, to her wet face. She was on the verge of speaking to him, of saying something fine. It seemed to her that on the tip of her tongue was something it had taken her forty years to learn, something wise or brave or beautiful that she could finally say. It would be just what Sonny

307

needed to know about life, and she would have said it if her own relief had not been so strong. She gasped with it, squeezed his hand, and somehow lost the words—she could not hear them for the rush of her blood. The quick pulse inside her was all she could feel and the words were lost after all.

In a moment she felt quieter. She put his hand on the table and stroked his fingers with hers. After all, he was only a boy. She saw that the collar of his shirt was wrinkled under his jacket.

"Never you mind, honey," she said quietly, reaching under the jacket and carefully straightening out the collar. "Honey, never you mind. . . ."